CW00350519

WINTERS HEAT

A TITAN NOVEL

CRISTIN HARBER

ISBN-10: 0989776018
ISBN-13: 978-0-9897760-1-1
Published by : MILL CREEK PRESS

Cover Design & Interior format by The Killion Group
http://thekilliongroupinc.com

DEDICATION

Much love to my family. Go TeamCT, and thank you CC girls.

CHAPTER ONE

His simple job just became complicated. Colby Winters watched the two men who had tailed him for days. For the first time, they weren't bringing up the rear on their cross-country caravan. Team Tagalong, as he had grown fond of calling them, pushed their way into the crowded airport ahead of him and beelined for the covert pickup location. Winters adrenaline and curiosity spiked.

He powered past a coffee shop, trying to catch Team Tagalong as they neared a jog. Business folks with rolling briefcases blocked his view for a second but cleared. His tails stood still, their faces tight and focused on the row of chairs that only Winters should've known about, where the package was hidden.

There was no doubt they'd learned about the pickup spot, and he needed a swift Plan B. He hated when the spy game changed in the final countdown.

Edging closer, he couldn't see why they stopped after powering past him. He followed their hesitant gaze. A woman, dressed in khaki pants and a cardigan sweater decorated like a pink Easter egg, was on the floor, pawing at the underside of the chairs.

That was their problem. And now, his too.

Plan B now needed to account for Miss Khakis-and-Cardigan. Team Tagalong advanced toward her. The woman remained oblivious to their approach while Winters pulled back.

This can't be happening. She had the small package in hand and was turning it like a Rubik's Cube.

His Plan B formed. Stay to the perimeter. Move in and extract the package at a location with fewer witnesses. Team Tagalong's apparent plan was a hand-to-hand version of engage the enemy. Manhandling the woman wasn't the smartest option, but they'd already proven not to be the smartest team.

Her eyes were as wide open as her mouth. One man had her elbow, and she buckled into his grip. Not the type of complication Winters needed. She couldn't look any more honest if she had a glowing halo.

Her eyes said she knew Team Tagalong would leave her dead in a dumpster. His instinct said the woman had no idea what she held. Then again, neither did he. The contents of the package were on a need-to-know basis only, and he didn't need-to-know squat in order to secure it.

She flinched again. Time for Plan C. Waiting to engage wasn't happening with Miss Khakis-and-Cardigan in the crossfire. His tactical pants and black shirt served as piss-poor camouflage, and their quartet didn't need the attention, but he stalked over and squared off.

The woman wrapped a white-knuckled grip around the package. She was scared, but that didn't seem to matter. Had he read the scene all wrong? She didn't yell or drop the package.

Was the unlucky female really an operative playing the innocent card? He didn't know. He didn't care. This op was a headache and a half. Time for the next plan: secure the package, and everyone could fend for himself.

Winters ignored the men and smiled as polite and professional as a gladiator on a bad day.

"Not sure what this is all about." He gestured to the men at her sides. "But hand it over."

"No, *pendejo*. She is coming with us." The man answered for her, flexing his sausage fingers around her bicep. Her mouth opened with unvoiced pain.

"Wasn't talking to you, was I?" He couldn't place the Spanish accent, and an international-fucking-incident wasn't his idea of an easy in-and-out. Next time he was offered a cakewalk assignment, Winters would ignore his sweet tooth.

Team Tagalong pivoted away, woman in hand, and merged into the constant flow of mindless travelers.

So, it's going to be like that.

She was dragged more than she walked. The second man hovered close, hiding her reluctance from any interested spectators.

Winters sidestepped in front again. He had orders not to engage. Extract and secure only. Extracting was a pain when he couldn't throw down. Besides, airports weren't conducive to altercations given their national security issues.

"Hold up. We have business to discuss. That package is leaving with me, *mi amigo*." Dickhead would have worked better, but the Spanish translation for that term of endearment slipped his mind.

The woman. She was an unknown, though she looked like she sat in the front car of the world's scariest rollercoaster. Pale color. Wide eyes. Pinched brow. He gave a once-over of the sugary outfit and superglue-grip on the package. She didn't act like an operative, but chameleons were tricky to spot.

One half of Team Tagalong pressed a blade into her torso.

Come on. You're pulling this stunt here? He rolled his eyes high to the terminal rafters. A legitimate coffee run would be needed after this hassle. Gas station coffee wouldn't cut it.

The operative let the woman's sweater cover his weapon. Maybe he *was* smart. When the blade pierced the fabric, she let out a quiet whimper. It was the first sound she made in his presence. Her pink glossed lips quivered, and her gaze ricocheted among the three men.

Winters rocked on the heels of his well-worn combat boots and lifted his hands. It took practiced patience to pull up short. But there were better ways to get that package than to engage in the middle of a commuter-swamped airport, where God only knew how many law enforcement agencies and security cameras patrolled.

He fell back and reached an alcove, ducked in, then flipped his cell phone open. Headquarters needed an update, and he needed intelligence. His boss picked up and grunted his usual hello.

"I got problems, man. Team Tagalong blew by my ass, snagged the package and a girl."

"Freakin' fantastic." Jared Westin had one inflection for all occasions, calloused, full of grit and gravel. Every day. Every time. "What do you need?"

Winters scanned the airport corridor. Nothing but business suits and carry-on bags. The trio was nowhere to be seen. "A clue where to find the fuckers."

Jared spoke to someone in the background and returned. "Pulling the parking lot footage, checking into their car rental. When'd they pick up a girl?"

Even his monotone questions had a hard-boiled splash. Jared could order a burger at a drive-thru and scare the employee clean out of her hairnet.

"We arrived at the same time, my tails leading the way. A woman had the package in hand. Shit got complicated. They took her. I backed off, figuring Boy Genius could work his satellite magic."

"Yeah, something like that. Parker's deep in the airport's system, hacking their programs. He'll send you info and screen shots ASAP."

"Hey, Jared."

"What?"

"Did I thank you for this job yet?"

"Nope."

"Good."

"Get to work, dick." Jared coughed his equivalent to a laugh and hung up.

Winters double-timed it back to his truck and jumped in. The tires squealed as he rounded the exit ramp. He tossed a handful of change into the payment kiosk and tapped his fingers on the steering wheel, waiting for the mechanical arm to lift and for HQ to hit pay dirt. His phone buzzed, and he checked the caller ID.

"What you got, boss man?"

"Parker traced their vehicle, a black, four-door Taurus, to a car rental company in Virginia. They used a credit card, which was also used at a nearby motel. Head there first."

"Roger that." As he exited the garage, the sun flooded the cab of the truck, and he pulled on his mirrored aviator sunglasses. "What's up with the credit card?"

He used cash on his jobs, as he assumed all operatives did.

"No idea. Nothing turned up."

"Huh."

"Sending the address to your phone now. And Winters?"

Winters received the address, programmed the GPS, and grunted in response. He picked through empty boxes of Dots, far more interested in crushing his candy craving than hearing a lecture from Jared. "What?"

"I scanned the parking lot footage. They put that girl in the trunk. And none too carefully. I don't think we're looking at two teams. No intel on a friendly or a female op. I'd tread with care."

He found some candy stuck at the bottom of a box and chomped down on it. *The trunk, huh? That's overkill.* "Got it."

"I'm serious, Winters. If this is a case of wrong place, wrong time, you dust off your kid gloves and use them."

That was more of an order than Winters would admit. He hated working with untrained women. They were always ready to bawl when it was time to tangle. It was better for all involved if he could hand her to a more sympathetic operative. But he was the only one here. Not much of a choice.

"I'll behave. I promise." He sounded like he was trying to get a crazy girlfriend off the phone. "When I have an update, I'll make contact."

Winters shuddered thinking about the red-eyed, tear-brimmed women. Finding the mystery woman dry-eyed was about as likely as him scoring a much-needed cup of joe in the next fifteen minutes.

The GPS showed the motel to be only miles away. Highway signs flew by, and cars shifted lanes to make way for him barreling down the road. He rounded a bend, saw nothing but red brake lights, and cursed. He tried to move to the left lane, but traffic was at a standstill. He slammed his hand on the top of the steering wheel. Maybe he could make a list of everything that could go wrong today and see how close he came by the time it was lights out.

He laid on his horn and crept toward the left lane. No one moved. Not an inch. Not even the moron he threatened to hit with his truck. Winters rolled the window down and motioned to the driver. Motioned may have been too conservative a description. He bore down on the man like a crack-addicted grizzly bear, ready for a fight to the death.

"Get over." He pointed to the shoulder of the highway. "Over. Now."

The man ignored the truck maneuvering its way into the crack of space. Winters blew the horn again and leaned out the window, ready to threaten life, limb, and loved ones.

"Move your car." Honking wasn't getting him anywhere, but he did it again. Then again and again. Still no help.

He dropped the gear into neutral and slammed the gas pedal down. The truck revved like a road warrior. The driver, who was fast becoming a sworn enemy, flinched, then tapped into the survival part of his brain and pulled over. Winters moved to the shoulder, pushed the pedal to the floor, and redlined it.

A half mile later, the source of the traffic problem appeared. Three lanes of a four-lane highway were closed for paving. Bright orange barriers and men with neon yellow reflector vests milled about machinery.

The one open lane had a fender bender. Two men with cell phones glued to their ears pointed at their bumpers. Winters hit the brakes in time to jet through the construction entrance, rumble over an unpaved section, and cross in front of all the stopped traffic. *Dear God, let there be an immediate exit.*

The GPS interrupted his prayer. "Exit highway in one hundred and fifty feet. Your destination will be on the right."

What do you know? He should pray more often.

He pulled off the highway exit. The motel was ahead, and he bounced over the rough entrance. The vacant lot had faded parking space lines and crater-like potholes. Knee-high weeds ran the length of the curb. A black Taurus was at the end of the lot. Fan-fuckin-tastic.

Winters parked his pickup truck around the side, ran through a quick ammunition and supply check, and closed in on the pay-by-the-hour room. He jogged by several silent rooms, then heard muffled words and a feminine yell. *Son of a bitch.* As much as he didn't like to work with weepy women, he would rain hell on anyone hurting them. Weeping or not.

One heel kick and the cheap door splintered off of broken hinges. Surprise was on his side. Winters held the Glock in his right hand and used his teeth to pull the pin from a tear gas charge the size of a cherry bomb. Nothing too serious, but enough for a distraction. Perfect for overwhelming a small room with a little smoke and burn.

He tossed it in with a shouldn't-have-fucked-with-me grin. The sparse room filled with the hissing smoke. The three other occupants clawed at their faces and covered their tearing eyes. In the smoky haze, their gagging noises, harsh sputters, and coughs littered the room like three teenagers wheezing on their first cigarettes.

Winters was trained for the gas. Prepared for it. Hell, the bitter taste in his mouth was almost pleasant, a Pavlovian effect tied to the adrenaline rush of throwing one of those babies into a room. Pull. Pop. Hiss. He loved it every single time.

He wanted to brawl, to clash, and take them down. Hard. They shouldn't have screwed with his day. They shouldn't have stuffed Miss-Khakis-and-Cardigan into the trunk of their car.

He moved with a single step to the closest man and punched, breaking the man's nose, which felt as gratifying as it sounded.

Winters smiled and beckoned for more. *Come and play*. The man staggered backwards in the haze, head in hand, blood seeping through his fingers.

The second man lurched toward him, arms swinging, as he jumped side to side. Winters jabbed an elbow into his attacker. The man reeled back, sucking in the acrid smoke in uncontrolled gasps.

Hopefully, one of them would hop up jack-in-the-box style, so he could have another round. Knees bent and body agile, he readied. The first man gained his bearings. Winters egged him on. "Try me."

The man charged. Winters landed a punch to his bloodied face. *Thud*. Knocked out.

The second man staggered forward, brandishing a switchblade with untamed, arching slashes. Looked like the same blade he pushed against the woman's midsection earlier. That was a mistake. Both then and now.

"You're going to wish you didn't bring that out to play today. Never should have threatened the lady. Never should have gotten in my way. Never, ever should have fucked up my job."

Winters grabbed the man's wrist and twisted toward the stained popcorn ceiling. A bone cracked. The knife hit the dirty floor. And all the while, a feminine fit of coughs reverberated from near the back closet. She was choking on the gas and hadn't moved to escape.

"Are you hurt?" he called to the woman.

No answer. Only gasps as she stumbled through the smoke.

"Where's the package?"

"Go to hell." Her words wheezed and faded.

Of course. What'd he expect? His lips upturned in a mixture of annoyance and exasperation, and his eyes burned as his tolerance for the gas neared its threshold. "Do you have it or not?"

The woman scampered and made a weak maneuver to escape. He stepped in front of her with a menacing grunt. This lady wasn't going anywhere.

She wilted without fresh air. As he countered her next move in their hasty dance, she backed into the corner again. He continued to question her, gruff and with quick efficiency, but only more coughs responded. She sniffled and wiped at her watering eyes. He felt bad. Almost.

"Stay put," he said.

He pulled plastic zip ties, his handcuff of choice, out of his back pocket and secured the unconscious men to a table. The woman jumped from her crouch in the corner. She fumbled toward the busted door, arms outstretched, wailing a determined cry. He hooked an arm around her waist. She flailed, arms pumping and legs bicycling the Tour de France.

He tossed her on the bed, clapped his hands on both her shoulders, and held her in place. "I'm not playing, lady. Don't move."

Winters took in the room. The cops might be there within minutes. "Last time. Where's the package?"

The woman hesitated with a sputter of coughs.

Damn, he didn't want to threaten her. He stood to his full height but didn't give an ultimatum. He watched her eyes flicking around the room, looking everywhere, landing on every possible hiding spot…except—bingo. He kept on eye on her and opened a drawer.

"No." She hacked again. "Don't."

The package.

The woman scooted to the side of the bed and jumped for it in his hand. The tear gas gnawed into his patience. What was she doing? His decision making skills weren't firing like they should. Not being able to think in this time constraint, he needed answers. Like who the hell she was, for starters.

He wrapped an arm around the woman and threw her over his shoulder. She was as light as she looked and losing steam with each gas-filled gasp.

"Wait. No. Let me go. Help. Someone help!"

"Pipe down," he said in a manner in which Jared wouldn't have approved.

Still, she continued a feeble holler. "Help. Someone. Help."

There wasn't anyone around, so her hoarse cries didn't matter. In joints like this, most everyone minded their own business. But still, she was a confusing headache. He didn't have to take her. He could've left her for the cops to figure out. But she looked more suited to sell Girl Scout cookies than handle thugs and cops.

She'd been hell bent on grabbing the package and couldn't have had a day of training in her life. She didn't make sense, and he wouldn't abandon her, his protective nature stoked.

Winters cleared the splintered door with her still over his shoulder. In the distance, the police sirens sounded. He made double sure the package was in his back pocket, then hightailed it to his truck.

Once he reached the four-door pickup, he set her down. "Stop hollering. I'm not a bad guy. We're getting the hell out of here, then we'll work this all out. Chill."

A determined flash glinted in her eyes, and he felt her muscles tense before she made a move. Gritting her teeth, she made a swift kick to his balls. *Son of a bitch.* Thank God for his reflexes. She was a handful, even when gassed.

"All right. If that's how you want to play, lady." He tossed her into the backseat of the truck. "I have the stupid package you're so worked up about. So don't think about jumping out of the truck while it's rolling. We'll make a deal. You'll get something, and I'll keep what I already have."

Winters scrubbed his face with the palm of his hand, then standing outside the open door, caged her in the backseat with his arms and torso. Why did he care if she bailed on him? He had the package. It was his only task. This mission was halfway done, and none of his task list included this woman. But why did she want it in the first place? It didn't make sense.

Propped on her elbows, she kicked at him, landing her feet on his abs. He rolled his eyes. "Well hell, lady."

She would make a run for it given the chance. He knew it. Winters looked at her, then the door locks. She was a liability that he didn't have time for today. He engaged the child safety looks, locking her in the backseat.

His seat punched forward every few seconds as she beat her heels into it. He dropped his head, suppressing a vicious string of swears. Before the cops could fly into the motel parking lot, Winters eased out the entrance. Unsure where to go for the time being, he pushed a button on his cell phone and connected to Jared.

"Got the package. And the lady." He glanced in his rearview mirror at her.

Fresh air had reinvigorated her, and she kicked his seat over and over, making his teeth saw together.

"Let me go, you jerk."

"Sounds like it," Jared said. "Clean up your mess and move it on home. And for God's sake, Winters, play nice."

Play nice probably meant no knockout juice or truth serum.

"Yeah, yeah. I'll figure out who she works for, and how she knew the pickup spot. Then I'll send her on her merry way." She kept kicking. He was so far past annoyed that it was amusing, in a he-must-be-out-of-his-mind kind of way. "She's a spitfire. It's entertaining."

She shouted, "You don't scare me. I'll kick you again. Get close to me and see what happens."

"Jesus Christ," Jared murmured before ending their call.

Winters sighed, resigned to the pounding in his head.

CHAPTER TWO

Not a bad guy? He seemed like one. The man wasn't law enforcement. He didn't have a badge to go with that gun he slung around, and his mannerisms were more lethal than reassuring.

This nightmare was the makings of a television evening newscast special. The news anchor would look into the camera, earnest and pensive, wondering aloud in a dramatic voice about Mia Kensington's last hours alive. Or maybe a reporter would interview her coworkers and family, everyone guessing about why she was in Kentucky or how she ended quartered into neat pieces that fit inside a handful of grocery bags.

Mia massaged the hammering in her head and tried to swallow against the raw burn in her throat. She sniffled again. Her nose still hadn't stopped running since he threw tear gas at her. Her eyes stung, and no amount of rubbing helped. Mascara smudges covered her knuckles, and her swollen lips were in desperate need of balm. Too bad the men who took her from the airport trashed her purse on the way out the door.

She had no phone, no identification, and no way to get help. The man driving the pickup truck apparently didn't care how many times she kicked the back of his seat. He just went about his business, making phone calls, and glancing at her in the rearview mirror. It was just as well. What would she do if he turned around? She shuddered. She was trapped in the vehicle with him and needed an escape plan desperately.

She studied him at the wheel. His dark brown hair was mussed from the fight at the motel room. Sweat dampened his short sideburns. His tanned neck was corded, and every few minutes, the man ran rough-knuckled hands to the back of his neck, rubbing his nape. He flipped the radio station at the end of every song, pushing the button several times in a row. Were those nervous tics? Interesting that someone so forceful, so brutal, was fidgeting.

Mia shook her head. Nothing she practiced as a psychologist could get her out of this truck. She needed to scrounge up every memory from the self-defense class provided to civilian women on base.

Too bad there wasn't anything on escape and evade. That would have been useful. Far more helpful than practiced groin kicks on a plastic dummy. She glanced at the front seat. Her groin kicks to muscle-man up there failed. She tried the tactic over and over, and he had laughed each time her knee jabbed his muscled thighs and abdomen. Laughed and rolled his eyes like she was the campy comic relief during an action movie.

The man adjusted his rearview mirror again. It worked to her advantage this time, giving her a direct view of him. Too bad his eyes were hidden by sunglasses.

"Want to explain your side?" He sounded rough but more interested in conversation than harming her, which was just as alarming.

Nope, nothing to share here.

He had a strong jawline. His lips were fuller than she'd noticed. She would remember every detail for the sketch artist after she escaped. She wanted his face all over the eleven o'clock news. Headline: Madman Proficient in Gunplay Saves Woman.

No. Not saves. Madman Proficient in Gunplay Kidnaps Woman. She was nowhere near saved sitting in this truck.

He had used the child safety locks. Those only worked on the backdoors. *Right*? If she could time it correctly, she could surprise him and get out the front passenger door. They were still in a residential neighborhood. Stop signs and semi-regular traffic. If she could get out, a cop could swoop in and save her. Soon as they slowed she would make her move.

He decelerated for a red light. *Deep breath in. Time to go.*

She lunged over the headrest. Her foot caught his sunglasses, and she used the leverage pushing toward the passenger door.

The man cursed and grabbed her calf. The truck skidded. A thunder started from the depths of her lungs and blazed past her raw throat. An adrenaline blast pushed her, and she launched away, her hand clawing at the door handle, the window button, anything to get an outsider's attention.

He still had hold on her leg, and she kicked, connecting with his face. Maybe his chin. Definitely his shoulder.

He cursed again. "Seriously, woman?"

Her free leg caught in the steering wheel, turning their trajectory. The truck jumped, then rocked back and forth. Mia's forehead hit the front console. She lost her bearings, and stars exploded in her head. He let go of her and slammed on the brakes. She fell forward again. Her eyes watered instantaneously. She crumpled shoulders-first on the floorboards.

"What in God's name do you think you're doing?" He was angry. She would've said he roared at her, but roaring would have been an understatement.

She turned to see his face and watched him check his rearview and side mirrors, then put the truck in park. A deep breath later, he looked down at her, still on the floorboard, and glared.

They had run off the road. *Where was the neighborhood watch? A helpful cop?*

He turned the radio off. The only noise was the hum of the air conditioning and the tap, tap, tap of his fingers drumming on the steering wheel. The floorboard was uncomfortable. The ridges of the plastic floor mat dug into her shoulder and elbow. She was eye level with a cigarette lighter knob and the new-car scent air freshener tied to it. The little pine tree with the rental company logo on it spun one direction, then the next, mocking her inability to move.

From her grounded position, the man above looked solid as a boulder. His long legs worked to tuck under the raised steering column. His slouch, more relaxed than poor posture, didn't hide the muscles in his broad chest and stomach. His tight cotton shirt did little to obscure his brawn. She saw the sinew in his neck, and…was that restraint tightening his jaw?

This maneuver had been the wrong tactic. Mia rushed to dry her watering eyes and scoot off the floor, but she was at an awkward angle, with her feet splayed in different directions, and her shoulder jammed between the console and seat. She couldn't reach the door handle, and she couldn't get up.

Oh, no. Claustrophobia grabbed her lungs and squeezed, driving her into a blood-pounding anxiety fit. She thrashed and kicked, shoving away from him, and pushed further into her console crevice, without a way to escape.

"You stuck down there?" This time the roar was gone, replaced by the tickle of amusement.

She wiped enough tears away to see his lips were upturned into a grin. Her face felt hot. She tried again to right herself, arms and legs churning in place, and failed in immaculate style. If she lived to tell about this, it would be the worst and most embarrassing day of her life.

After running a hand over his chin, he checked the mirrors again. "Need a hand up?"

Silence was the best answer. She couldn't get out of this predicament without a smidge of help, but the heck if she would engage this kidnapping maniac.

He offered one dangerous hand. The gesture wasn't threatening. Still, she had nowhere else to go. If she had to be stuck with him, she didn't want to be upside down on his floorboard.

Mia wriggled her wedged arm toward him, and he clasped it. His hand was strong, coarse, and overwhelming. With a swift pull, he righted her next to him. He raked a gaze over her that made her shiver.

She returned the obvious once-over. He dressed straight out of an action movie, except she knew there weren't blanks in his firearms. He crossed thick muscled arms across the expansive plane of his chest. Dang. She took on GI Joe and lost.

Avoiding his stare, she looked out the front windshield straight into a ditch, semi-near the red light she'd been hoping to escape at. They were at an impressive angle. The hood pointed down and the tailgate up. The horizon was higher than it should have been. Not one single car drove by. They were alone in their one-car accident.

She scooted toward the door, and his hand landed on her thigh.

"You've gone through hell to stay with that package. You're just going to bolt now?" He shook his head. "I already told you I'm not a bad guy. Believe me. Don't believe me. I don't care. Maybe we can work something out. I don't know. But I've been told to be on my best behavior. So, let's just pretend this whole thing never happened."

That was his best behavior? Gassing her in a motel room, tossing her over his shoulder, and locking her in a truck. His worst behavior was unimaginable. Definitely the stuff that kept FBI profilers busy. He was powerful, all-male, and awareness flushed through her. Her blood ran thick, pulsing in her neck, washing away the panic, replacing it with a stomach-knot.

But he was right, she'd put her life on the line already, and if there was the chance she could get her hands back on the package…

Without a second thought, Mia scampered back over the seat into the second row. Her moves were awkward and uncoordinated. Her butt stuck in the air longer than she thought it would as she pulled herself over, legs fluttering behind her. It took several seconds to move from her unintentional downward dog yoga position and sit upright on her bottom.

Why did she do that? Her face flushed again, and her stomach re-tied its knot. She pressed her knees together and hoped to lasso her unease. She needed to be clearheaded to survive him and *work something out* with the package.

He looked into the mirror and slapped the truck into gear. "Comfy back there?"

The man placed his mirrored sunglasses back on, fed the truck enough gas to rumble onto the road, and ran his fingers through his dark hair.

Mia tucked a fist under her chin and caught the smell of him on her knuckles from when he helped her up. He smelled red-blooded and robust, a mixture of soap, sweat, and gunpowder. She caught herself sighing.

What was that? Madmen kidnappers shouldn't smell that memorable. This case of Stockholm Syndrome might've started earlier than normal.

She needed to think her next move through. Why did she try to escape without that disk? It brought her to Louisville and got her into this mess. She couldn't abandon it now. It was too important.

Another option had to exist, and Mia decided to sit in the backseat until that opportunity arrived.

CHAPTER THREE

Cartagena, Colombia

“Find out who took her.” Juan Carlos Silva bellowed into his satellite phone and hung up. Standing poolside under the fierce Colombian sun, he dabbed at his brow with a freshly pressed linen kerchief, then smoothed his tailor-cut silk shirt.

It was bad enough his men traveled all the way to the United States and couldn’t complete their mission. The job was to collect a simple package containing a disk. But they ran halfway across that country, only to lose it again? Appalling.

He inspected the pristine pool water for a speck of dirt. He wanted to find something wrong. An excuse to yell at the knobby-kneed boy charged with his gardens and pool. Not that he needed one.

His neck pain flared, as it did when inept employees prattled their excuses. If he thought the job would be so complicated, he would have sent more men. Men experienced in American subterfuge. His judgment call on this one was foolish, and while it was his fault, it would be easier to take his frustrations out on someone’s hide. He cracked his knuckles and called out for the pool boy.

The phone chirped again, and he thought to ignore it. If those idiots couldn’t find a simple woman who escaped with the disk, he would kill them to prove a point. Maybe string them up by their necks and hang them from the front gate of his estate. Perhaps he would make them pick out a machete from his collection and select a limb to lose.

He never should have assigned junior members. But at least two of his men still trailed the woman and that wretched package, and Juan Carlos would grace them with another opportunity to make it right.

Answering the chirping phone, he didn't listen to his man on the phone. "Retrieve what is mine. Take the woman. Both are more valuable than your life."

America wasn't Colombia. The practice of kidnapping was frowned upon more so in the States. Though much of his high-end product originated there, usually his men showed more finesse. Kidnapping was a practiced art.

Perhaps, he should give some direction. It was imperative both items were presented to him. He inspected his manicured fingernails. What advice would help? No, advice was wrong. Incentives were most effective. "Pray to the Blessed Virgin Mary for guidance. For if you fail, I will hand your mother your head."

He disconnected the phone with a decisive click. Irritation made him sweat. The damp beads pooled along his cropped hairline. It was already hot enough outside. He didn't need this added aggravation to sully his appearance. There was a certain look he expected of himself. Sweating was beneath him. He paid people to sweat for him.

Juan Carlos dabbed his brow again. There was work to do. Fresh inventory arrived earlier. Young women to inspect prior to their auction. Easy, untraceable money.

Winters rolled his head left to right, cracking his neck, and directed his attention to the woman behind him. "I'm Colby Winters. Most people call me Winters."

He sounded flat and bearish when he wanted to be trustworthy. Trying to make her talk while balancing his irritation made this job more complicated by the mile.

The woman didn't acknowledge him. Again, he glanced at her in the rearview mirror. She wrinkled her nose at him, which was an improvement over the kicking and shouting.

"And you are?" His temples throbbed. Parker could easily pull her identity from any number of security cameras, but he wanted her to open up. Who knew why?

"None of your business. I don't introduce myself to my kidnappers." She gave him the snake-eyes, pursing her lips to complete her pissed off quip.

"Should have expected that." He gave her a once-over, taking in her swollen lip and puffy cheek, and wanted to bend steel. "Those guys roughed you up?"

"What does it matter? I'm not saying anything to you either. So you'll just do the same."

"Aren't you a tough one?" Intrigued, he gave a half-cocked smile. She was stronger than he gave her credit for. Must've been that deceptive sweater set she wore. The pastel colors lessened her bite.

As best he could from the driver's seat, he studied her face and the slope of her neck to her collarbone. His backseat passenger was, by all standards, attractive. A little vanilla. Like a teacher or librarian, if he ignored the mussed makeup and hair.

"I'm not going to hurt you." He swallowed his gruffness. "Let's try this again. My name is Colby Winters. You can call me Winters. And you are?"

No response.

"Tell me your name, and I'll share a little about me."

She narrowed her eyes. "Fine. Mia."

Their gazes clashed, and his chest warmed. Winters chewed the inside of his cheek before he turned the AC on high.

"Nice to meet you, Mia. We've made some progress here, haven't we? Let's jump to it, doll. Why were you at the airport?"

She shifted in her seat. "I had things to do."

Evasive. Not scripted, but not careless enough to give him any details. "Who do you work for?"

"No one."

"How did you know where that package was? That was mine."

"Yours?" Her chin jutted up. "I don't think so."

Finally, a reaction. She was resolute. Strong. Strident. Even angry. She glared at him in the mirror.

"Well, it sure as shit isn't yours."

She sighed. "That's not true... It is now. But it wasn't before."

Her forceful rebuttal dissolved with a drop of her shoulders. What was her inflection? Unease or... Sadness? Whatever she felt it made him uncomfortable. He was out of practice with souped-up emotional interactions. She didn't even make sense. Nothing but a carnival ride of crazy. "Lady, I don't know what you're talking about. But we can work something out, *if* you stop being so cryptic."

He flexed his grip on the steering wheel. What the hell did he care anyway? He had the package. For the time being, that was his only objective, and he'd accomplished it. But his curiosity was another thing. Why did a sweater-set-wearing, librarian-look-alike want anything of Titan's?

As if reading his thoughts, she piped up in a hoarse whisper. "The person who owned that package told me to get it."

She wasn't giving him a lot, and the vagueness did nada to pacify his interest.

"You're wrong. I was tasked with the pickup." He didn't want to scare her and summoned any empathy he might have squirreled away. "The owner hired my company to retrieve that package."

"Well, Mr. Winters, that's the difference. Owned versus owns."

Mia didn't elaborate, and he tried to decipher her meaning. What was she talking about—owned versus owns?

He ran his hand through his hair. It was too shaggy and unkempt. He needed a haircut and a shave. The scruff on his face was a scant thicker than usual, though he liked to keep a menacing shadow. Men backed off, and danger-junkie women gravitated toward him. Win-win.

He adjusted the sunglasses and focused more at her than at the road while he drove. "Why don't we start from the beginning?"

"Why don't you?" Her smirk was still defiant. She didn't carry herself like a professional operative and didn't act like someone on a job. But her challenging attitude took some major cojones.

Given the last hour or so, she had reason to act that way, but it was still unfamiliar. Not a lot of people gave him shit. Not a lot of people questioned him. Never a petite woman dressed like an Easter egg. But Mia doled out the brashness by the bucketful.

"Answering my questions with questions isn't going to get us anywhere. Though you entertain me to no end."

She scrunched up her face. "What do you want to know?"

"For starters, where are you from?"

"Alexandria, Virginia. Right outside DC," she said.

"Well, so am I. How about that?"

Her eyes flashed.

His sarcastic quip was too much. He still needed to calm it down. Why couldn't he handle this simple interrogation? "What sent you to Louisville?"

"A client needed me to help him with something."

"And your client is…?" He let the question trail, hoping she would answer. But she didn't. Instead, she focused on smoothing her shoulder-length hair, which stuck out in various directions. Her messed hair was his fault, after he grabbed her like a bag of tactical gear. "Doesn't seem like a good client, sending you to do his dirty work. It's actually a jackass move."

Silence from Miss Cardigan-and-Khakis.

"You walked straight into a bad situation. Two professional teams had the same goal. Secure that package. Or was it three teams, Mia? At least own up if you're working this op, too."

Quiet minutes passed. Mia neither acknowledged him nor the situation. She concentrated on a few strands of hair, twirling them around a finger.

"What do you mean by professional team?" she asked.

Was she screwing with him? Red flag after red flag told him this woman was some innocent who just stepped in a huge pile of crap.

"Assuming you're not acting the part of blameless bystander, I'll play along." He threw a handful of Dots into his mouth, needing to release some tension. "A pro team, a professional team—it's a group of operatives trying to complete a covert task. Every operative knows their role: good guys or bad ones, or a confusing mixture of the two, but they know. And it seems like you've spent some time with both today."

"And you're the good guy, huh?" Mia acted interested for the first time in anything he had to say.

"I'd like to think so, though I'm sure many would disagree." He smiled, showing lots of teeth. It was too much. Too fake. He knew it and was sure she knew it, too. "If I were going to hurt you, I'd have done it by now. You're baggage I don't need. But we seem to want the same thing, and I'm curious enough about you to slow my return until I get a few questions answered."

"Why are you curious? You have what you wanted."

He didn't know what to say next. Awkward wasn't his thing, but today, he aced it. "What do you do? For work. What type of business are you in, Mia?"

"I thought we weren't answering questions with questions."

Smooth move. He needed to change tactics.

"We should get ice for your face." He pulled into another motel parking lot and turned around in his seat to stare at her. "Stay put. Please."

Mia nodded and remained in place, though he wasn't sure why. Nor was he sure why he tacked on the *please*. He placed a handful of zip tie cuffs on the dashboard.

"I don't need these. Take it as a show of trust you'll sit and stay."

He wouldn't tie her up, and she wouldn't run. He could tell by her body language. In all likelihood, that was because he still had the package, and she wanted it. Whatever her motives, he didn't care. As long as she listened.

He moved fast, secured a room, grabbed an ice bucket, and returned to the truck. He held his breath, hoping she was still there—and she was. He ignored the smile tugging at his cheeks.

Through the window, she studied him as though she had something to say. Her eyes moved from his head and drifted the length of his body, down to the asphalt, and up again. With each sweep, she analyzed him: his chest, his arms, his legs, even the scar on his face. He was feet away, but her intensity made it feel like mere inches. She held his gaze, mouth poised to speak.

Mia broke their stare and focused on the empty parking lot. So much for getting into her head, learning anything about her. He rounded the hood and hopped in the truck.

If she didn't look like saccharine personified, he'd assume she was just checking him out. But nah. Not this one. This one didn't cross men like him, and he didn't hang out with women as soft and touchable as her. He shook his head clear. Soft and *sweet*, rather. Touchable wasn't something he needed to ponder.

He pulled the truck to the rear lot and unlocked the doors and disengaged the child safety locks, then gave her a nod. Her clothes were dirty. The cardigan set was dingy. Very unlike a librarian. Bruises grew darker on her otherwise flawless complexion. He should have killed those fuckers in that motel room instead of tying them to a table. But there wasn't a point in focusing on the past. Training should have kept regret from his head. But he continued to think of ways those men should've paid for hurting her.

She got out, ignoring him. He grabbed his box of Dots and dumped a handful into his palm, downing them with a mind-clearing gulp.

He threw open his door, got out, and locked the truck behind him, then he leaned on the hood. Mia stood there, feet planted amongst the parking lot weeds. He lofted the key over the truck hood. She grabbed it from the air, surprising him, and looked at the room number. Her fingers played over the plastic card, and she gnawed on her swollen lip without moving from him.

"Go there. Room 102. Right at the end." He held up the bucket. "I'll get some ice."

Mia nodded with a half-hearted smile and turned toward the room. The way she walked, the way she swayed... He noticed. Big time. His pulse beat faster, and his eyes tracked her movements. Nothing to do with watching out for her, and everything to do with taking in the sight. He rubbed the scruff on his face and stalked to the ice machine.

With a full bucket of ice crooked in his elbow, he knocked on the door and pushed it open with his steel-toed boot. She sat stock-still on the bed, palms flat against the floral comforter, ankles locked, knees pinched together. Her face was paler than when he left her. Now that her adrenaline had worn off, it looked like shock wanted to take its place.

Shit. Shock. Something else he didn't want to handle.

He trained one eye on her and fashioned an ice pack from a bathroom towel, then moved close to the bed to examine her cheek and lips. Vacant eyes stared to the blank wall in front of her.

As gentle as he could manage, he turned her face upward for an inspection. Mia's skin was velvety but bruised and scratched. Broken and damaged. Winters pressed the makeshift ice pack against her cheek with his softest touch. Soft wasn't his thing, but she didn't flinch. Maybe he did okay.

"You doing all right?" He tried to replace his normal edge with tone to show he wasn't the enemy. He needed her to know that for tactical purposes. She was an asset. Something he needed to take care of. If she was pleasant to look at, well, that was a bonus.

Her shoulders pinched up in a stiff shrug, and she snatched the ice pack from him. Her gaze flicked to him, then away. And again, she flashed her eyes to him and stole them away. For a brief moment, they weren't numb or exhausted. They were… beautiful.

That flash of prettiness tore at his insides. His blood ran cold just as fast as he felt white-hot. Sweat dampened the back of his neck. He worked to keep his palms from sweating and rubbed them up and down his pant legs. It was as unfamiliar a feeling if there ever was one.

Someone so striking shouldn't be so scared. Was she deteriorating? Falling apart in his care? A valid concern given her borderline-catatonic state, but that wasn't the basis for the twists within his stomach. He swallowed against the lump in his throat.

"Mia, are you okay?" He drew out his words, enunciating each syllable, trying to attract her attention. Her distance worried him. She repositioned the ice pack and crawled toward the headboard.

"I need to lie down for a second." She dropped her head onto a pillow.

The detachment in her request made his heart drop. It wasn't right. The cruel world dumped on Mia today. She never saw it coming, and he hadn't made it much better. Did he have to throw her over his shoulders? Couldn't he have subdued the men without blasting tear gas?

She peered from the pillow and gauged him. A slow bulge crawled down her throat, the tension visible from across the room.

The military might have trained him how to survive if captured alive by the enemy, but nothing prepared him for her unblinking hesitation.

"You're not my type, and this room is safe. Just get some rest."

She nodded. Her eyes fluttered, long lashes drooping heavy. They locked onto him, then sealed shut. She was out. His anxiety washed away now that she rested, lessening his concerns a degree. He must need sleep as much as she did.

The room was much darker with the setting sun and only a desk lamp was on when she stirred. Hours passed since Mia collapsed against the motel room bed, and she didn't alert him when she awoke. But he knew. Her slight body shifted and tensed under the blanket he'd thrown over her. The even beat of her breathing hitched and reverberated in his ears. Silence thundered. Did she worry—or worse, was she scared—because he was in the room?

"Sleep okay?" Stupid question. His thumbs drummed on the table. He'd been watching her for hours except the minutes he ran out for provisions. But even then, he could see her in the back of his mind. The imprint of her bruised body tortured him.

She cleared her throat. "How long have I been out?"

"A while. I grabbed some food. Got you a few things from the store across the street if you want something clean to wear. Like sweatshirts and stuff."

Playing the gentleman card sounded like a solid plan earlier, now it felt fake and foolish. Normal information-eliciting tactics weren't appropriate, and he had no idea how to proceed with her.

This was why Jared never paired him one-on-one with the untrained or the guiltless. Winters didn't have a careful touch, and he was unsuccessful when he tried. Case in point. Mia acted beyond apprehensive as she picked at her dirt-streaked sweater and pants.

"So…" He turned to the table. "Food? Clothes?"

"I'm starving." Her tongue ran over her lips. Maybe he should have bought some lip gloss or something like that. Women liked that stuff. Needed it. Didn't they? He blew out a frustrated puff.

"I didn't know what you liked, so we have everything from peanut butter and jelly makings to fried chicken, but it's not hot anymore. And candy. I have a bad candy habit. Though I'm more than willing to share if you promise to stop kicking me for the rest of our trip."

She tucked her legs beneath her and inched toward the shabby spread on the table. "Thanks, Mister—"

"Just call me Winters." He needed something to do with his hands. All of the sudden, his arms were gangly and awkward. He stuck his thumbs in his pockets.

She nodded, slid off the bed. After two glances over her shoulder, she made a plate of food using a pile of napkins. She conjured images of movie nights and Sunday pot roast dinners. Safe, responsible activities non-operatives did in their normal lives. A tightness in his throat surfaced as he tried to swallow away confusion.

"You ready to answer some questions for me now, Mia?"

"Not really."

"We could start simple."

"I'd rather just eat." She polished off her sandwich and picked up a drumstick.

"The airport. Why were you there? Hell, how did you know where to go?"

Something changed in her. And just that fast, he regretted pushing her. The fresh color painting her face was gone. Her fingers tore at the chicken. She stared at him with sad eyes.

"You said my client *is,* and I said my client *was*. You said *owns*, I said *owned*."

"So you aren't working together anymore?"

"He's dead."

Her reaction hurt to watch. Heartbreak. Fallen eyes. Aching tonality. The corner of her eyes pinched, and she swallowed a few times. She needed comforting, an emotional poultice. Both were things he knew zip about. Why was it so hard to conjure up a soothing word? Nothing came to mind. He didn't know how. He fell back on what he knew. Interrogation.

"How'd he die?" He worried he'd just made her pain worse.

"*They* say he killed himself. But he wasn't suicidal. He was scared for his life."

"How would you know that?"

"Because I was his therapist. And, whether I should have been or not, something like his friend."

Winters sat there for a moment and watched her eyelashes flutter. Her eyes grew moist and tears welled. Agony overtook her innocence. He reached out to her arm, trying to soothe away the pain in her. Her skin was so warm whenever he brushed it. And each time, it shocked him how fragile she felt. His fingers traced down her bicep.

Mia's downturned head shot up, panic flashing across her face and a clear warning to back the hell off.

He snatched his hand from her as fast as he could. His finger singed, the tips tingled. Why the hell did he reach to her? Thinking of him as a good guy only recently began to solidify. At least he hoped.

"Sorry about that." Erratic behavior wasn't his norm. "I don't know what that was. Sorry."

"It's okay. Anyway…" She rubbed her arm. "My client said something would happen to him. That if he turned up dead, I needed to go to the airport. To those chairs."

"And when did he die?"

She put the chicken down on the napkin and wiped her fingers. "Two days ago."

Winters's jaw flexed. He'd gotten his marching orders two days ago and had headed out from DC. She bit her lip, uncertain maybe if she'd admitted too much.

The woman needed reassurance. Comforting. And he itched to provide it, but instead forced his hand to keep away from her. He needed to keep his paws off of her. Christ.

Think about work. "Do you know what's in the package?"

"Yes, do you?" Her hesitant eyes said she told the truth. No abnormal pupil dilation, no increase in her respirations.

"No."

"Well, that's probably why you haven't killed me yet and dumped my body." There wasn't a hint of sarcasm.

"You're having a hard time seeing me as one of the good guys, huh?"

"You don't look like a good guy. You look like a killer. You look like you enjoyed that whole thing back at the motel."

"I'm going to take that as a compliment, doll." He drew up a half-smile in an attempt to lighten her mood. "And truth be told, it was fun."

The window cracked. The wiz and thud of a bullet smacking the back wall took him by surprise, only inches away from Mia's head. He dove on her, shoving her to the side of the bed.

"Get down!"

CHAPTER FOUR

Winters rolled across the bed, drawing his Glock from his back holster. He pounded off two rounds, holstered it, and snagged his M4 assault rifle perched against the wall. He drew it up to his shoulder. The smooth metal and solid weight in his hands was grounding and washed away the awkward, apologetic mess he was earlier. He scanned through the scope, giving off short bursts of semi-automatic fire into the parking lot, in the direction the bullets came from.

Whoever was out there was messy. They should have been able to take both of them out with a clean shot. Hell, they should have gone after him first.

There. One man dropped. Another scrambled into an old Lincoln and screeched out onto the main drag.

Winters lowered the rifle down but held it close. Without the assistance of the scope, he scanned the parking lot again. Nothing else seemed out of place. Someone shouted from an adjoining room and gunpowder burned in the air.

"Dinner's over. Come on. We need to roll out of here." He yanked Mia's arm, pulling her off the glass-covered carpet. She stood on shaking knees and nodded but remained frozen like a statue.

"Let's go, Mia." He reloaded his handgun with a quick slam of the magazine, threw the rifle over his shoulder, and tucked a combat knife into his boot. She still hadn't moved. He wrapped his arm around her waist and carried her out the door.

He took one more look around, crossed to his truck, and put her in the passenger seat. She clutched the bag of clothes he'd bought for her. When the hell did she grab that? He rushed to his door, slammed the keys in the ignition, and squealed tires.

"Glad to see you appreciate my shopping." She slowly turned toward him. "Time to give it up. What's with the package?"

She shook and stared numbly out the vehicle's tinted window. Her teeth chattered as if an arctic breeze blew from the vents. White knuckled, her fingers splayed, and nails dug into the seat.

He snapped his fingers twice in a row. "Mia, honey. You can't go into shock on me now. Come on, girl."

That got her attention. She scooted closer to him, appearing thankful for the pickup's bench seat and leaned against his arm. "They're trying to kill me. I'm going to die."

"And we're not going to let that happen. But you have to let me know what's going on. You have to trust me. Can you do that?" He checked his mirror to change lanes but also inspected her for chattering teeth and white knuckles. Both had disappeared. Progress.

Hell, she felt good against his arm. She locked eyes with him, and for a moment, he forgot where they were and what they were doing. It was those dark, sultry eyes. How did he miss those earlier? They were as dark as his, but hers were still bloodshot from the tear gas bombs.

He pulled his gaze back. That didn't last more than a second and scanned her again. He didn't notice the sweater or the dirt or her terror but rather the supple mounds of her breasts.

Where was his mind? Sure as shit, not paying attention to his surroundings. He'd been concerned about getting her fresh clothes and some food. He should have known they'd be tracking him. Or her.

"Mia, tell me what you know, and I'll figure out the rest." Her warmth pressed against his arm.

"I'm a therapist at a military base outside DC. I'd been seeing a patient who recently returned from a covert op in South America. Mostly routine stuff. But overnight he became…" Her voice cracked.

"You're okay. I promise. Just trust me."

She took a deep breath. "He became what I thought was paranoid. He said he had a file."

"A file?"

"Yes. He hid it at the airport. A human trafficker was after him. He said if he turned up dead, I needed to get that file to a contact in DC."

Winters saw a cop ahead and slowed down to the speed limit. "Why didn't he just pass on the file himself?"

"I don't know." She leaned against his arm.

"Okay, then what happened?"

"Military police showed up at my office to ask questions. They said he jumped off his apartment balcony. He lived on the 14th floor." Tears brimmed, and she blinked rapid-fire. "That's not possible. He wouldn't have."

Winters looked down at her in the crook of his arm. "Do you know what's on that file?"

She shrugged, silent.

Oh, she knows.

"It's worth killing for?" He accelerated through traffic again, growing more anxious with what she might say.

Mia nodded. "If you're the South American human trafficker, warlord type, then yes. It'd be worth killing for."

"Which you know I'm not, so tell me what's in the file." He tried to give her his most trustworthy face. It wasn't a well-practiced look for him.

Seconds ticked by. Her eyes narrowed, her fingers fretted, and she sucked in a long breath. "He said it was a list of covert agents in deep cover in South America. Names, faces, identities of those infiltrating the cartels."

"Good God. We're talking spies and undercover agents? A nonofficial cover list? You pursued a NOC list? On your own?" She obviously had no idea how dangerous that was. A death wish for the untrained, and Miss Khakis-and-Cardigan was definitely untrained. Determined, yes, but that wouldn't keep a bullet from stopping her dead.

"He bought it off some local tribe leader who was more interested in cash than outing a US agency."

"And now someone traced the file back to the States and wants it. I need to figure out how my client plays into this. And how they knew where the package was. Hell, how the other guys did, too."

"I had notes." She grimaced.

His fingers drummed on the steering wheel, and he waited for more.

"I made notes in my file on him. I didn't think there was any merit to what he said. I wrote it down so I wouldn't forget about it, in case I needed to reference it in our sessions. I honestly thought he had delusions."

Winters pressed a button on his phone and connected to Jared. After he recapped everything to boss man, he nodded and hung up. "The other team must have learned the location after reading your notes."

"They have my client notes?" Mia grasped his forearm. Emotion ran visible across her cheeks. He couldn't tell if it was anger or embarrassment. She needed him to say something, anything. He had no idea what though.

Fuck it. He wrapped his arm around her shoulder, hugging her. It was some form of comfort. One he hadn't much practice at, but she needed at least that much and, though he had no idea how to ease pain, her sigh seemed to say he made an okay first attempt. Well, second if he counted the last motel room.

"Kensington," she whispered.

"What's that?" He held her, punctuating the question with a slight squeeze.

"My last name. Mia Kensington."

He smiled at her. It was a genuine smile—not used to illicit information or coerce a mark. Not all that uncomfortable but alien to him. He could get used to though. "Pleasure to meet you, Mia Kensington."

"How'd your guys find out about my notes if you didn't know my last name?"

"That's how an ops team works. My job was to get that package. But I picked you up along the way. The team at home watches my back, feeds me intel, et cetera. So they probably picked your headshot up from the security surveillance at the airport and compared it against a few databases. Since you work on a base, I'm sure your picture hit as a match with one quick search. From your civilian employee badge."

"Oh."

She smelled like vanilla and sugar, even after the hell she'd been through that day. Her soft hair brushed up against his bare bicep. Unsettled need prickled down his neck. His throat tightened, and fire ran to his groin.

"Mia…" Distraction and anticipation stole words from his lips.

His heart pounded loud in his chest, fighting for his attention. With each flutter of her eyelashes and innocent movement against his skin, his tension spiked. It was shocking. He was on the job. There was no time for distraction. Losing control was unheard of. Unacceptable.

His arm was cemented around her shoulder, and it wasn't moving. He stared as the broken white lines on the highway passed in quick revolutions, one right after another. The hum of the truck's engine poked at his concentration.

He needed to get out of this truck. He needed cool, fresh air to cover him. Right now. Deep, mind-clearing breaths were in order as soon as possible. Anything to get his disciplined mind back to what it did best—analyze, act, accomplish.

Winters made a sharp exit off the highway onto an unlit ramp. He jammed on the brakes. Gravel spit from under the truck. The back end skidded and fishtailed before it came to a stop. His heart thumped. His throat tightened. The faint scent of burned rubber filtered into the pickup cab.

Oh, what the hell. No way was he getting out of this truck.

As fast as he pulled off the road, he brought her close to his face, and without even a second to hover over her, he crushed his lips onto hers. Her tense mouth gasped a breath, then melted. The hot caress of her tongue sent explosions from his chest to the palms of his hands. The pounding in his heart didn't get any better. It only pushed his racing pulse faster, making it gallop wild, as intoxicating rockets flamed inside him.

Insanity. She was delicious insanity.

In between breathless pants, wicked want fired. Her lips were full. Her kiss was better than he expected, and hell, he expected a whole lot. She stoked him faster than he could ever remember. A kiss unlike any other kiss. There was no denying that.

He knotted a hand in her hair, held her to him, and devoured her. The press of her silken flesh made him hunger for more. His breathing deteriorated into a desperate rasp of torture. With each inhalation, he smelled, tasted, and consumed feminine beauty. This angel was a vixen in disguise, and God help him, he wanted her.

Her small hands wrapped into his T-shirt, then she stroked his stomach, flexing her fingertips against the fabric and straining against him. He dropped his lips to her neck, and she moaned. That perfect purr fanned his desperation. Her goose bumps flashed under his tongue's caress, and she shuddered with each whipping kiss.

She tasted of sweat and tear gas, of soft woman, and carnal ambition. There wasn't a timid thing about Mia. Who was he to assume what she wanted? To think she needed soothing and caring? It seemed all she needed was him. Hard. Tough. Possessive.

Her grip on him flexed again against his taut muscles. She looked so fragile, but good God almighty was he wrong. She strained to spread her legs. Their position on the front seat didn't give them a lot of room, but he was all over her, making the most of their confinement. Her head dropped back with a deep gasp, leaving her neck open for his teeth to rake against the delectable skin.

After forging a path up her neck, he ate at her lips again. She pushed toward each rough kiss, begging more of him. He leaned into her, hungering for the sweetness of her flesh. His swollen cock pushed into his pants zipper. And the hell of it was she knew it. Little Miss Khaki-and-Cardigan, the same one who looked like a preppy librarian, wanted him and wasn't keeping it to herself.

Her hand dropped from his abs, slow and deliberate, to his hard-on, rubbing him through his pants. A rumble escaped his throat. Her nipples peaked harder, pressing through the fabric to tease him in the pale moonlight. He'd die to pluck at them, to thumb each in seductive agony until she cried out for more.

He tugged at the shoulder of her shirt with his teeth, pushing the bra strap down a delicate slope. Slow lashes of his tongue blazed toward her firm breast. Exquisite and supple.

Sharp lights flooded the interior of their pickup truck. Bright like a warning beacon. A car exited on their ramp. It sped too fast, nearing them too quick. With one deft move, Winters dropped her down to the bench, beneath the exterior line of sight, and held her in place. He heard the harsh intake of her unsuspecting gasp and felt her body go rigid under his palm. Winters narrowed his eyes to study the car as it passed. Nothing suspicious. Just the cockblock timing of a lead-footed driver.

Hell. What if it had been trouble? Here he was pawing at a woman he should protect. Some shithead wanted the package he was responsible for securing. And he wanted the woman who was now also his responsibility. Winters ran his hands from the heavy stubble on his face into his shaggy hair. Danger had never before been a powerful aphrodisiac. Why was it driving him to the edge now?

For the first time since he burst through the motel room door with tear gas, she didn't appear to be scared or angry. Instead, she shined with lust, want, and reckless need, most likely, a mirror image of him. Hot desire pulsed through him like a dangerous toxin. Losing focus would get them both killed.

She tilted her head away from him, laughed to herself, and pushed off the seat. "Deal with stress like that, huh?"

What did she just say?

"Stress? I don't get stressed out, doll." She thought he needed a release from *stress*? How about a release from her continuous feminine hum and sweet fragrance that she radiated? Or the breathtaking way she wrapped her hands in his shirt, pulling him close? Never mind how she struggled to open her legs to him. *Heaven help him.*

"So that was just…?" Mia fingered stray strands of her hair.

"C'mon, Mia. Don't psychoanalyze me with your therapy stuff. That was what it was. A hell of a kiss."

"That was more than a kiss."

He needed a release, preferably by working out, pounding pavement, or engaging in a hell of a spar. Any type that didn't come in the form of Mia Kensington. Instead, he threw an argumentative glance her way, pushed the truck into gear, slammed his foot on the gas pedal, and burned rubber as they ate pavement.

CHAPTER FIVE

Mia studied Winters at the wheel as he drove. He acted relaxed with one hand thrown over the steering wheel like they hadn't been someone's target practice all day long, just as he had the moment before his lips met hers. She never saw it coming. Maybe wished it. Wanted it. Thought about it. But never anticipated it.

The kiss was hot and wet. Needy. His tongue slashed across hers, and his cheek stubble rasped her skin. With each graze of it, her stomach flipped. His raw masculinity rolled through her like a bulldozer. The sudden onslaught set her nerve endings afire. Her body ached for him, craving more. The whole thing lasted only moments, but it felt like a wonderful eternity. She had been lost in him. And when he drew away, a coldness slapped its frosty fingers across her skin.

She hadn't been thinking, only feeling. And she wanted to crawl back onto him. Her blood still boiled for him, but heck if she'd let him see that. He was cool and collected, and focused on the road.

She glanced at him from the corner of her eye. Oh well, she could at least pretend to be in the same ballpark of awareness. She could do disinterested and bored. Her interest was purely a subjective awareness of him as a virile man, and the result of enough adrenaline to kill an elephant. Psychology was on her side for this one.

His arm, no longer slung over her, rested close as they drove in silence. This would have been awkward if he acted like he gave a damn. Which he obviously didn't. She pouted.

He coughed, interrupting her self-diagnosing pity-party. "That *was* more than a kiss. You're right."

More than a kiss. She didn't expect him to bring it up after his understandable reaction. They were driving down the highway at breakneck speeds, and he bobbed through traffic like a man with something meaningful to prove. Tough guys like him don't get stressed? *Bullshit.*

He glanced at her, his eyes dipped down, and she felt the hot caress of his scrutiny. His foot hit the gas pedal, and the engine revved before he maneuvered to a steadier speed along the straightaway.

"I didn't mean to offend you, Winters. I understand, in your line of work, stress would be considered a fatal flaw." The jab came out as a snicker before she realized her mouth was moving.

"My line of work?" This time, he turned his head to do the once-over. His smile was hitched on one side and made his eye crinkle at the corners. Even at night, in the dimmed cabin of his truck, his steely dark eyes shined bright.

"Yeah. Whatever it is that you do." Mia flipped her wrist and rolled her eyes to the darkened passing landscape. It was useless when all she wanted to do was watch him.

"What about your line of work? A therapist, huh?" He stretched back in his seat, readjusted his long legs, and rolled his broad shoulders. Would he not do that? It was distracting. "You've been psychoanalyzing me?"

"There's always the chance." She sucked on the side of her bottom lip. Did he know his muscles flexed when he stretched?

"And the verdict?"

His timbre was so bottom-of-a-canyon deep that she wanted to slide into his lap, closing the minute space that vibrated between them. That couldn't have been less acceptable. She shook her head to clear away her distraction.

"Mia?"

Oh, right. Her verdict. Where to begin?

"You're less dangerous than you initially seemed." She tried to sound unaffected. Didn't work.

"That's your professional assessment? I seem less dangerous?" He bunched his forehead. Yup, her softball judgment was a big, fat fail. "That's like saying your trip to the airport was a nuisance, or your visit to the motel was unplanned. You can do better than that. Come on, girl. Give it to me."

He was trying to tempt her. She was sure of it. She narrowed her eyes. *If that's what he wants.*

"My professional assessment is... Well, other than your propensity to fight, your behavior doesn't deviate from normal culture. Nothing appears to be pervasive or inflexible about you. That's if you discount when you kidnapped me." She smirked. "I assume you're former military. It's obvious you're trained. And despite this save-the-day type action, you aren't narcissistic, avoidant, or paranoid." Mia took in a deep breath. It all came out so fast, who knew if it even made sense. "How's that work for you? Professionally speaking?"

He gave a curt nod. But she wasn't going to let him off that easy. Not when she wanted a reaction from him as much as she hated needing it.

"But that kiss. I don't know if you want me analyzing that. Do you?"

He grimaced. The tough guy couldn't stand the metaphoric heat. But then again, maybe she didn't want to think about it either. Because when she did, she longed to taste his perfect lips again, though she was well aware of why he kissed her. He might not call it stress, but it was a reaction based entirely on their day of bullets and bruises.

"So, Winters, what's the deal with you anyway? Who does Mister Save-The-Day Hero work for?"

He concentrated on driving and strummed his fingers across the steering wheel. His hands were rough, fingertips calloused, but they reminded her of the careful touch at the motel when he offered her a bag of ice. She jumped when he had caressed her cheek, both panic and anticipation coursed through her. It was an immediate assault to her senses. He stayed on her skin, and she…liked it.

"Should I revise and add avoidant to my assessment?" Mia struggled to keep the smile to herself.

"I'm not avoiding anything. But it's not something I normally share. That's all."

"I'm supposed to trust you. And you haven't shared a single thing." *Other than that kiss.*

"All right, already. I was a SEAL. My last deployment was Afghanistan." Winters's jaw set hard, ending the conversation.

That wasn't going to happen. She had questions. She needed to know something more about him. She needed to keep the conversation going. Otherwise, her mind had its own agenda.

"Bet you saw brutal stuff over there."

"Yeah. Guess you could say that." He shifted again and ran his hand across his face.

"So what did you do overseas?"

"Strategic and operational targets."

"Vague. A little predictable, too, I suppose."

"Oh yeah?" His eyes flashed to hers. He cocked his head, placed one fingertip on her knee, and snaked it up her thigh as fast as ice melted on a chilly day. He stopped at the junction between her legs. "I've been predictable?"

There wasn't enough oxygen getting to her lungs. She had no idea what to do, so she changed subjects with the smoothness of sandpaper, ignoring the blooming heat near his fingers. "Who do you work for now?"

He gave a hushed chuckle, drummed his fingers on her leg, and pulled his hand away. "What's it to you?"

"You're so testy." She mocked him. Childish, yes. She knew better but couldn't help it.

He cracked the knuckles on the same hand that left fire blazing on her thigh. An unbearable need to take that hand back screamed within her. Mia closed her eyes, sucked in a breath, and sent off a prayer for strength. No fortifying breath helped right now. She needed a brick wall in between them.

"Titan Group," he said. "I work for a tactical operations firm named Titan Group. We're just a bunch of ex-military and former agents dickin' around, taking on the world." He chuckled. "Normally, I wear a cape, but it was at the dry cleaners today."

Did he just make a joke? She loved that. "How about one of those spandex bodysuits?"

"You could always dream."

A quiet giggle escaped her lips. A very nice dream. "I thought you were more like GI Joe, but now that I know about the cape, you sound more like Superman. You fly from one job to the next when there's a light in the sky or the cops aren't around?"

He didn't look amused at her comparison. *Guess the jokes are over.*

"We work with clients when the normal channels of business can't get the job done. Or hell, when they won't even consider it."

"How noble of you." She smiled. "And decidedly more GI Joe."

He smirked. "You think you're cute, don't you?"

"Maybe." She could flirt a little with him and learn something. "So this bunch of guys you work with, I assume you're all deadly, virulent, and...antagonistic?"

"Nah, I prefer effective."

"And do they all rescue women and kiss them at the end of the day, too, or is that just you?" Her heart thumped in her chest, threatening to jump into her throat. *Where did all this boldness come from?*

Winters swallowed hard enough she saw his throat bob. The adrenaline was gone. All reactions should have long since fired and ceased. They should have, but she still wanted to taste him again.

Mia turned and leaned toward him, inches away from the side of his face. The truck smelled like man and guns. His raspy cheeks beckoned, begging her to nuzzle against them. The pinpricks of stubble were so close, but she stayed away.

"Nothing to say, Winters?"

Heat emanated between the scant space separating their bodies. Their gazes clashed. Her throat constricted, and the heavy beat of her heart pounded. Seconds passed, loaded with anticipation.

"We need gas." He tore his gaze from hers and eyed a tall gas station sign illuminating the night ahead.

What had she been doing? She needed to say something. "Where are we headed?"

"Virginia."

"Virginia? We're driving home? That's like another twelve hours," she said an octave higher than normal, giving an incredulous glare. She scooted to her side of the vehicle in two side pushes.

"Don't like it? Find another ride." He stopped the truck at the pump and jumped out without looking back. The harsh slam of the door echoed in her ears.

What just happened?

That was cold. He set the gas pump up and ambled into the store. No way was he off the hook after that. He would have to explain why they were booking it cross-country instead of hopping a flight home. Mia jumped out and followed behind him.

He had his phone to his ear, Dots boxes in hand, and now, he ignored her. Mia went to the drinks cooler and watched him. He had to be talking about her. She puttered around the beverage coolers, trying to listen, picking up a handful of words. *Won't be home. Work. I love you.*

Her hand flew to her mouth. *Oh my God. He's married? He has a girlfriend?*

She grabbed a soda and met him in the snack aisle. He stood awkward, pressing his phone against his ear. Mia grabbed a bag of pretzels in a big show and slammed both drink and snack into his stomach. The same rock hard stomach she noticed when he pressed against her.

"I need these." And in a flash of fury, she stormed back out to the truck.

The heck with Colby Winters.

The humid evening air clung to her. The smell of the gasoline radiated from the dirty concrete. The parking lot was empty, the pumps vacant other than Winters's truck. The distant chug, chug, chug of his pickup still filling up was the only sound she heard. No birds singing nighttime songs. No crickets calling out.

Once a safe distance from him, she turned. His steely eyes followed her. He put the phone into his pocket in a slow, deliberate move, and stood there.

He seemed skyscraper tall, just as broad in the chest, and his pants were well-worn in all the right places. A longing buzz escaped from her lips without permission. Any sign of his earlier arousal was long gone, but the pants still cupped him in a way that she could imagine. His T-shirt clung tight against his narrow waist, somehow hiding the gun she knew was tucked into the back of his jeans. How did someone so menacing come off as sexy? She shook her head. No, there would be none of that.

She didn't become a psychologist only to analyze other people's problems. She could do a serious analysis of herself and knew exactly why he was attractive. It was a simple reaction to her tumultuous day. Any other day, he would just be a jagged-around-the-edges man that she should bypass. One she might even cross the street to avoid.

She needed sleep, a couple of meals packed with carbs and calorie dense desserts, and a lazy soak in her oversized bathtub, glass of white wine in hand. She didn't need him, no matter what her body swore. After serious pampering, the chemical reaction that was her attraction to him would be an afterthought.

She looked at him again. His dark expression was analytical. No, he didn't study her, but rather, the area around her, surveying her surroundings. A feeble gas station sign illuminated the dark night. No moon or stars. A flashing neon sign in the store window advertised the lotto and smokes. Bursts of brilliant color decorated the greasy lot.

Surveying was still all wrong. He wasn't surveying. Anticipating, perhaps. He walked toward the cashier without moving his steel hard gaze from her direction.

The unnerving glare sent butterflies swarming in her stomach. As if he knew what evil lurked in the shadows. He grabbed the bag from the store clerk, then his long legs carried him back toward her. He was hurried. Distressed. His face turned darker, to something intent on destruction.

A large hand slapped her mouth, shoving a rancid rag into it, burning her swollen lips. Coarse fabric abraded her tongue. It tasted foul and smelled like the gas station—gasoline, perspiration, and stale tobacco smoke. Bile rose at the back of her throat. The urge to gag pushed at her, and her stomach convulsed. Her head was thick and groggy, her arms and legs weighted. The dim parking lot lights blurred and swirled like a Tilt-A-Whirl, and she fell into a stranger's arms.

She wanted to turn and pull away, but she couldn't fight. Her limbs were glued to her side, as if she'd drowned in cold molasses. She was suffocating and couldn't reach for Winters. He was miles away as her vision skewed sideways, blurring buildings and pumps and with now dimming colors. Bright yellows and greens turned soupy orange and tan. The dark and inky sky mixed, and she didn't know which way was up or which way was down.

The arms around her compressed her lungs, moving her against her will. Mia's feet dragged on the ground, and she couldn't lift them. One shoe slipped off, and her heel scratched over the greasy ground. Pain blossomed at her heel and ankle, radiating up her paralyzed legs.

Her attacker struggled, wheezing and stumbling. It had been easy enough for Winters to throw her over his shoulder. But now, with these rawboned arms wrapped around her tight chest, he dug into her armpits. Maybe there was still a chance Winters could get to her.

Help. Please, Winters. The thoughts were slow and hazy. Her eyelids became too heavy to hold open. The humid night air suffocated her. There were loud noises in the background, but nothing distinguishable. And it all faded to black.

CHAPTER SIX

Something felt wrong when he entered the store. His honed instincts flared. He knew it, feeling the tingle of expectation, and he was right. The clerk eyed him with more than a hint of curiosity. A hesitation. Winters always caused a little apprehension, but there was more to it. An alarmed awareness. He failed to act on his gut feeling—that intuition of danger ahead and to get in gear. He was off his game.

Few routes existed from Louisville to Northern Virginia. He chose Interstate 64 East. Safe, fast, and apparently predictable. It took them through the middle of nowhere into the Appalachian Mountains before returning to the buzz of DC's outskirts.

He pulled out his cell after returning the Glock to its holster. Two bars of service. Not bad.

The phone rang once before Jared picked up.

"What's your problem now? Let me guess. The lady landed one of her kicks." Jared laughed.

"Screw you. We had a snatch and grab. I have the package but lost the lady. They're on foot. I'm headed after them."

"Jesus, Winters. She wouldn't be your responsibility if you'd left her in the first place."

"But I didn't, and she is." His chest ached as he tried to keep his patience. Now wasn't the time to blow his shit.

"Fix this. I better not hear about Titan in some local news report."

"Just reporting in, boss man. I'll go radio silent if you want."

"What I want is to know how the fuck this happened."

The storefront windows were shattered. Fragments of glass still hung in the window panes but most of it glittered on the sidewalk in front of the store. A small fire skimmed across the gasoline soaked parking lot. At least the sparks hadn't ignited any pumps. A burglar alarm screeched, and flashing lights spun in bright distress. There wasn't another store in miles, and traffic was minimal. The lights and siren served to alert no one.

"I'm in the middle of nowhere. They anticipated our route, maybe canvassed the stops along the way, and I'm convinced the clerk called them. I don't know. Maybe they pulled the bounty hunter routine. Offered big cash." Bet the clerk regretted that phone call now. "I got a few shots off and took cover from return fire. And I thought you'd want to know what the fuck was happening. That package, this job, it's hot."

"Parker's running the scanners. We've got nothing. Doesn't look like that alarm is tied to a monitoring system. No 911 call out. And best we can tell, those security cameras are for show. We cut the phone lines. You have a quick minute to find your girl."

"10-4." Winters blew out and ended the call. *Simple package extraction, my ass.*

Seconds ticked by as he planned his next move. The clerk lay curled in a ball on the floor, hands over head, whimpering near the soda cooler. He didn't move, didn't speak. At least that wasn't a headache he needed to worry about. Winters crunched over the shards of glass and maneuvered back outside to an offensive position.

He crouched behind a thick telephone pole, weapon in hand. There had to be two additional men in the wooded area behind the gas station. It was the only way to explain how the third man had enough cover to drag Mia's limp body into the woods.

As if he asked for their locations, they fired at him. Amateurs, giving away their position. That was unexpected after the pros at the airport.

Winters peered from behind the pole and squinted toward the woods, narrowing his kill zone. Triangulating. He couldn't see the men, but he could predict beginner mistakes. Two more shots pinged out. One sparked off a nearby dumpster. The other one splintered a piece off a telephone pole.

It was exactly what he needed. Those greenhorn gunslingers should've stayed home.

He fired. Pop. Pop. One short cry. Another gurgling cough. No return fire. His shots were accurate. But were they lethal? Both shooters were down, he was sure, but he needed confirmation. He waited. One, one thousand. Two, one thousand. He wanted to wait until ten, but he got to nine and about gave up. Giving them a chance to move was torture. He shook his head, forcing himself to focus. He'd be no help if he needed a toe tag. Every second, each passing heartbeat, was too long to wait.

No sounds disturbed the night other than the now hysterical store clerk and rhythmic screech of the alarm system. Winters ducked from his safe position and ran to the dumpster. No one shot at him. He crouched to reload from a clip at his belt, then moved toward the tree line, heading down the same path as Mia.

Her kidnapper wasn't trying to hide his trail. Thirty yards to the left, Winters saw a downed man. He might have been shooting blind into the woods without a target to set his sights in, but damned if he didn't have a laser-pointed sense on where to take the fuckers down. He continued to follow the trampled brush. Mia's second shoe was in the leaves. Anger rolled through him.

Someone stepped on a branch. Seconds passed. Not even the blaring alarm sounded now. The clerk must have disarmed the system. It would be only a few minutes until police arrived at the gas station, assuming the clerk got his shit together and called 911 from a cell phone.

Another cracking sound. Winters's body jerked toward the sound and launched into motion. The kidnapper shuffled, panting hard, struggling to move with his load. This didn't make any sense. It was amateur hour. All of the noise from the man acted as a homing beacon. What happened to the professional level of the earlier team? The man sweated whiskey and tobacco. Even if he weren't making all that noise, Winters could smell him.

I'm coming, honey. Don't you worry. I'm gonna kill this fucker for you.

Silent as a breeze, he closed the gap. Winters pressed through the thick Kentucky backwoods, zeroing in on his target. Her perpetrator panted harder now. Cigarette smoke and cheap booze poured from his sweat. The man circled the same few feet, unsure what direction to commit to. He seemed disoriented, unsure of the path to his getaway vehicle. The woods were blindingly thick. It would be easy for a novice to lose focus.

Mia gasped. She sucked air like a woman hell-bent on coming round.

He saw movement through the trees, less than forty feet away. *Target acquired.* The man struggled. He was overweight and panic-stricken, glancing in every direction, knowing he was the hunted.

One stealthly step after the next, Winters drew closer. He would sidle up behind the man and snap his neck. He was the Grim Reaper right now and had never been happier to own the role.

Ten feet. He crossed a downed tree. The man stalled. Mia stirred again, registering a croaky cry. It hit Winters in the gut, blazing a fury in his blood.

Five feet. The man had no idea just how close he was to death.

Mia roared out. Her palm flew straight up, connecting with her captor's nose. Winters heard a clear crack of a nose breaking. A smile crossed his face. *That's my girl.*

Her attacker released her legs to cover his nose. She slopped back a kick that rang true to the man's nuts, doubling him over. He let go and covered his crotch. Gravity did its job, and she hit the ground, flailing, but then righted herself.

Hell, yes. No doubt. That's my girl.

Not that he needed the distraction, but Winters took full advantage of it. He snapped the man's neck and let go. His only concern was gathering Mia against his chest. He tried to calm her, brushing off the leaves and sticks clinging to her. She thrashed wild. Each limb fought for freedom.

"Let me go." Her speech was slurred, but it didn't keep her from shouting.

With one arm around her torso, he attempted to put a hand on her cheek and direct her gaze to him. To assure her that she was safe again. She bit down hard on his finger.

"Son of a bitch!" He didn't let go of her waist, but her struggle lessened a degree as she recognized him, trying to piece it together.

"What?" Her confusion evident in her unfocused eyes.

"Calm down, Mia. It's me. Colby." He hushed her, whispering in her ear and trying to counteract her reaction to whatever drug had knocked her out. His lips danced across her temple. Her silken skin was like heaven. "You were drugged, but you're okay."

She hung limp in his arm. Her hard breathing regulated, and her shaking slowed to a gentle shiver. "I thought you liked to be called Winters."

He laughed. The comment was absurd. Her mind didn't work like other victims, and it fascinated the hell out of him.

He placed her on bare feet, holding her shoulders to keep her upright. As he murmured to her, he smoothed a stray strand of hair. They had to get a move on. But he needed one more minute to confirm she was alive. That she was his. "You're a funny girl, you know that? Are you okay?"

"That's a ridiculous question." She scowled at him, trying to get her balance. Her arms counteracted her sway, outstretched and wavering. Her words slurred, but she didn't try to dust him away like a pestering fly.

Winters laughed again, a smile staying on his cheeks. *This is my kind of woman. No bullshit and plenty of sass.* She impressed him, and it wasn't the first or second time she'd pulled that card.

"Ready to get out of here, doll?"

She nodded, but still, she wobbled, bracing against him. Her palms on his chest, though unsure and drugged, did a hell of a thing to him. He ran his hands over her forearms and dropped to her waist. It was more possessive than steadying.

"Then let's go. I just need to figure out where their car might have been."

She slipped her hands over his and turned to walk. He took one step in the direction of the highway, then dropped his gaze to her bare feet and the underbrush. With an easy swing, he lofted her into his arms. She didn't fight him and fit perfect against his chest like the missing piece in a jigsaw puzzle.

She rubbed against his shoulder, bemoaning her lack of strength and judgment. He ignored her words and focused on her nuzzling him. There was no denying how satisfying it was to hold her.

"Why *their car*? I want our truck."

Her rasp wasn't meant to be seductive. He knew that. It shouldn't have done a thing to turn him on. But it sounded like a *morning after* rasp, all scratchy and grated, and it made him twitchy and turned-on.

What the hell was his problem? Awareness was key to their survival. Her survival.

Tonight, he was out of character, starting with missing the signs of impending assault, all the way up to here and now. He shouldn't be running around with a hard-on. His concentration should've been laser-beam focused on their safety and the disk in his back pocket.

He cleared his throat and foraged a path through the woods. "I have to assume the cops are seconds away from the gas station. So, forget our pickup truck. It was rented with an alias anyway. No biggie."

"Colby?"

"Yes, doll?"

He stepped through the thicket and pushed low-hanging branches away from her. She nestled against his chest.

"Thank you for saving me. Again." She paused for a heartbeat. "Is it going to stop?"

The innocence in her words killed him. He growled with heated emotion. Anger. Lust. Possessiveness. "Hell, yes, it's going to stop. So don't worry about it. I'm going to fix all of it."

Winters dropped his chin to her silky, tangled hair and breathed her in. Her hair pressed against his skin, tempting his control. Despite the day, she still smelled like butterscotch and vanilla. He heard a sigh that caught him off guard. It was his sigh. He rolled his eyes but sighed again, kissing her forehead and letting it linger.

She tightened her muscles in his arms and stiffened. "Please don't do that."

"What? Kiss you?" He knew he shouldn't have. He stepped over more branches and pushed another thorny branch away from her. Why did he kiss her just now? She was scared, and he was on the job. If there was a better reminder of that than a shootout at a gas station, he didn't know what it was.

"Yeah, just don't." Her body remained as still as a sniper blending into brush.

"I'm sorry about that. I don't know what came over me." That was the hundredth apology for the day. It had to be a record considering he apologized… never, whether he should have or not. Strange. Mia tested him in a way he didn't know possible. Hell. Strange didn't even begin to describe it.

"You should be sorry." She looked tart. Her lips parsed together, and the bridge of her nose scrunched in a wrinkle.

That was one confusing look. This was why he shouldn't mix it up with her. Why he didn't mix it up with any woman who wanted more than an exchange of first names. Then again, he liked knowing that Mia was Mia Kensington. *Whatever*. His blood sugar must've been low or something. He continued to cover ground in search of the car.

"Wanna explain the attitude?" Was he auditioning for Dr. Phil's job? Christ.

"I heard you back at the gas station. *I love you?*" She mocked. "I heard you talking to your wife or girlfriend or whatever."

He laughed. *This shit's funny.* Of course she heard him. He knew she was too close. This was funny, but he kept that to himself, instead opting to tighten his hold. More of a hug, really.

An abandoned car sat on an access road, closed the distance like he just saw a sign screaming it was two-for-one freebie day at Glock and Company. She fought the hold, pushing her shoulders away from him, but he couldn't have cared less, and he worked to not chuckle out loud.

"You're cute when you're jealous," he said and kissed her nose.

She hissed and squirmed in his arms again. Her backside unintentionally rubbed on his forearm.

Christ, he might not live through this day. "Mia, would you cut that out? You're distracting me."

"No. I'm out of here." Rub, rub, rub.

"Right. And where you going?"

"It doesn't concern you."

She was too much. Enough with all the snark and scoots. They killed him. With each sway of her backside, he was digging his grave. Each time he hit the rocky bottom, he'd just start over fresh.

He stopped at the car. "Here you go. Down as you requested. Your chariot awaits."

She crossed her arms and tapped a bare foot.

"Fine. We can do this again." He scooped her up, jacked open the passenger door, and plopped her in, then moved to the driver's seat. The keys were in the ignition. *Excellent—easier than hot-wiring the thing*. He twisted the key. The sedan turned over and idled. The radio came on. Elton John's "Can You Feel the Love Tonight".

Funny. So very funny.

"I can feel something." Mia pressed buttons on the radio. Static and garbled stations filtered in through the speakers.

"You're testy when you're like this. It's cute." He repositioned his chair and chuckled. "This whole jealous thing is adorable."

She jammed the buttons on the radio harder. "Jealous? You're a piece of work. Stop talking to me."

"You're mad that we kissed. That *you* grabbed *me*. Not used to the whole white knight thing? Or are you upset that you were turned on in the truck?" He slid the tip of a finger from her cheek to her chin. She batted it away, hard.

"White knight? Are you insane?"

She glared at him. Oh, if looks could kill, Winters would've been on the next bus to Morgue City.

"Some would say yes to both white knight and insane. But from you, I'll take strategic, operational genius. Handsome man who keeps saving you. Take your pick."

"There's something wrong with you."

"I thought you analyzed me already and turned up empty-handed."

"That was before I knew you."

"And where is all this coming from again? Oh yeah, cause you were eavesdropping and heard me say I love you."

She turned up the static on the radio loud enough it hurt his ears. Calling her out wasn't the best move he had in his arsenal but better than ignoring her.

He turned the volume down, steered them back on to the road with one hand draped over the steering wheel, and followed the road's turn as it passed by the gas station. As expected, blue and red flashing lights flooded the area. Local troopers combed through the store and his truck, wondering what the hell just happened in their one gas station, two stop light town.

If they hadn't found the bodies already, they'd be stumped. Podunk Kentucky didn't see a lot of shootouts, and it didn't have a regular body count.

CHAPTER SEVEN

After the gas station debacle and two separate motel incidents, Diego Cortes didn't have the disk or the lady. She was on the run with a proficient partner. Sweat soaked through his shirt. If El Jefe knew of his failures, it would be a writ of execution. Juan Carlos Silva was as vicious as he was creative. This was bad, but he could salvage it. Diego's reputation and beating heart were on the line, and if ever there were a chance to prove he was worthy, it was now.

Representing the Silva Cartel was an honor. He wouldn't fail.

The Lady of the Rosary medallion under his collar stuck to his chest. He pulled it out and flipped the medal between his fingers. *Santa Madre de Dios, please help.*

Diego was the last man standing and, like he was told by Senor Silva, he needed to use his brains. He should have done that before, but, no, his head was too big. Hiring local criminals was a mistake. More than a mistake. They were amateurs. And now, they were dead. He'd handed them a handful of bills after trolling for sordid men jonesing for an American dollar. He should have found an investment instead of a quick fix.

He knew Senor Silva better than most. Diego slaved under his tutelage, earned his trust, and swore to the Virgin Mary his loyalty. If he didn't complete his task, Senor Silva would take immense pleasure in his death. He would nurse a crystal glass of high priced liquor, bleed him out, and delight in calling his mama. Senor would torture her, recounting how Diego failed the Silva cartel. Their family, his legacy obliterated. How his mama would weep, mourning for so many reasons.

No. Success must happen. The holy medallion slipped back under his shirt, tangling in his chest hair. It pulled, ripped a hair loose at the root, and reminded him this sting was a mosquito bite compared to what could happen.

He prayed for strengths and triumph. *Santa Maria, Madre de Dios.*

Winters eyed Mia. She rolled the window down, slapping the button as it shorted out, twice. He needed to do the same, anything to air out the stench of leftover fast food and stale smoke. The car was disgusting. The steering wheel was sticky, and empty beer cans rolled on the floorboards. He needed to wash his hands pronto. This clunker was foul, but according to Titan, not hot.

"So who do you love, Colby?"

Her question swung him out of autopilot. He wouldn't tell her the truth. "What's it to you?"

"Never mind. You're such a jackass." She huffed, pushed further away from him against the car door. Her foot shoved a beer can aside. She sucked on her lip, and he could all but taste the resentment. Mia had mastered the art of a first-rate sulk, and it tested his resolve.

"Wow. You come off as so put together and analytical. I'm surprised you've resulted to name calling."

"You don't know me."

"Obviously," he said.

She turned to face him. "I have no idea who you are. I have no idea who you love. And I have no idea why…"

"Why do you care?" That was way too harsh. But he didn't want to answer her question. He couldn't. He needed to protect himself. He should have stuck with the brilliant plan of lies.

"I already said never mind. Just leave me alone."

He didn't want to leave her alone. That was part of the problem. Winters checked over his shoulder before changing lanes, stealing a glance at her pouting lip and tight eyebrows. Tears brimmed on her bottom eyelids. *I'm an asshole.* He looked again. Yup, tears were idling up for a free fall. *Oh hell. Don't do that. I can't stand your tears.*

But as soon as he thought it, he cringed. He didn't need her in his life. He shouldn't share anything personal. It was easier to fight with her than speak the truth, but the bickering wasn't worth her hurt feelings.

Winters shook his head at what he was about to say. His secrets were bubbling free. His typical MO abandoned him miles ago. Right now, he'd do anything to get rid of those wet eyes.

"Don't get your panties in a twist, Mia. I was talking to my *mom*."

Could he not keep his mouth shut? Work world. Personal life. Two very separate things. The two worlds didn't comingle. They shouldn't. For a million reasons, they simply could not. Loose lips sink ships. His *ship* was far too precious to make vulnerable. But here he was, unable to keep his lips sealed. All because some beautiful babe pouted? He glanced at her. Yeah, her angelic face would do it.

Days ago, that revelation was implausible. Today, no other choice existed. He'd knock out her hurt and jealousy like he took out the enemy who attacked her.

He opened his trap to again to explain. "My—"

"Your mom? Are you kidding me? Big, tough badass calls his mommy when he can't come home from work? You're worse than I thought. I didn't think my asshole meter was this far off."

Like an attacking rattler, she had drawn back and fired with spitting accuracy. Given this once in a lifetime bout of honesty, he didn't see it coming. But now that she'd made her move, it was game on.

"My, my, Miss Mia. You're about to get a taste of foot in mouth syndrome."

"Try me."

"With pleasure, babe. My mom *babysits* for me, doll. I have a daughter. A baby. Tiny tyke. Cute as she can be. And my mom watches her when I work."

Mia's jaw fell wide open. Ding, ding, ding. That was what he wanted to see. Mia was dumbstruck—and pretty as hell—

but with nothing sassy to say. One of his prouder moments of the day.

Still, his gut churned, anxious over his revelations. He was stupid to say this much. Yet, somehow he needed her validation. He cast a glance her way, hoping for her reaction to justify his trust.

"I didn't know." Mia shifted on the vinyl car seat, crossing her ankles, and crunching an empty fast food wrapper.

"Why would you know?"

"You don't seem like the fatherly type."

"I bet I don't seem like a lot of things."

She gaped. Score one for Team Winters. He couldn't shake his grin. Hell, if he'd known he could smile this much. His cheeks hurt. They were possibly the only muscle he didn't work out on the regular.

"And the baby's mother is?"

"It's complicated." The answer was an automatic defense mechanism. His mouth again spoke before his mind gave it the okay to proceed. His attitude was meant to protect his baby but served only to deflate Mia.

She sat still, hands folded in her lap, awaiting a simple explanation. Her therapist brain must've been in psychoanalytic overdrive. Simple was the furthest thing from the truth. He was already facing deep waters. Time to swan dive. "My line of work leads me straight to hell on a better than average day."

Mia watched him in the dark car. He changed lanes needlessly, rubbing the back of his neck, then checked all his mirrors again, adjusting the rearview even though it was fine. Nerves punched, and he thought about backpedaling. "I like to keep my private life private."

She still didn't say anything. Must've been the therapist in her working him over. And, boy, she was good. He could barely keep the story contained. He fidgeted with the temperature controls and scanned the radio stations. Nothing but static. *Stupid mountains*. Mia remained quiet, and he couldn't find anything to do other than recount the story. Ears over asshole, Winters dove into the truth.

"We busted up a very bad situation. Human traffickers, sex trade fuckers. There weren't a lot of girls we could save, but we got some safe, back to the States. Everyone picked up new identities. Except one lady. A girl, in all honesty. She wouldn't. Her name was Vanessa, and she was a beauty queen look-alike with a brass set of— She was a tough one. Kind of like you." He paused, pissed his mouth ran off again before the brain gave a thumbs-up. "Anyway, she wasn't going to give up her life. College. Friends. Though she had no family to speak of. Little did I know, she was pregnant. No idea who the father was. They did bad things to her."

"That's horrible." Mia was a thousand notches quieter than when she doled out her quips.

"Vanessa went back to college in Cali, and that was the last time I heard from her. A few months later, California Child Protective Services showed up on my doorstep, newborn and diaper bag in tow. Vanessa died *mysteriously*. She apparently listed me as the father. And in her will, she left a key to a safety deposit box."

Mia didn't say a word. He wasn't even sure she was breathing.

"You tell me how many college girls write out a will. None. She knew those fuckers tracked her. She knew if anything happened to her that baby would be safe with me. I found a note in the safety deposit box explaining everything to me. So that's who I love. My mom and my daughter."

Static played on the radio. He didn't make a move to change the dial, concentrating on the road. It was the first time he told the story to a stranger. Right now, she was anything but. Anxiety gave way to relief. Somehow, he was content in his decision to enlighten Mia.

She slid both her warm hands over his nearest forearm. His skin tingled and the rush carried into his chest.

"Colby, I was way off base. I'm sorry."

"There's no way you'd know. Anyway, Clara's single-digits months old. She's my world. And I'm lucky to have my mom and trustworthy peeps around. That trust now extends to you. It's better you know anyway."

"Why's that?"

He'd have to clue her in to his op plan eventually. What a plan…if it could be called that.

"'Cause I'm bringing you to my place until we figure out what the hell is going on. It'd be a shade past awkward if I roll up, and all of the sudden, you have to hang with my family."

"We're going to your home?" Her fingers clenched, her nails biting into him.

He ignored her reaction and smiled in the dark. "It's the safest place I know. I have to stash us off the grid. I've never brought anyone there before, other than family and the team, so this is an adventure for both of us."

If Mia had guessed what type of person Colby was, she would've been wrong. If she guessed what would transpire after deciding to get that disk in Kentucky and go for a cross-country ride with him, she'd have been wrong on that account also. No, actually, she'd have been dead.

They barreled down the highway, on the way to his home. To his *family*. She shook off a shudder. No one would describe her as family oriented. Family conjured up the worst memories, and even in her therapy practice, she held her nose when discussing it. What kind of psychologist did that make her? Not one worthy of the distinctions she somehow pulled off.

Then again, her family wasn't on the agenda. He wasn't trying to enmesh her into his, nor was he *taking her home*. He was keeping her safe. Keeping her alive. Right about now, that was worthy of a champagne toast and kiss on the lips. Or cheeks. Cheeks would be safer around him.

Exhaustion clouded her mind, but still, she studied him, thinking of their kisses. He concentrated on the dark highway, only the dashboard lights illuminating the chiseled hardness in his jaw. It looked more than capable of taking a punch. He was none the worse from earlier. And those lips. They promised to keep her safe. The whole act was… attractive. In an evolutionary sense. Women were attracted to alpha males for biologic reasons.

Besides, he wasn't her type. Safe and stable worked just fine. Though his callous, foreboding act was interesting. She'd give him that. Add that to his impermeable wall breaking down, well, it made her want to curl up in his arms. *This is insane*. But psychologically speaking, her reaction made sense.

Dang his bad boy charm.

Heat crawled up her neck, and her nipples tightened. What she wouldn't do to feel his kiss again. She brushed her fingers over her mouth. It tingled with his memory. The adrenaline had disappeared, but the desire stayed alive. Too bad he wouldn't kiss her like that again. Men like him used women to expend energy. The action was gone, and his interest in her morphed into the sexual equivalent of oatmeal. Tasteless, colorless, and only appetizing if starving. With that understanding, her want froze and eyes sealed tight against the sight of him in the dim dashboard light.

CHAPTER EIGHT

Each s-turn on the sharp mountains road swayed Mia into her seatbelt. Her head bumped the window, waking her. With a sleepy yawn, she rubbed her eyes and fingered her knotted hair. He'd been watching her for hours, just as long as he'd observed the passing white lines speed by in a blur.

Damn if she wasn't something to stare at, even in the dark, and she made cute noises in her sleep. Precious breaths and sleep-drenched murmurs. He'd remember those long after this op was over.

He had fidgeted with the temperature gauge, not wanting her to be too cold. He kept the radio quiet, just loud enough so he could hear it and stay awake, or to distract his mind from her. Whatever. It didn't help.

"What time is it?" Her slumber-soaked question didn't sound rested. It was the same tired keel as before she passed out. Mia needed real food and real sleep. She needed to get away from this road trip from hell. His on-the-job lifestyle was pragmatic. Sleep when necessary, and down gas station purchased protein bars and Dots. The Dots alone could suffice him, and sleep was overrated. But Mia needed more. Hell, she deserved better.

"Colby? Is that clock right?" They'd be much closer to their destination if that console timepiece was anywhere near correct.

He checked his wristwatch. "Nope. We should be further along, but with our adventure at the gas station, we lost major time." He paused. "So I've been thinking, you handled yourself well today. Not many people have your aplomb."

"Aplomb?" She asked in a deadpan voice.

"Oh, big word. Didn't think I had a brainy side, huh, doll?"

"I'm sure you do."

"That's all right. You just think of me as all brawn, saving that cute ass of yours from thugs. What was it, once, twice? After the airport. A shootout at the motel. I'll be your hero." He nudged her shoulder, anything to touch her again. "If that's how you see me."

"Well, don't forget the gas station." She bumped her shoulder back against him. "I've had a very tough day. The least you can do is remember *all* my near death experiences."

"Of course. It slipped my mind." He nudged her for a second time. Christ, what was this? A grade school playground? Should he pull her hair next? He laughed, his smile teasing. "Let me get this right. Not many people are kidnapped, gassed, shot at, and grabbed. Basically, rescued over and over."

He winked at her through the darkness.

"Yeah, my day sucked. But it's a typical nine-to-five for you?"

This drive flew by when she was awake. Hell, it did the same when she slept. He'd never had an entertaining operational road trip. Nor had he ever shared. Fessing about his daughter was mindboggling. He never admired a victim before either. She handled it all, airport to gas station, unlike a wimped-out casualty.

"I think you're strong, Mia. Way stronger than I gave you credit for at the airport, when you looked all librarian-like." He waited, knowing there was more to be said, and it would kill the mood. One knuckle at a time, he made them crack, then shifted in his seat.

"What aren't you telling me?"

How did she read his mind? "Why do you think I'm keeping something from you?"

She faced him, but he kept his eyes on the broken white lines. "You know guns, and I know body language. Spit it out, big boy."

He checked the rearview mirror again.

"Colby."

"All right, I'll level with you." She was a mind reader of sorts. That could pose probs. "We're in the middle of nowhere, and there isn't another town for a hundred miles. Only truck stops and motels line this highway."

"Stop with the tour guide routine. You aren't telling me anything I haven't noticed. I thought I was full of aplomb and stuff like that. Please, go on. Tell me."

He needed more time to feel her out. But if she thought she could handle it…he guessed he agreed. Fine. Whatever. He'd give it to her straight.

"We picked up another tail a while back. I'm surprised it took them this long to find us, but they did. And so this is what we've got to deal with now."

She didn't check the side view mirror. Smart girl. Nor did she panic. Her breathing didn't change, and as best he could tell, she remained calm.

"Why didn't you just tell me that?"

"I didn't want you plastered to the windows like I promised you Gucci was falling from the sky. If you did that, you might as well have hung a sign up that said *we see you*."

"I'm the Gucci type?"

"You're a woman. I don't know." He shrugged.

"Typical." She laughed. "You should have said don't look, but we've got a situation."

"Put your shrink hat on. You still think that's what would have happened?"

She shook her head. "No. I would have checked."

"That was my dilemma. Though you weren't a problem." He snuck a glance at her. Picture perfect composure. "I'd run them off the road, but these dog-leg turns are tricky, and you're in the car. So we don't out run 'em. We draw them out and eliminate the problem."

"Eliminate the problem?"

Winters tilted his head. Spelling it out wasn't going to happen. She could use her imagination if she needed further clarification.

"Extrapolate, Mia." He massaged his neck, pushing away tension. "They've sped past us, dropped back, and paced us, maintaining a variable visual since we crossed the state line. Next time they drop back, I'll pull into a truck stop. They'll find us. Guaranteed. I'll deal with the situation, and we'll hit the road again. Sound like a plan?"

She jutted her chin up. "Whatever you need me to do, I'll handle fine. I'm not helpless."

"I noticed that about fifteen hours ago."

He reached over to put his hand over hers, interlacing their fingers. Tingles skipped up his arm. He hadn't pulled a move like that since he got a set of wheels in high school. His end goal had been trying to nail some action. Her hand squeezed his, cascading another rush of sensation along his skin. Maybe his goals hadn't changed that much, but it felt a little bizarre. Less about the end goal and more about the moment. Or some shit like that.

Mia turned in her seat, still keeping her hand in his. "You're so casual."

"You want me to get all triggered up?" He checked the mirror for the tails again. He'd be ready, even if the woman next to him was distraction-worthy.

"You're acting like someone isn't trying to kill us."

"It's not the first time, and it's sure as hell not going to be the last. I won't let anyone hurt you." God help the men chasing her. "And I don't scare."

His thumb caressed the top of her hand. Engaging the enemy was an expected part of his operational to do list, but it must have been a nightmare for her. He wanted her to feel safe with him. He wanted her to trust him.

"But I'm scared, Colby." Mia chewed her bottom lip.

"I know you are. Don't worry. I promise you, it'll be okay." He tightened his grip and brought her fist to his mouth. He kissed her knuckles and pressed her folded fingers against his lips. She was sweet, but under it all, she was a woman who could hold her own. He should have known that when she wielded her kneecap as a weapon. Mia blasted every one of his preconceived notions. Untrained women in the field weren't weak as he assumed.

A motel sign illuminated the night with a flashing neon sign. Vacancy. Truckers welcome. Free cable. Karaoke bar. He eased the car off the highway and into a parking lot lined with a handful of big rigs.

He put the car in park in front of the motel. "You're coming with me. I'm not leaving you alone again."

She crunched her feet against a fast food bag. "I don't have shoes to wear."

"Them's the breaks, doll. Barefoot and safe. Come on now. We'll be fast." The plan he was piecing together didn't allow much time. Convincing her to move wasn't in the plan at all.

"I'm going to stand out. My clothes are tattered." She stared down and rubbed her hands over the shirt.

His lips pressed into a tight line, and he resisted the urge to grab and carry her around again. They were past that type of interaction. But it would've been far more expedient. Coaxing wasn't his forte, and he had to make fast work of it. He took a deep breath.

"Honey, this truck stop has seen far worse. Trust me. And if someone pays too much attention to you, I'll distract them. Hell, I might just pummel their face."

She tilted her head, her hair obscuring part of her smile. "I thought you were always calm in the face of danger."

He tried not to blow out a frustrated breath but failed in grand fashion. Time was speeding by, and she still hadn't moved. "Undue attention at your expense is their mistake. As far as anyone is concerned, you're mine. You're *with* me. And I'd consider it a personal affront if they looked at you any way you don't like. Or any way I don't like."

His blood felt thick in his veins. Given their day, he would've considered killing someone who even offended her, and he wouldn't have been sorry about it. That was who he was, a warrior, and she was… Mia was a priority.

"Oh." She opened her door a crack, signaling her willingness to make a public appearance, and turned back to him. "All right. Let's do this."

She smoothed her hands over her sweater. Even barefoot in mussed up clothes, she personified grace. Check that. The woman defined understated sexy. He didn't know why it wasn't so apparent at first.

The torn shirt worked for his attention. It'd be so easy to finish the rip, tearing it off of her. Fuck, man, he couldn't tear his eyes from her body. She might have been a priority, but she was the best looking one he'd ever seen.

"Colby?"

He blinked, more than aware he was busted staring at her tits.

"You're distracting, Mia. You know that? Every time I look at you—never mind. Forget it. Let's do this."

He jumped out and walked to her side, pulled the door wide open, and she slid out. With her hand in his, they made their way to the front desk. The freckled-face clerk eyed her up and down. Mia buried her cheek against his chest. She fit perfect. Their bodies were the right mix of spark and C4. Together, there was the potential for explosions.

He made a specific room request, handed over a few Benjamins, and watched for incoming assaults.

"Sir, your receipt and room key. Are you sure you want a backside room? There's a karaoke bar back there. It's loud, and the drunks are nasty. Nothing will slow down 'til after five in the morning."

Winters grunted his lack of concern. It was time to loiter and keep a visual on the incoming traffic. The only flaw in this plan was the proximity to a private room and bed. But that wasn't why they were there. He should repeat that mantra until the tangos arrived.

The clerk directed them out the reception area. "King-size bed. Non-smoking. Your room is back out the front and around the side. Just follow the music from the bar."

King-size bed. His dick went semi-hard, and he stifled a groan. *Stop thinking about her naked.* It wasn't the time.

Winters nodded his appreciation to the clerk and leaned close to Mia's ear. His mouth brushed her lobe. It took more strength than he expected to keep from nipping her earlobe. "Come on, doll. Let's draw 'em out."

CHAPTER NINE

Winters's plan wasn't perfect, but it was a solid start. Mia padded barefoot with her hands clasped tight in his grip. The soft slap against the tile floor took him away from the dirty reception area. The sound was pure, echoing against the seedy undertones of the motel. It was a complete contradiction, just like her genuine presence in his less than stable life.

They walked outside to a starless night. The faraway sounds of cars were almost drowned out by the thump of tunes pouring from the nearby bar. Winters made a beeline for their car and idled them to the darkest corner of the motel.

"You ready?" he asked. Man, did he not want to put her in this position.

"Not much choice."

"True. Let's get this shit over with." He opened the door, and she did the same.

He scoped out their locale. Shadows noted. Vehicles cataloged. Nothing out of place. She stood by the hood ornament, bending it down and letting it bounce back up. She was nervous. He couldn't blame her. This was an offensive attack. Her first with him. Probably her first ever.

"Mia, you ready?"

"You already asked me that." Her voice was tense. He wished he could wash it away.

"This is going down easy. I don't want you to worry. You got me?"

She put her hand on his belt buckle. "Yeah, got you."

That wasn't what he meant it, nor how she probably meant it, but it was fine by him. *Hold on to me anytime*. "Let's move boots, babe."

Winters brought them to a vacant corner of the motel and drew her in front of him. He pressed against the brick wall, pulling her close to his chest and could see all entry points here. The driveway. Front and rear entrances of the bar.

She laid her weight against him and let out a long, tired breath. Nothing left to do except wait. And breathe in her vanilla and butterscotch. Their enemy could roll up anytime, and he'd fight fast and furious, but right now, he needed this. Mia leaned against his hooked arm and looked up, tilting her chin.

"You okay?" he asked. Peppering her with the same questions was pointless, but he couldn't stop.

"Tired. That's all."

"I'm sorry I've had to push you so hard." Soon as this was over, he'd make sure she had anything she needed. The woman would be pampered. No doubt.

"I didn't mean to complain. I hate… All of this. You wouldn't be here if it weren't for me."

That was her concern? "Hell, Mia. It's not like that."

What was it like? *Oh, man.* He had a thing for her in a bad way. Winters bent his head toward her. Their foreheads kissed, and there was no question. While she was with him, she was his. His to protect. His to savor. A woman like Mia was rare. At least he had brains enough to notice.

He never should've put her in this position. He could've packed her off in a plane, back toward the East Coast. Someone from Titan could've kept her safe while he finished his original job. But selfishness and curiosity made it so he wouldn't push her away. He couldn't, because an irrepressible desire consumed him, powering lust through his veins.

"Colby." Her hushed whisper tickled his skin. "What are we going to do?"

His pulse thumped in his neck, and he tightened the forearm wrapped around her waist, melding her onto him.

I'm on the job. Serious danger ahead.

He'd missed it before and couldn't let that happen again. No time for arousal. No time for fantasies.

Images flooded his brain, searing his senses. He remembered the taste of her tongue. Red-hot cinnamon. A sweet, delicious burn of aphrodisia.

What were they going to do? Where to begin... A million ideas popped to mind, starting with making good use of the wall behind him.

No woman had pressed against him like this, so pliable, supple, and luscious. They had always draped him like sex kittens on steroids. Those other women were as over-sexed and one-dimensional as they were obvious, all self-fulfilling prophecies, and they were the definitive opposite of Mia Kensington.

Before Mia's hands explored him, before her beautiful body had even disrobed, she toyed with his mind like it was the first of many playgrounds. And he wanted to play so bad.

"I've started a list." His lips flitted over hers. "Want me to share?"

Her eyelashes fluttered. "What kind of list?"

"I have you thirty feet from a bed. What kind of list do you—" A drunken couple stumbled out of the bar. Actually, more likely a john and a pro. He should have seen them before he heard them. "More on the list later, doll."

Men were coming to hurt her, and his hard-on could pick another time for games.

"Okay, Mia, here's what we're going to do. When they pull up, act like we let loose. We had too many drinks." He motioned to the karaoke bar with a tip of his head, then dipped his lips to her neck, lingering under her ear. "I'm convincing you to come to my room. You're not putting up too much of a fight. Just enough to keep it fun."

He nipped her earlobe, and she took a tiny gasp. It made his gut jump. Her taste drugged him, intoxicated him. Temptation was a cruel mistress. Giving him a little and making him wait.

"That's your plan?"

"Not my whole plan, no. But that's the part you have to play." He traced the slide of her neck. "Think you can act mildly interested?"

"You're crazy." Her voice was husky. "Men are trying to kill us. How can you think about sex?"

"You're not?"

"I'm... I'm—"

"You're what? I'm getting into character. You should give it a try."

"You're rubbing your hard-on against me, is what you're doing."

"All part of my cover. Believable, huh?" Her innocent act was toast. She was far more like Jessica Rabbit than Snow White. "If I tried to drag you off to bed right this second, you wouldn't join me?"

There was only one answer. He knew it. Felt it as sure as he felt her body mold against him. She couldn't fight their hunger either.

Her breaths escalated. The quick rise and fall of her breasts fueled him. Winters cupped her chin in his hands, palms caressing her cheeks. Sweet Mia. If he could freeze this moment, it'd be one he'd put on repeat.

"I would," she whispered. "But..."

"Forget everything else. It's just you and me." He thumbed her lips, dragging the bottom one down.

Slowly, his hands drifted into her hair. Lust hung heavy in the cool night air. Her dark lashes fluttered, and her hard nipples pressed against his chest.

How beautiful would she be naked? How would she feel? Impossibly smooth. He would whisk across her sensitive spots, watching those succulent breasts rise and fall in anticipation. He would make sure she ached for him. As much as he ached now.

His fingers tangled into her hair, and Mia leaned her head back, heavy lidded and heady breaths.

"Shouldn't you watch for the bad guys instead of torturing me?" Her eyes were sealed shut, defenseless.

His lips grazed her neck, and she purred, the sinful sound acting as a deft stroke to his already engorged shaft.

"You don't think I can multi-task?" He kissed behind her ear, dancing his mouth down her neck. It was a tease. A simple promise of what was to come. When he had a moment to concentrate on her, he'd do whatever it took—lick, kiss, caress, and suck—to make her cry out for him.

His fingers slid to her nape, trailing to the front of her shirt. The fabric felt fragile under his palms. He was losing a battle to a ripped shirt on a pretty girl, but revenge would be amazing.

"How can you do this," she nudged her head down to where he nuzzled his erection, "and pay attention to anything else?"

"Can you imagine what it's going to be like between us when I don't have to worry about anyone but you?"

A smile bloomed but before Mia could respond, the faraway sound of tires crushing gravel flittered through the parking lot. She tensed in his arms. Her body now rigid as the brick wall he leaned against.

"Did you hear that?" she asked, all arousal siphoned away.

"I've got it. Don't you worry about a thing."

He closed his eyes and inhaled deeply. Time for his game face. He would fight and maim, whatever the hell it took to end up in that motel room alone with her.

A vehicle moved to the far side of the lot and idle. "That's our guy. Just relax and stay with me."

"I can't relax. I don't know what to do."

"Yes, you do."

Her eyes darted toward the night sky, panicked, and her muscles morphed into cement slabs.

"You handled yourself just fine earlier." He watched their enemy over her shoulder and gave her a squeeze. *It's in you to pull this off.* "You were a fighter. Just do what you did before."

"Tell me what's going on, Colby."

"You want a line by line?" Knowledge was control. That made sense. He fingered the tear in the fabric at the top of her shirt, playing his part as a distracted drunk. The shirt was toast very soon.

She nodded. His ears strained to hear an engine cut off.

"Two guys. They see us."

She tensed again.

"Come on, girl. Relax with me. They can't know we see them."

His hands ran down her back, massaging her not-so-imaginary knots. Her tense muscles began to relax, melting all over again.

"There you go. We're going to walk around the corner soon and disappear from their line of sight after they get out of their car. I need you to play it up. Remember. I'm seducing you. You're caving. When we round the corner, I'll have to let you go to take care of this."

"Don't get hurt." She locked eyes with him, complete seriousness clouding her face.

Really? She didn't mean to lob insults, right? He choked out a harsh laugh and shook his head. "Mia, I'm taking offense to that, so you know. You need to say something like *go get 'em, killer* or *my, your muscles are big.*"

She moved her palms over his arms. "My your muscles are so big."

Her nervous laughter electrified him, making him want to prove she was protected. Nothing would harm her. Ever.

"Now you're getting the idea."

"Just don't forget you're not invincible." Her smile faltered. "Okay?"

What was up with the challenges? Her timing wasn't spectacular. He'd have to bring that up when a better moment presented itself.

"I'm a lot of things, doll. But worried about getting hurt ain't one of them. Now, if you don't mind, feed me macho shit or shut that pretty trap of yours."

Crazy woman. Worrying about him. Questioning him.

"All right, here we go." He pushed them from the wall. "Time to convince our audience we're headed to bed."

She took a step back, pulling from him, batting at his bicep. He mirrored her dance, tugged on her shirt, and tried to close the distance toward the corner of the motel.

It wasn't a hard role to play. He wanted in that motel room more than he'd ever wanted a woman in a bed.

Her head dropped back. Fake, flirtatious laughter floated in the air as she played her role well. Their game ignited

Winters's contempt for the men watching them. Watching her. She was a sight to see, and he'd hurt them for their mere enjoyment.

He lifted her in one fluid motion, her bare feet fluttering inches over the ground, and he walked backwards, one slow step at a time, nuzzling the rasp of his cheek against her skin.

Training was his savior as she moaned for him. If he didn't have a pinpoint focus on the enemy, he'd be out of control, attempting anything and everything to hear that sound again and again and again.

They rounded the corner, and Winters pinned Mia against the wall, caging her. She had nowhere to go, yet his breath caught in his throat at the sheer power she held over him.

"You're sexy as sin." He placed a finger over her mouth in a show of silence.

His rough finger looked harsh against her lips. He wished her tongue would flick out and run the length of his finger onto his palm. He imagined the wet heat wicking across his skin, and it shot all the way to his cock. Talk about inappropriate timing for a dirty fantasy.

Mia untangled herself from his hold without complaint and without any more ludicrous questions about his safety. She had no idea what thoughts crossed his mind. He had to laugh, then turned toward the corner.

Winters heard enemy footsteps fast approaching. He held his hand up to her, reissuing the order to stay put and mum.

The first man came broadside. Winters struck out at him, fist balled with lightning-like wrath. Like a shot of caffeine, it rushed through him with energizing satisfaction.

The second man rushed into the fight, uncoordinated. Winters's punch plowed into doughy flesh. It gave a dull thud as the man stumbled back and dropped.

Man number one reappeared, and Winters grabbed his throat, forcing his carotid artery closed. He needed another ten seconds until the man would go limp. It'd be great if man number two would take longer than that to rebound. Trying to keep the other man down, Winters heeled number two's face onto the pavement. Just a little more time.

Five. Four. Three. Go to sleep, fucker.

Man one gasped against Winters's hold, eyes bulging and veins popping. Sweat poured off him, strings of saliva running out the side of his open mouth. *Shit.* Man number two rolled loose and jumped back to his feet, jabbing with a knife.

Winters kept his hand on the man's throat. Waiting for lights out. He evaded a stab, jumping to the side in this game of Swiss Army hopscotch. The need to kill crawled through him. He wanted them to pay but didn't need the overkill. Mia shouldn't witness the aftereffects of it.

And goodnight. Man one was definitely out. His legs stopped flailing. His arms hung limp. Winters dropped him onto the ground. *One down, one to go.*

Man number two tried for another stab. Winters snagged the offending hand, twisting an arm back and up. The knife clattered to the parking lot. The man's shoulder popped. He howled. Winters landed a punch to his head, knocking him silent, then dropped him on top of the other. *Assholes. You shouldn't have fucked with my girl.*

CHAPTER TEN

Winters toed the bodies, rummaged through their pockets, and pulled out a set of car keys before he turned to Mia. Frozen in place, she hadn't moved from the wall, manning her assigned spot. Her jaw was tight, her lips pressed into a straight line, and her eyes as round as the backlit O in the motel sign high overhead. Her skin had paled in the dark night.

Ah, man. He'd worked so hard to make her trust him. To make her think he was safe. Now, her face screamed stranger danger, and her stance said the woman was about to beat feet. All in all, she'd reverted back to when he pulled the shoulder toss move on her post-airport.

"Mia, honey."

Her jaw dropped and hung wordlessly. *Not good. Not. Good. At. All.*

"It's a really bad time for you to go into shock."

"Not. Shock."

"Whatever it is, I need you to snap out of it."

"I'm safe. You… Took care of them, just like you said."

He jangled the keys to catch her attention. Mia focused on him, dazed. He lofted the key ring her way. She caught them one-handed while still plastered against the wall. Not a bad catch.

"Get their car and drive it over here."

She nodded, peeled away from her brick support, and obeyed without question, parking it in the unlit spot he pointed at. Winters popped the trunk and tossed the first man in, then the second. He eyed the parking lot in a quick sweep. No other cars struck him as suspicious. No one exited the karaoke bar. They were all alone.

Violence had never before been an aphrodisiac. Hell, it wasn't now. But protecting her, isolating her from dangerous men, that shit was downright carnal. His blood rushed to his cock. A savage possession reared up.

Her dark eyes flicked over him, making his cock ache for her, and she hissed. "I told you to be careful. You could've been hurt."

He was by her side in an instant, pinning her against the wall again. God, he should be careful with her. But the temptation on her face, the flash in her gaze, promised it'd be impossible.

"You doubted me?"

"No. No. I didn't doubt you. I just…I didn't know what else to say just then."

Not giving her a second to make the same mistake twice, he slanted his lips over hers. It'd been too long since her lips covered his. Everything in the parking lot was a game. All part of the dance.

He needed her embrace to wash away the violence coursing through him. The need to battle dissolved as soon as she opened her mouth wide, wicking her hot tongue across his.

Mia knotted her hands in his hair, pulling him to her. Her mouth molded onto his, her body molten against his hands. Mia was just as hungry as he was. If that wasn't one of the hottest things ever…

Her legs snaked up his, and she pushed against him, firing everything he tried to ignore. Her hands clawed his neck, making him hard within seconds. Miss Khakis-and-Cardigan had been so deceptive. Dressing sugar sweet but with an inner temptress.

"Maybe I am invincible. What'd you call me, GI Joe?"

"Shut up, Colby." Her mouth punctuated the command with a kiss.

Their room was steps away, the key in his pant pocket. Both her legs encircled his waist, grinding her onto his erection. Christ, he needed to make it to that room. He needed privacy right this second. Winters pushed the door open, supporting her tight ass on his forearm, and kicked it closed behind them. Seclusion couldn't have come fast enough.

He paused in the dark room. His free hand slid across the wallpaper. He had to find the light switch. There wasn't a chance in hell he'd miss watching this.

He flipped the switch.

Two bedside lamps illuminated the cheap room in an amber glow. She deserved better than this, but there wasn't anything he planned to do about it now.

Winters leaned forward over the bed, placing her on the mattress as quickly and gently as he could manage. Given the circumstances, it wasn't a tender moment.

Her nails dug into his back. *Nope*. She didn't need gentle. What the hell was he thinking? Just like that kiss in the truck. She wanted. She needed. And the wicked glint in her eye told him just as much.

The showy rip in her shirt that had tested him all day was done for. He grabbed the edge and tore. It split but gave him no relief as the air rushed out of his lungs and his mouth watered. She was gorgeous.

"I hated that shirt anyway."

"I'll buy you a new one. That shirt teased me all day. It was payback."

Her pink lace bra was sheer. Her full breasts begged for his tongue, his lips. He thumbed one through the lace, and she arched her back, rolling her head to the side. "There was no teasing."

"The hell there wasn't." The bed sank down as Winters nudged her legs apart to kneel between them. "You're beautiful. Breath stealing, knock me on my ass gorgeous."

She laughed and turned away from him.

"No, you don't, Mia." He bent over and cupped her face, pulling it back to him. "You okay? You need me to back off?"

"I never said I wanted you to stop."

He smoothed a palm over her flat stomach. Torn fabric lay at her sides, framing her. He leaned over and brushed her nipple, teasing with his lips. She groaned, and her hips rocked. Her khaki pants. His tactical pants. They were so opposite, but right now, so connected.

With each swipe across her pebbled nipple, she twisted, offering approving cries, and pushing her breast into his mouth. Her backside lifted off the bed, making his insides corkscrew tight.

"You like that?"

"Uh-huh." She nodded, doing great things for his ego.

"I've wanted you naked and underneath me since we squared off."

"Pretty sure," her eyes danced, "that's why I tried to kick you in the balls."

"So it's like that, huh?" He closed down on her nipple, giving her more tooth than tongue.

Her fiery purr escaped on a breath, and he wanted her lips around his dick worse than he could have imagined. He traced a path up her arms, letting his fingers crawl across her creamy skin.

He'd take everything he could, anything she would offer, and relish it. This would all go away too soon. The tightness in his chest, the attraction to his opposite, it would disappear when they arrived home. He needed to make the most of it, and get her out of his system. Out of his head.

Winters grabbed hold of her wrists, pinning them above her head. She resisted and met him with a kiss that short-circuited his head. Her hips thrust toward his, then she bit his lip. *Hell yeah.* Not the reaction he expected. It was so much better.

"Give me my hands back, Colby." She screwed her legs tight on his thighs. Her hair splayed out on the bed, wild in every direction.

"Not a chance, doll."

"That's not fair."

"Mia, honey, if you find yourself in a fair fight, you didn't plan your mission correctly." He wanted her to tear at his grip, to come apart while he held her in place. He wanted to see her, from head to toe, rocked in a cataclysmic orgasm.

His legs held their ground, and he undid the top button of her pants. As if he hit the slow-mo button, he dropped Mia's zipper one stilted frame at a time. The pleasurable torment made his cock strain for its release.

He wedged his fingers past the tight opening in her pants, between her legs, and smiled in satisfaction when he found the damp underside of her lace panties. Her zipper bit at his wrist, but it didn't matter.

She rubbed her sex against him and struggled to shift her pants down.

"That's my job. These will come off when I say you're ready."

Moaning exasperation betrayed her. "Colby, now."

He moved to her side, and she kept her legs open, rocking her against his touch. Winters immobilized her. One hand above her head. The other pressed against her mound.

He pushed the damp lace aside. One finger, then another, slid across her. If he thought he'd know how smooth and silky, wet and wanting she'd be, he was wrong. Stroking her was so far past pleasurable.

Her pants shifted over her hip bone. A small tattoo caught his eye. A symbol. Artful and delicate.

"You have a tattoo."

"Hm-hmm."

"What's it mean?"

"Survivor."

"Didn't expect that."

"It seems like you haven't expected me at all."

So true. His fingers dipped into her, then withdrew. A small shudder coursed through her body. He encircled her sensitized bud of nerves, so slick with her juices.

Mia struggled to lean up, straining against the wrist hold. *She wants to see?*

And like she read his mind, she said, "I want to watch you."

He was wrong if he thought he couldn't get any harder, and he'd never been so close to losing it before.

"You can see." His throat hurt with guttural vibrations. He didn't recognize its sound.

"Not as much as I want to."

He released her hands, and she arched into him, digging her nails into his shoulder blades. She clawed for blood. Marking him as hers. She could leave scars for all he cared. He'd own that constant reminder.

Her legs opened wider, straining at her pants, then she pulled from him and unclasped the front opening of her bra. Her swollen breasts fell free and taunted him. She was intentionally trying him. It was a game of who could distract who more. And it was fucking awesome.

"I told you I was calling the shots here. That's the only reason you got your hands back."

"I got my hands back because–"

He stopped her with a suck on her bare nipple.

She bucked against him, then ran her hand over her breasts, massaging. "You were moving too slow."

Too slow? He was worried about moving too fast. His mind spun circles. Christ, if he died on this op, she'd be to blame because she was killing him.

He gave her ass a swift lift and tugged off the pants and small scrap of lace covering her, tossing it aside. She lay naked before him, a smile lighting her face. She wanted him. Trusted him. That was no small feat after the days she'd had recently.

He wicked his fingers over her wet folds with more pressure, tightening his attention on her clit. Arousal poured off of her, musky and mouth-watering.

"Stop teasing me, Colby."

"Honey, we've only just begun."

"I can't handle it. I need release. Now."

"You will." It was a promise he would keep more than once.

"Please."

He tried to shush her.

Mia reached for him. "Don't make me beg."

He rolled between her legs and kissed. She tasted extraordinary. Sweet and memorable. Her pleas broke off. Harsh breaths forced past her lips.

"You'll come so hard, you'll forget the hell you've endured." *He'd do anything to wipe the attacks from her memory.*

"Promise me."

"Promise."

He spread her wide, lashing his tongue over her. Her juices wept down his chin. Mia flexed toward him, calling his name.

Damn straight, she could wear out his name. He loved hearing it pour off her tongue.

She fisted the comforter in one hand and drifted her other down her stomach. Her fingers met his tongue. The sensation whipped lightning-fast down his spine. She grazed, dancing with his kiss, and moved him swifter and harder. Her cries were louder, her legs spread further, heels digging trenches into the mattress.

He paused to watch. She wasn't shy and thank God, because this worked for him in ways he didn't know. A possessive need flashed, and he joined back in, his tongue comingled with her fingers.

"More."

Sure thing. He'd take orders from her. He speared her tight entrance with two fingers. Mia clamped around him. Such a tight pussy. Liquid fire coating his fingers. He'd explode if he entered her. She deserved better than an eight second rodeo, which was all he'd probably muster at the moment. He tried and failed to recount the steps of cleaning his rifle. He tried to list the phonetic alphabet. Backwards. Zeta. Yankee. Xray. Nothing helped.

"Colby," she said breathlessly. "Don't stop. Harder. I need more."

Harder. He could do harder. He could do whatever the hell she told him to do. He grabbed her ass, holding her tight against his mouth. She pulled from him, pushed toward him, but it didn't matter.

Finally, he couldn't handle anymore and rumbled into her sweetness, the vibrations tearing the last shreds of her climb into an untamed climax. She bucked hard against his mouth, her hands ripping through his hair. She could pull every last strand out if it meant that orgasm was as strong as it sounded. She cried his name and cursed him. He forced her through it until the last of her ripples crossed his tongue, and she went limp.

One deep breath, then another. He released her from a grip that may have been far too tight. Marks outlined where he held her in place, but the satisfaction on her face did something barbaric to his need for her.

CHAPTER ELEVEN

Their break didn't last long. Mia lifted her head from the mattress and snagged him with a look. "I need you. Now."

Yes, ma'am. That'll work for me, too.

She reached for his hair and ran her fingers through it. Nice to know he still had some. Directing him from his knees, she tore at his shirt. "Get this off."

It was only then he realized he hadn't disarmed. *Very gentleman like. Shit.* He stood, and un-holstered his Glock from the small of his back. The smooth metal was cold in his hand, a violent contrast to her sizzle and warmth.

One-handed, he pulled the slide, released the clip, unloading it in one swift move. The magazine hit the floor. He emptied the round in the chamber and placed his concealed carry on the nightstand.

"Show off." She laughed, looking impressed.

"You liked it," he said an octave lower than normal, saturated in arousal. He wanted to impress her. Needed her to see him as something beyond a street fighter, even if it was only a quick trick.

The gun holstered under his pant leg was still loaded. No way would he leave them vulnerable. Her fingers brushed over his belt clasp, working the buckle. His erection pressed hard into his pants, wanting her touch.

"I wasn't complaining." She rounded her hands onto his ass, encouraging him to step out of his pants and boxer briefs. He unstrapped the remaining holsters, set his backup and his tactical knife on the nightstand, and dropped trou.

His hard-on, freed of restraint, reached for her, and she didn't hesitate. Mia clasped her hands around him. He grabbed a condom from his pants pocket. She stroked him, thumbing the crown of his cock, then took the condom from him. She tore it open and slid it down. One surprise after another.

"Come here." He growled into her ear, praying he wouldn't have to beg.

They moved to the middle of the bed, and he loomed over her. Had there ever been a more beautiful face looking up at him? Her bottom lip quivered. Her cheeks were flushed. She was stunning.

He guided his cock against her tight entrance. The tip teased, dipping in and pressing against her accepting muscles. Heaven help him. This minx could steal his soul if he didn't put up a barrier.

As he inched in, she pulled him down to her, urging him. Waiting any longer wasn't possible. He took advantage of her offer. He filled her. For a hot second, he almost lost it at first full thrust.

Deeper, then deeper again. Still it wasn't enough. All of him, hugged tight by her. It shouldn't feel this good. She shouldn't be as accepting as she was, melting around him. Her muscles tightened, and she crushed a kiss on him, taking his lip and sucking hard.

Sweat slid down his shoulders. Moisture poured between their skin, from their kisses to their slick connection. Her legs wrapped around his waist, clinging to him. Her entire body hung on him, taut with a rabid hunger.

He pounded into her harder. Almost too hard. The sound of their slapping flesh burned his ears. She didn't fight it. No, she seemed to crave it as much as he did. Her hips moved with him, begged him to keep up the intensity.

The lights were on. His woman was wild. They were out of control and completely in sync. *Sweet addiction, have mercy.* He struggled for more, struggled for restraint, but reveled in the complete lecherous abandon.

"Colby, please." She begged, muscles constricting on his shaft. "Make me come again. Now."

It was all he needed to push into overdrive. Palming her ass off the mattress, he gripped tight, fingers flexed, and aimed to please. He needed to explode, but not until that beautiful face had unraveled again. She'd come on his cock if it killed him.

A low growl choked from his throat. It was the desperate plea of a man waiting to detonate. Her head dropped back with a hoarse howl. Her pussy tightened, rippling over him. She called his name from some bottomless depth he'd never heard from a woman before. Her body bucked into his thrusts, her arms wrapped strangle-hold tight around his neck.

He came right after her. Every muscle in his body strained. He flexed the last thrusts, then collapsed over her. She was saved from crushing death by his caging forearms. Their sweaty cheeks pressed together, mouths agape.

Hard pants burned from his lungs. His chest heaved, shoulders rising and falling in sated, breathless satisfaction. Strands of her hair stuck to her forehead. To his forehead. Her eyelashes grazed his temple. Tonight defined world-stopping, better-than-amazing sex. And the only thing he could focus on was her.

Mine.

Possession blazed, shaking its fist, shouting into the night.

Minutes passed and neither moved. Their breathing stabilized together in painstaking slowness. One finger at a time, her hands relaxed from their death grip, and her legs unhooked.

She didn't say a word. And thank God, because he had no idea what just happened.

CHAPTER TWELVE

Colby's hard body held her still. Mia just existed. No thinking. No worrying. Nothing. She felt her limp, loose body sprawled on rumpled sheets. Numb satisfaction pulsed. Her fingertips tickled. Blood slowed its screaming rush in her ears. The taste of his kiss lingered, robust and vibrant, on her tongue.

That incredible ride was more than memorable. Repercussions of Colby ricocheted up, down, and all around her mind and body.

It felt like a night of firsts. The first time a man hovered over her, his stomach damp with their perspiration. Though it wasn't. The first time a man made her cry out his name. No, that *was* a first. She truly lost control and begged. She cried his name in need and thanksgiving without thought or motivation. *Yes, definitely firsts*.

This night was different. His piston-powered force drove her to the edge and fell with her. She shuddered, recalling the pained look on his face, his teeth gritted, and muscles contracting around her. He held out for her.

He looked Herculean and chiseled, scarred and battle-ridden. The most handsome man to ever lay eyes on her was now lying *on her*. And if he stayed like this much longer, Colby could ask her to gun down a bad guy, and she'd pull the trigger without question.

His harsh stubble grazed her chin, his forehead meeting hers. The air was hard to breath, and she sighed.

This is too much like... Something more.

And she didn't want *something more*. She could go with this tonight, letting her fantasy run to its full potential. But *more* with him was unrealistic. More might very well kill her.

It was dangerous, far more so than gunfights and secret lists. Men like him needed physical release, the clinging of a woman crying out his name. It was good for the ego, good for his game.

"Are you okay, Mia?" His tenor raked a level lower than a rumble.

And then he asked about her feelings? It was too much. She nodded his question away, discounting the weight in his voice, and the tightening in her chest.

The room smelled warm and potent. Like the virile man enveloping her. She'd savor their encounter, but it wouldn't last nearly as long as she needed it to.

Their breaths and the hum of the air conditioning served up the white noise. A quiet intensity. The calm after the storm. Heck, the calm after the hurricane.

Colby picked his head up and locked eyes with hers. Their fire, the deep brooding that burned in his irises, ignited a heated tremor in her all over again. Shivers ran across her skin. He leaned down to kiss her. Hard and deliberate. The harsh scruff on his face, and the supple slide of his delving tongue made her want to sign up for another round.

"Good. Me, too." He broke from her but lay close on his side. An arm hung round her waist, hooking their bodies together, maintaining their link. A soothing finger toyed with her belly button, rounding in and out of the shallow indentation.

He loomed like an ominous mountain chain next to her, and she couldn't help but admire the compact definition of his shoulders and the corded grooves between each ripple of muscles. Solid everywhere, even while relaxed. He was a warrior's warrior. It made her mouth water.

Colby rolled off the bed. An icy earthquake wicked across her skin. He lumbered toward the bathroom, stretching his arms high overhead, making every muscle from his neck to his ass flex. Her lungs hurt, and only then did she realize she forgot to breathe.

His body was of a caliber that action movie heroes aspired to attain. He leaned over the bathroom sink, twisted the faucet on, and covered his face. After a second splash of water, he let it run, steam rising, framing his profile. Hinged at the waist, folded arms resting on the bathroom counter, he hung his head lax in the flickering bathroom light.

Uh-oh. That wasn't a good stance.

That seemed a whole lot like regret. And she wouldn't handle his remorse well. He'd gone hot and cold on her before. She didn't expect it then, and she didn't now. What was that saying? *Fool me once, shame on you. Fool me twice, shame on me.*

She stared at the ceiling again. Maybe he realized he was stuck with her until Virginia. The one night stand that he couldn't leave. *Whoopsie. Sorry about your luck, Rambo.*

"Why are you here with me, Mia?" His head still hung over the running water.

She'd called it, and here it came. He would push her away, his repentance bubbling to the surface like a hot spring. It was so dang cliché. She kept a laugh to herself and pressed her lips flat.

"Don't worry about me. I'm not the clingy type." She didn't want to play the bedroom equivalent of Twenty Questions.

"Christ, Mia. That's not what I meant." He tilted his head toward her, raking his eyes across her face. He looked mad, or was that annoyance?

"Well then, Colby, what did you mean?" Sarcasm wasn't her friend right now, but the snarky shake of her head said otherwise. "That type of question. Your timing. It's clear to me. No need to backpedal."

"I meant why haven't you called the cops? Why are you okay with everything that's happened so far? Asking why you're here wasn't supposed to be an inquisition until you made it one."

The heck with his interrogation retreat. He knew the answer. There was one reason he was so sure she'd go with him, forcefully or not, in the first place.

"I told you. It was my client's dying request."

"No, bullshit. That's not an acceptable excuse, and you know it."

"All right. Several people are trying to kill me. Bullets whizzed over my head earlier. I don't want to be stuffed in a trunk again. Is that acceptable?"

"Nope." His eyes danced, an eyebrow raised. He needed to back off. He was already ruining her post-coital moment.

"So what do you want me to say?" She rolled her eyes. Why was he pushing her? "You'll do a better job protecting me than the cops could, and, I don't have to explain how I came across a secret government document." *Besides, I'm too busy thinking of you naked.* "Does that work for you?"

All her climatic residuals were gone, and she blamed the undressed detective running shop from the bathroom.

"You've got serious walls built around you, doll. You know that?"

Oh yeah, she knew. Years studying psychology had clued her in. But all the money spent on higher education didn't matter. She'd known since grade school that parents screwed up kids, and that a bad home life was a serious detriment for normal emotional health.

Walls were a concession for never finding a magical cure. But that was okay. She'd done just fine with her closely guarded psyche.

Well, that was the truth until Colby kissed through all her barriers. She needed to build those up again. Fast.

"I'm a realist. A pragmatist. You're a one-night-stand man. I can tell. And I got carried away with the moment."

"You've got it all wrong, and you don't even know it. It's simple: You're the deceptive one." He hung his head back down, facing into the sink. "You look one way. You act another. You say one thing, but I see the wheels turning in that clever head of yours. What you say isn't what you think. Hell, honey. I know the deceptive deal. But that's cool if that's how you want to play it."

"I'm not even going to dignify your accusations."

"I didn't say it was a bad thing." His half-smile made her stomach rocket into her throat. The man dripped testosterone. It was the freakin' grand rapid of pheromones in this room. Mia flushed, remembering their bedroom showdown. Her palms itched to run down his strong back. *Still carried away in the moment, it seems.*

"I saw it in your eyes. You're just as triggered up as I am. You want the same thing I want. But you don't know it." He paused, studying her. "Nah. You know what you want. Don't you? I admire that. It's sexy as all hell."

No way, not-uh. She wouldn't give him the satisfaction of calling her out. Her stomach might knot, her jaw might lock, but no way would she admit anything.

She looked back at him. It had been so easy. He didn't judge, only acted. She trusted him from the moment he carried her into the room, until the second he leaned over the bathroom sink. Then it all came to a screeching halt.

Except, wait. Did he just call her sexy? Whatever. She must ignore him. Turn the tables. Something. Anything. Because he wasn't throwing on his clothes. And him, naked, was dangerous. Lord, so very dangerous.

"Now who's psychoanalyzing who?" Why did she sound like that? Oh, no reason. Just because her body was betraying her. She needed it to stop reacting to him.

"Do you ever give honest answers?" He laughed into the towel as he dried off his face, then nailed her with a stare. "When it comes to you, *to Mia*, not your work or your clients, are you ever sincere about what you want?"

She was earlier in bed. That was about the most honest she'd been. Ever. But she kept that little secret to herself and rolled onto her back. There was no denying that she felt something. But it didn't matter. Adrenaline. Chemicals. Hormones. They were all arousing. And *they* were deceptive, not her.

She could psychoanalyze this…their behavior, their glances, and the oppressing emotion that tugged at the edge of her consciousness, but she didn't want to.

He turned the shower on, and she expected he'd close the door on her any moment now. She earned a door slam. She was being a bitch. And there wasn't a reason for it, other than to protect her hide.

A shower would be amazing. Hell, right now, it would feel light-years past unbelievable. Steaming hot water would wash away her bitterness and confusion. But for now, she'd wait until her wet noodle legs could carry her to the bathroom.

Mia held a leg inches off the bed, testing it. Limp. Loose. Lax. *Yeah, it might be a while.*

His hands clasped on her ankles. She jumped, but didn't get far. He was as stealthy as he was silent. She didn't have time to stay startled. With a fast tug, Colby slid her to the edge, dropping her feet to the floor. His eyes flared, dark and aroused, a hard line set to his jaw. That, she didn't expect. Nor did she expect to see him hard for her again.

"Can't get enough, huh?" And there was the bitch again. She needed to sew her mouth shut because clearly her brain had given up monitoring duty.

"Christ, woman. Major defensive walls. You've gotta work on that."

"Says the big badass who leads a secret life."

"At least I know what I want, and I'm not afraid of it." Colby hooked his forearms under hers, dangling her above the carpet. "And I want you. Again."

She felt weightless, as if her worries fell off when he lifted her up.

His hard-on rubbed against her stomach, instantly welling a heat in between her legs. He walked back into the bathroom, put her down, and stepped into the steaming water.

"Nothing to say, Miss Mia?" His head tilted and gave her a look hotter than the scorching stream behind him. Dark stubble. Dark eyes. Dangerous scar under his eye. A triple threat. But nothing she was scared of.

Water sprayed around his head, but she was stuck in place. He was a risk. A delicious, enticing risk. But one nonetheless.

Colby extended his hand from the shower. Rough and calloused, and damn if she didn't already know how perfect it would feel against her.

"Come here. I need you next to me." His voice was an embrace to her fears.

Where she'd been sarcastic and standoffish, Colby was honest and contemplative. Those weren't the attributes that she knew of him, yet they made perfect sense. She was losing the emotional battle that he didn't realize she was waging. Without questioning him again, she stepped into his embrace.

"That's my girl. Such a beauty." He pushed the hair off of her cheeks, tucking it behind her ears.

The water burned. It was a shade cooler than unbearable, and she pushed into his protective broad chest to escape its sear. His hands trailed from the nape of her neck to cup her bottom, his fingers curling along her backside. She softened into him, lips brushing his chest. He spun them around in one flash move, shielding her from the boiling waterfall, and pressing her against the cold, wet tiles.

The man was on a mission of seduction, and he was winning. Every cell, every inch of her skin readied to beg for him. Ravenous hunger shredded her mind. Her nipples were so hard they hurt, and they pressed into his scratchy chest hair for blistering relief. Her ultra-sensitized body swayed against him for the full effect of his firm physique and heavy cock. She was sore from earlier, but it didn't stop her most intimate muscles from firing to life again.

His breath teased her ear. His perspiration washed off, and she caught the taste of it on her lips. Strong arms wrapped around her, enveloping her. He smelled of their climaxes.

"Christ. I can't get enough of you." His words cracked against her neck. His teeth rasped her, shooting sparks down her spine.

She fingered his cheeks, the rough stubble of the day's worth of growth abrading her palms. She wanted to explore his chest, his abdomen, but he was pressed so close she couldn't. Instead, she savored the engorgement rubbing between them. She needed to feel this. To feel him. On her. Inside her. However she could get him.

Water sprayed the back of his head, and it dripped over her. The faint scent from his hair teased hints of sandalwood and amber. Humidity and ecstasy flooded the shower stall, steaming a hazy fog around them. All she could see, all she could feel, smell, and taste was Colby Winters. And she was lost in it all. Deliriously, completely lost.

"I'm telling you. That's all stress. You wanting me like this—" He bit against her neck, and Mia almost couldn't finish her thought aloud. "It's adrenaline. Isn't this how you normally relax after…doing what it is you do?"

His tongue ran gymnastics down her neck. She tried to ignore it but failed with exceptional flare.

When he stopped the kiss, he said, "Just when you start to relax, you get all keyed up again. I already told you I don't get stressed." Colby tightened his grip on her bottom, massaging his fingers into her skin. "But you're going to keep psychoanalyzing me. Making your educated guesses about what makes me tick, aren't you? Go on. Build self-protective walls. Practice your frigid glares. I'll blow through them. Again."

Hiding her quick breaths was a lesson in the unfeasible. She panted against his chest. "But this is how you relax. Right? I'm trying hard not to get lost in the moment." Her words came out so muted, she wasn't sure he heard her.

"No, doll, this," he slid a testing finger between her legs and teased her, "isn't normally how I relax. And I'm doing something very wrong if you don't get lost in the moment. If you're thinking about anything besides us right now, I've got work to do."

"I *am* thinking about us." She tried not to moan, but his fingers gave her no relief. He was doing everything right. From the curl of his caress to the long-suffering in and out, Colby knew how to make her need him.

"In the wrong manner. You're over-thinking this. I can tell. You're holding onto something, somewhere. Let it go. Unravel, like earlier. Come for me." His fingers quickened their pace, blazing within her. "But no, Mia. I don't do this after my ops. I don't shower with women and ask about their feelings. I'm flying blind here, babe. No idea what I'm doing, but I'm doing it for you."

Oh shit. Not what she expected. Not at all.

She tried to breathe. She was so close. "You know what you're doing."

"I'm not talking about getting you off. Though I'm loving every second of it."

"Aw, you make me sound special."

"Making you moan is special. I like it." His finger pushed into her aching pussy. Her muscles tightened around it, her jaw fell open and, like he selected the option from a menu, she moaned on cue. "So come on. You were lost in the moment before. What's so different now?"

This needed to be about adrenaline-driven reactions. No feelings. No emotions. *Oh, who's she kidding? This is perfect, whatever the reason.*

Mia lifted one foot and trailed it up the solid muscle of his calf, the scratchy coarse hairs tickling her foot. She widened her stance, allowing him further entry for his erotic assault. Her head rolled against the wall, her cheek turned onto the cool tiles, and she fought the flutter of her eyes. Good God, his fingers did nothing short of the Devil's dance.

She wanted to answer his questions and meant to explain herself. To say once in bed was fun and uncomplicated. Twice in his arms was too much. But it came out a secretive growl. Wordless and embarrassing.

"That was fucking beautiful." He slid his finger from her opening, then with two fingers, he repeated the same internal stroke. In and out, over and over again. The pad of his thumb encircled her clit. "Moan for me again."

He chipped away at her unseen walls, fighting his way into her head.

"I can't." She heard the betraying ache as she struggled to speak.

"Liar. I made you scream before. I want to hear it again."

"Please don't make me. Please."

"Why, baby?"

"Cause I'm going to get hurt."

Dang. It came out before she could stop it. His hand stilled for a heartbeat. *No, no.* This was why she fought him. He made her more honest than she should be. More than she knew was possible.

"I'm not going to hurt you, Mia."

"Of course you will. Unintentionally, but hurt just the same."

"You don't trust me?"

"I do."

"Then just relax, and let it all go."

He raced his thumb against her swollen nub. It was all she could do to keep from grinding on his fingers. The constant push against her tender flesh, still raw from earlier, sensitized every nerve ending. All her senses fired. Including her mind.

With every steam-filled breath, her want multiplied. Mia didn't remember his arm moving round her to support her. Her legs were open, her bottom resting on his forearm. She leaned back against the tiles. She was so close.

Colby flexed his fingers into her. The press of his palm against her clit challenged her to erupt. She clenched around his fingers. An all-masculine grunt poured from him, its timbre catapulting her closer to explosive orgasm. It revved from her clit, into the far reaches of her limbs. She sucked in the falling water. His name fell from her gasps. She thrashed side to side under the spray, and he kept her firmly in place against the cold wall. Her body jerked, suffering through every last wonderful ripple of her orgasm.

"Fuck yes, Mia. That's my girl."

His girl. He sounded possessive and greedy. And that was exactly what she needed.

Colby crushed his lips onto hers, easily forcing her mouth open, and lashed his tongue across hers. As she came down from her high, Mia circled her hands around his shaft and stroked one hand on top of the other.

He pulled back from kissing her. A this-really-sucks smile played on his face, and she had no idea why. "I'm aching for you again."

"What's stopping you?" She kissed a scar under his collarbone, trailing her tongue along the ridge of his shoulder.

"I don't have another condom."

Talk about a mix of disappointment and frustration. His voice matched his this-sucks grin.

Mia tightened her grip on his substantial erection. "Not a perfect solution, but I'm nothing if not inventive."

She grabbed the travel size soap and sudsed her hands, raising a do-you-wanna brow.

He nodded, chin jutting hard. "Hell, yes."

Bubbles coated her hands, foaming to her wrists. She ran his length, the small bar of soap still in one hand, before cupping his tight sac. He flexed against her motion and an approving groan broke free. *Now that was special.*

The soap bar slipped from her hands, landing on the floor, and spun with the draining water. She traveled her hands to his head, then thumbed his crown with each stroke.

Colby covered one strong hand around hers and pumped in time with her. His abdominal muscles tightened, and his hard thighs contracted. The already taut skin on his body stretched, gleaming under the water. His toes dug into the tile floor. His bicep flexed as they shared the stroke. His fingers wrapped so tight around her hands on him, she thought it might hurt. But it did nothing more than make him harder.

It was her turn now. "I want to hear you."

He gritted his teeth, an intense look of concentrated enjoyment plastered across his face. "I haven't exactly been quiet."

"Come for me." Tonight was liberating. He was liberating. She said what she wanted and went after it. Let the sky high walls tumble, and apprehensions vanish. "Right now, Colby. Come for me."

A curse escaped his mouth, and his entire body clenched. She massaged him against her wet stomach as he came, pulsing his seed across her belly. His cock jerked and spurted again, hot streams jetting on her. He leaned his head on his forearm above her head, his chest heaving.

"Mia." He sucked in a raspy breath.

They stood there, not moving until the hot water began to cool. Colby turned the shower off and grabbed a towel from the nearby rack. He wrapped it around her, moving his hands down her back and sides. She was jelly. If he hadn't held her upright, she'd have melted into the floor.

He held her close, maybe sensing her complete fulfillment, and found his own towel. He ran it roughshod over his body, wicking the wet drips off him more than drying himself.

They hadn't really bathed, but the hot water more than made her feel clean.

"You're unbelievable," she whispered against his shoulder. "I've never come like that before. I've never…said what I wanted."

"You did in bed earlier tonight."

"That was heat of the moment. Here. Now. I was cognizant of it."

"You and your therapy words. Honey, you've been cognizant of us since we first kissed." He pushed a wet strand of hair behind her ear. "I've never wanted a woman the way I want you."

He wanted her. Simple as that.

"You wore me out." She smiled at him, a tiny laugh escaping. "I'm exhausted. More than exhausted, really. Are you tired?"

He caught her eye, evidently proud to have done so. His smile threatened his mulish exterior. "You want to stay here?"

Mia nodded. "Where else would we go?"

"We could keep driving, if you wanted us to head home."

"I want to sleep next to you, with you, in your arms." Saying it aloud took her breath away. Bravery was a good fit.

Colby stilled and didn't respond.

Oh no. Maybe it was a very bad fit.

Mia pinched her eyes closed, embarrassed. Why did she confess her secrets to him? That wasn't smart. No. It was flat out stupid.

"Come on, doll." He dropped his towel on the floor, standing gorgeous and naked in front of her, and he pried hers loose from her talon grip. A chill danced across her skin. "Dry sheets will be so much better than these crappy-assed towels. Let's warm up under the covers."

She took his hand, plodding behind him, dumbstruck. He threw back the comforter on the already rumpled bed, adjusted a few pillows, and lifted her onto the mattress. Before Mia could crawl through the rough fabric to the far side of the bed, his warm body sought and found hers. He pulled her against his arm, flipped another pillow behind his head, and nuzzled against the back of her wet hair.

"That's not what I thought you were going to do," she said.

"Welcome to the club."

"What does that mean?"

"You haven't done a single thing I've expected of you either."

"Oh." *Oh?* That was all she could say? But her mind was exhausted, and he was a puzzle she couldn't figure out.

CHAPTER THIRTEEN

Winters was more than aware of Mia curled into the crook of his arm. More than aware of her melodic breaths and the occasional quiet snore that played wrecking ball to his convoluted thoughts. She was beautiful and enticing, guarded and tortured. Hell if he'd let her use her excuses tonight. *Heat of the moment, I don't think so*. He didn't fall for that bullshit. No, when they'd been in bed, they'd been on fire, and it wasn't just an adrenaline high. He didn't know what the fuck it was, but it was more than a fast and furious lay, his typical pump and dump.

Warmth continued to roll through him even though she had long since closed her eyes. His tongue was thick, and his jaw was clamped together so tight he should have a headache. *Heat of the moment*? The accusation killed him.

He had her earlier, in a way he'd never experienced before. Sex, yeah, that was fantastic. But it was iced with a little something more. Something with a flash and bang to it. The hell of it was he wanted more. Like an addiction. And then in the shower… What did he expect going in there with her? He was short a condom, and only by some amazing grace did she give him release. Even now, he craved Mia again. Once wasn't enough. Twice wasn't either.

He should have put them in the car, driving to Virginia. But there wasn't a chance of kick starting the road trip again if she wanted to sleep next to him. She was his for the moment, all gathered up in his arms like an innocent angel.

He smiled, remembering her panic in the bathroom. It took him a stupid second to realize he wanted her fast asleep in his arms. That realization shocked him clear out of his towel. Her adorable face was alarmed, and she tried, in vain, to scurry away from him in bed. It was cute to watch her try but far more fun to ease her worry.

This was a memory to keep. A memory to store for dark days when he needed hope and belief to survive. He was smart enough to know once in a lifetime when it smacked him across the face.

Winters eyed the oversized fuel and food signs passing on the highway. "Coffee?"

"No."

"Are you hungry?"

"Nope."

Daybreak turned into harsh afternoon glare, bearing down at him through the windshield. Hours passed in the trashed-up car, and other than a sideways glance, Mia had all but disconnected herself from him like he was a plague-infected pariah. He was ready to pop red smoke and call in for an extraction team. *What the fuck did I do wrong?*

She was distracted, disengaged, and detached. More focused on the passing scenery and overhead road signs than any amicable gesture he lobbed at her. He could've sung show tunes acappella, and she wouldn't have noticed.

Shit. He didn't know the first thing about the morning after. And, as by evidence of her withdrawal from him, he didn't always ace everything he tried. So much for thinking he was a stud.

What did it matter if the woman didn't live for his every thought? So what if she wasn't hungry? For food or for him. What did he even want from her anyway? Doe-eyed looks or good morning, let's-go-again kisses? Well, he got none of those. Just a curt good morning, and a very matter of fact re-dressing in her dirty, torn clothes. He chuckled. She did a hell of a job piecing her shirt back together. If she hadn't been so formal, teetering around like a proper marm, he might have told her so.

"Are you going to tell me what I did that was so wrong?" He scrubbed his hand over his face, hating that he even asked.

"You didn't do anything."

"Yet, here we are. One-syllable answers and the silent treatment. You don't seem like the type to play games, Mia." He paused, waiting for any sign of life. "I'm glad to see the glacial attitude has returned."

Sarcasm wasn't helpful, but screw it. He exited the highway. The last chance for fast food would be a passing memory in seconds.

"I'm not. Look, Colby…never mind. Nothing is wrong. I'm just tired." She shrugged and dug at her fingernail like her life depended on it.

"I call bullshit, but you can fess up to me later or tell me why you're ignoring me. Either way, you'll tell me."

She didn't say anything. Her hands were crossed in her lap, and if he didn't know any better, she was a tight squeeze away from white-knuckled.

Winters let her ignore him. It gave him time to plan his afternoon with Titan. They had a shit ton to hash out, starting with the NOC list and ending with Mia's sweet ass no longer in the line of danger.

He barreled down the familiar roads, tapping the steering wheel. Her safety was paramount, and there was nothing they could do to protect her without engaging the enemy. They needed to cut the head off the beast, not deal with the pansy teams that kept up their mediocre attacks.

He cleared his throat. "You've got about five seconds, Mia, to fess up. Three. Two. One. All right, we'll talk later."

The car slowed, and they pulled up to a brick fenced property with a wrought iron gate. Old, thick trees lined the property, and a green canopy was draped over the driveway. It was nice to be home, but even better that she was there with him. Though that struck him as odd since she hadn't strung a sentence together with more than three words in it since she fell asleep in his arms the night before.

"When you said home, did you mean *estate*?" Mia's jaw hung open.

"The good guy business pays well. I like my privacy, and it's safe."

"I can tell." Her jaw still gaped.

It would've been a lie if he denied the masculine pride coursing through him at her reaction. She was impressed and, for the first time when it came to a woman, he cared.

"You can make yourself comfortable while I meet with the team for a while. I promise you, there's nowhere safer. And my mom will whip up a mean meal. Fried chicken, mashed potatoes. The works. You can meet Clara." He snuck a glance at Mia. *Open up a little, would you?* He shook his head. Now, he sounded like a whiny teenage girl. Awesome. "Are you overwhelmed yet?"

"No. Not overwhelmed. Just do what you need to do so I can get back to my life. Please."

He shook his head again. Her life would never be the same for the simple fact that she'd been kidnapped, and she saw violence firsthand. She was a psychologist. She should know that. That stuff messed with minds. He lived through it all the time, and it was a heavy, dark burden.

"I'll get it figured out."

Winters rolled up to the front of the white colonial house. His mom opened the door with a baby on her hip, waving the young child's arm. She was mouthing hellos for Clara toward the car, but the baby looked more interested in tearing her silver-haired bun out of place.

He caught Mia cringing, and her hands ran the length of her thighs. "Oh God, Colby. This is a bad idea. Horrible. I don't even have shoes on. What is your mother going to think? I've worn these clothes for days. I can't let her see me like this. I can't let anyone see me like this."

"Well, you can't hide in the car. And she won't care. Hell, she won't even notice."

"Of course she'll notice. I'm not wearing shoes. My shirt is basically scotch taped together. Anyone would notice."

"This is the most you've said in hours. Since you woke up."

A flush crossed her cheeks. All he wanted was for her to lean into him. To kiss him. He wanted her to stop torturing him. That wasn't too much to ask.

She was the therapist. Maybe she compartmentalized or whatever. Boxed up their night and forgot about it. Other than the blush on her face and neck, Mia didn't seem the least interested in him or having another go at it in the future. It was infuriating.

Unable to hold back, his hand glanced off her pink cheek with a caress. Something he was getting much better at since they'd met. She was so soft, and whether she'd acknowledge him as a man or not, he couldn't stop from stroking her.

He took her hand, squeezed it, then got out of the car. He kissed his mom on the cheek and swept the baby into his arms, holding her up over her head. Clara giggled and kicked in excitement. Her blonde curls and smile warmed his heart every time.

He heard Mia walk up from behind him. Her bare feet shuffled on a few loose stones on the driveway, and her arms wrapped across her stomach.

"Mom, this is Mia. Mia, my mom." Winters made the introductions, momentarily ignoring both women and focusing on Clara. It'd been far too long since he held her. It was an automatic; he held the baby, and the world sank away. His eyes slipped shut, and he drank in Clara's hug, her innocent scent of shampoo and baby powder.

After a long hug, he saw his mother extend her hand to Mia, confusion and surprise on her face. Funny how similar the expression was to when he knocked on his mom's door, baby in tow.

"Mia, nice to meet you. You can call me Judith."

Judith flashed an inquisitive eye at her son, having never met any client or woman in his life before. Most certainly not at his house, with his daughter. A flush heated his face, imperceptible to anyone but his mother. He wasn't a mama's boy. Never had been. But their relationship had changed to friend-like, or even mentor-mentoree, after he arrived on her doorstep, holding a baby two-handed like she was a nuclear bomb, and kicking along the bag of diapers Child Protective Services gave him.

He had been terrified. And his mother, bless her heart, didn't call him on it. She simply started to help. She could diaper the hell out of a baby, showing him that while it seemed duct tape was the only way a diaper would stay secure, the tabs on the side did just fine.

She knew Titan Group skirted the edge of legal. She knew that he was in danger each time he left for a job. He told her as much. But hell, he'd made some major changes after Clara arrived. Decisions were now made on more than mission-critical information. He had to base them on a baby. He had to get home to Clara at the end of each op. He had to establish routines and schedules. And he had to plan for a babysitter. It was comical. Shopping for formula and smashed peas while wearing tactical gear was quite possibly his latest favorite pastime. The looks he got were nothing short of alarmed. If he were feeling particularly in need of a laugh, he'd smear on camouflage face paint.

Nothing in his life had been stable until Clara came along. And even now, stable was a stretch. But for Clara's sake, he did what he could to provide her a settled home. And his mother was his saving grace.

She didn't appear to notice Mia's bare feet or tattered clothes. But, oh, he knew better. She was discreet. That was for sure. The woman didn't miss a beat. Lord only knew what she thought, and he was certain to hear about it later. Would she go the interrogation route, or infiltrate behind enemy lines, asking Mia subtle questions?

Maybe he should have placed a warning phone call. Right now, that was a blinding flash of obviousness. *Too late.* He hadn't wanted to do that in front of Mia, and after everything that happened the last time he left Mia alone to call home, he sure as shit wasn't going to do that again.

With the baby on his hip, Winters watched Mia stand next to his mother. His mom's head tilted a degree sideways. One eyebrow raised slight enough so that only he noticed. It was a warning sign of the impending Q & A session.

Mia, on the other hand, had to work her blinkers and fight off her wide-eyed observation of him and Clara. Her demeanor made him uncharacteristically warm and hazy. Or was that fuzzy? It was such a bizarre feeling. He couldn't define it.

"Mom, would you mind cooking up some lunch? I'm dying for something home cooked, and I think Mia could use a real meal. I think she's had a bag of pretzels in the past twenty four hours."

Mia's face flushed. "Oh, I can help. I don't need to be tended to—"

"You'd never know it, but Mia's been shot at a few times, not to mention a nasty bout with some tear gas. Though that was my fault." Truth be told, he was proud of his girl for taking it like she did. Winters winked at Mia but still spoke to his mom. "I think she could use some of your famous cooking. And, Mia, you need to rest. I'm going to need your help later. So eat, then sleep. I have to head out for a while, but we'll take care of it all. Is that okay?"

Her mouth opened, closed, and opened again, but nothing came out. Her fingers touched her lips, a gesture as lost as the words she couldn't find. She shuffled a bare foot back and forth on the driveway, then nodded. Pebbled rocks bent to the will of her painted toes.

His mom started back into the house. "Colby, I'll let you get your friend settled, and I'll be in the kitchen. I might have some clothes that'll fit, Mia, if you want. I'll leave them at the foot of the stairs. I'm sure Colby will direct you to the nearest shower."

"Yes, thank you." She smiled, conveying her appreciation.

Winters balanced Clara on his hip, and, with his free hand, took Mia's chin, directing her gaze to him. His stare tracked her, despite Clara's every attempt to remove his sunglasses. "You need to relax. You're not an imposition or a headache. If anything, you're a pleasant surprise."

"Pleasant isn't how I'd describe myself right now." She swallowed hard enough that he could see it. Her fingers pleated the bottom of her torn-and-repaired shirt.

"Here I go. I'm an old MP3 stuck on repeat. What's wrong?"

Mia sucked her bottom lip and remained quiet. Had she been through interrogation resistance training?

"All right, doll. I'm going to show you around. You have the roam of the place, comfy bed, and a hot shower. Mom will stay here with Clara while I'm gone. She's more than happy to help you with anything you want. Really, she's easygoing. I promise."

Winters dropped his hand from her chin and interlaced his fingers with hers. Clara squealed and grasped at the rough hair on his face. With a lesser degree of hesitation in her drudging gait, Mia followed him into the house and into an expansive foyer with marble floors and rich colored wallpaper. She immediately eyed his security system panel next to the front door and security cameras.

"Don't let it bother you. It's for safety and protection. I can be paranoid about my family's safety. I'm a big believer in 'you can never be too careful'."

"Colby?"

He turned to face her, squeezing her hand tight. "Yeah?"

Mia sighed, but it sounded like the nervous whimper of a scared puppy. A scared, cute puppy. "I don't do *family* well. I don't have one. I don't know how to handle one. I—uh—can't remember the last time I held a man's hand, walking around his house, with his mom in the kitchen." Mia's palm went clammy in his hand. Her gaze bounced round the room, maybe looking for an escape route.

Well, shit. That was her problem? Never in a million years would he have guessed that. But he'd keep that to himself.

CHAPTER FOURTEEN

"I warned you this might be awkward." Winters gave a reassuring laugh and winked. Anything to help bring her out of her shell. He needed his Mia back. Not the silent, stone-cold Jane Doe who'd ridden in the car with him the last hundred or so miles. No, he wanted the spitfire, crazed woman who'd run them off the road and tried again and again to nail him in the balls.

She turned to him and gave a placating, unsure-of-her-survival smile.

"No one's asking anything of you. This is just my reality. And like I said, it's also the safest place to keep you until all of this is sorted out. My two worlds collided. Work and non-work." He shook her hand with a slight swing. "There's nothing to overthink. Can you shake off the nerves?"

He was hot again with a pleasantly uncomfortable, terribly unfamiliar feeling that had him questioning his judgment. Fuck it. He squeezed her hand with more want than comfort. He'd been squeezing that hand over and over since they'd gotten out of the car. He couldn't help it.

"It's simple. Everything collided back on that exit ramp. And in that motel room." His heartbeat galloped. Was that trepidation or lust? "I don't know what to tell you. And you haven't said much. So let's start simple. Do you want me to let go of your hand?"

His heart thumped in his chest. Once. Twice. If she didn't respond soon, he'd punch out of this conversation with more than a little wounded pride.

"No." She shook her head.

He didn't care if she looked like she was going to puke. He wasn't letting go of her hand. Someone would have to put crosshairs on him before he would break away. Even then, the move would be duck and cover, not catch and release. She was here, safe from the world, and until he knew what to do with her, that was where he wanted her.

"Outstanding. I wasn't in the mood to let go." His thumb caressed her tight grip.

It would've been easy to hand Clara to his mother, drag Mia to his room, and tear her clothes off her. But it wouldn't have been right. Besides the absurd awkwardness, his first responsibility was to Clara. He wasn't about to pawn her off whenever the mood struck. And the mood was always striking where Mia was concerned.

They walked down the hallway and up the stairs, grabbing the clean clothes, a sweatshirt, and flip-flops that Judith had laid out as promised.

Mia looked at him, the most interest he'd seen all day. "I'm going to change now."

"Anything you want." Guess he'd have to let her go.

He directed her to the bathroom. After a while, she came out squeaky clean, freshly clothed. The woman squared up quick. Over her shoulder, he saw her clothes stuffed in the trash can. *Bet slamming those in the bucket was like scoring the winning basket of a championship game.*

He took her hand and led her up the stairs. "So you saw that bathroom."

"Check."

"Here's the toy room."

They walked into an ice-cold room, only illuminated by a few computer screens. No windows. No furniture. Only shelves with his workstation in the middle.

"Toy room?"

"Grown up toys. Though not the kind that you may think of." He gave her a devilish grin. "Tools of the trade. Gadgets and gear. This is a tiny listening device. This one looks like a pack of gum, but push two pieces together, and you've got a slow burning smoke. Nothing explosive though. All show. I try to keep the C4 far away from the baby."

She laughed, acting less tense. "Makes sense."

"This one's pretty cool. It can make anything safe to drink. And this thing appears to be an outlet cover, but it has a high res camera. Motion activated."

"You're a kid in the candy store."

He shrugged, knowing he shouldn't show her anything in the room. Covert wasn't covert if others knew what secret weapons were available. But he wanted to distract her. Hell, he wanted to impress her. *Again?*

"Now this one." He peeled a microscopic translucent piece of fabric off wax paper and pressed it to her arm. "The material is a bio-agent. Soon as it comes into contact with your skin, it'll begin to destroy itself. It's a tracker. If activated, it's like a homing beacon."

"I can't see it anymore."

"That's the point. The enemy can't remove what they don't see."

"Oh." She giggled, inspecting the near invisible patch.

"That's funny?"

"No. It's just all I need for work is my DSM-IV, and you need spy equipment." She shivered. "Why's it so cold in here?"

"I like my gadgets, guns, and vehicles a precise sixty-six degrees. I work better when it's chilly. But you both have to be cold. Resuming our tour..." He walked them into the hall and pointed toward the doors. "There's my room, across from Clara's nursery."

Mia paused at the baby's room and stared at the lilac colored walls and bright white furniture. It was unlike the hardy décor of the rest of the house. Dark furniture. Thick leather. Heavy carpets. The nursery was as bright and carefree as Clara's smile. It suited the happy baby. He'd made sure that it was perfect for a precious girl. He would've made the walls out of cotton candy and hung twinkle, twinkle lights from the ceiling if he could've.

"Guest room. Guest room, again. You can stay here, if you want. It's got a gorgeous view of the lake out back, and it has its own bathroom. There's a Jacuzzi tub in my room. Feel free to use that if you want. Lots of whirling, jetting bubbles I hear chicks might like."

"You hear, huh?"

"Yup."

"Never had one of your lady friends compliment you on it?" She raised an eyebrow. "Or witness for yourself?"

"Sorry to disappoint. You're the only woman to step foot in this house who's not a blood relation."

He studied her for a second. His skin crawled with the need for her to stay with him, in his bedroom, in his bed. He longed to feel her skin against his again, to watch her sleep-heavy eyes flutter closed while she lay naked against him. But after ignoring him all day, he wasn't nearing that hope without much more serious consideration.

"Okay, then. A hot tub soak sounds amazing. Your house is gorgeous. Colby, thanks for taking care of me through all of this," she whispered.

He blew out. There it was again, that indescribable emotion that hit him under the collar and deep in the gut. It was a variation on adrenaline, nothing like a headache, and closer to heartburn.

"You need to relax. Do whatever it takes, all right?"

"I will. But I'd be just fine on a couch with some fast food. I hate that I'm burdening your family. I'll be out of your hair the moment you think it's safe."

Mild disappointment pecked at the thought of her not wanting him. Hell, not mild. Not by a click or two. They were short, slicing stabs of irritation. He wanted her jonesing for him like he was sweating for her. Pure need mixed with something he couldn't quite put his finger on. Enjoyment. Or infatuation? Whatever that sensation was, it was more than welcome and had nothing to do with his couch or sending her packing the second the all-clear rang out.

The ring of his cell phone interrupted the cacophony of thoughts. Phone calls were once in a blue moon. Only when it was a member of Titan or his mother. Without missing a beat, Mia reached over and lifted Clara from him, freeing both his hands in an instant. With a quick nod of thanks, he answered the phone in a curt manner that could sand plaster, then walked to a nearby window.

"I'm glad you finally got your ass back home. Took you long enough," Jared said.

"Really not in the mood for it, boss man. What did you learn about our client?"

"They're legit and made contact through our CIA friend. That NOC list is heavy-duty. They'll keep those operatives' identities safe. You just have to bring it in."

"Heavy-duty? I could've told you it's hot. I'll bring it over this afternoon. We have to talk about securing Mia Kensington's safety. The men after her and that disk are making some risky moves. It's not going to stop."

He didn't want Mia to hear him, and she wasn't paying attention to him. She had Clara close to her face, pointing out another window. The baby pulled at her hair, and Mia encouraged her in whispers, talking to Clara, tapping on the window to show her a bird. Or tree. Or something.

"Jared, I have to call you back."

He holstered the phone without waiting for a response and moved to Mia, threaded his fingers into her hair, and pressed his lips to her now agape mouth. She closed her lips onto his, and the intensity shot straight to his groin.

Hell, he couldn't help himself. His woman and his baby. It looked right. It felt right. Like it might have been if he had a normal life, and he wasn't a man who went to work strapped to the hilt like a warrior, and she wasn't a job gone rogue that he'd brought home.

He could kiss her all day long. Her plump lips fulfilled him. The kiss washed away the pining that ate at him when he didn't touch her. Thank God she kissed him back. He'd be completely messed up in the head if she didn't.

With his eyes still open, he stared at her, so close, so beautiful. Hers were closed, and he absorbed her warmth as she teased over his lips. His heart beat faster when she relaxed, molding into him while still holding his baby. Clara played with her hair with uncoordinated jerks, and Mia didn't stop her. It was picture perfect. Straight out of a Disneyland fairy tale. He couldn't have closed his eyes if he wanted to.

He pressed his forehead against hers. "I don't want you to stay in the guest room."

"And I don't want to." She locked eyes with him, and his gut tightened.

"I'm not asking you to play family. I get it. You don't *do* family. And I… can't. But I also can't see you across the room and not want to hold you. You're a crazy woman for even suggesting the couch." He grazed a finger down her cheek. "I can't sleep in the same house as you and not hold your sweet-ass body to mine."

Actually, he wouldn't be able to sleep knowing she was anywhere else in the world. He needed her under his roof, under his watch. While this job was a go, he would make sure she was by his side.

Weighty seconds ticked by. Each heavy lungful of air burned in his chest, and his heart felt thick. After she ignored him all day and played down every attempt at his strained subtleties, he should have been apprehensive about bearing it all. But he wasn't. It was a simple and basic need. Her with him.

"Lunch is ready. I'll heat up a bottle," Judith called up from the kitchen.

Rich smells drifted down the hallway. The spice and grease of fried chicken. The doughy aroma of biscuits fresh from the oven.

Mia smiled, tranquil as his lake at sunrise. Nothing stirred. No hesitations. Only a calm, peaceful serenity. It was a small miracle. He'd have to start all over if she freaked out on him.

"Are you hungry, Colby?"

"Starved." In more ways than one, but that wasn't important.

"Me, too. Let's go." Still carrying the baby on her hip, she laced her hand in his, and pulled him down the stairs and into the kitchen.

It didn't go unnoticed by his mother that Mia walked in with the baby on her hip. Her stomach swirled at the woman's barely raised eyebrows and dawning realization of her and

Colby's questionable circumstances. His mother didn't say anything to her or, as far as Mia could tell, to Colby.

Plates heaped high with food sat on the table. The spread should have been displayed on a cooking show. Picture perfect, and she was much hungrier than she realized. Famished, really.

The bottle warmer buzzed on the counter. Judith grabbed it, tested the bottle on the inside of her wrist while eyeing Mia. "You must be starved. But you're more than welcome to feed her if you want."

Mia's cheeks heated at the offer. "I don't know the first thing about feeding a baby." That, and she was sure the baby in her arms would call her bluff and jump if Mia so much as moved.

"It's simple. She does all the work. Just hold her like this." Judith moved Clara into a cradle in Mia's arms and passed her the bottle. "And hold the bottle upright like this. Support her head. She'll stop when she's done."

Mia looked at Colby. He smiled, encouraging her. All right, maybe holding Clara wasn't like snuggling an escape artist.

Big, bright eyes blinked. Fat cheeks plumped then caved with each suck. Clara was mesmerizing. Enchanting. She made Mia believe in familial happiness for a flash. This was why women spoke incessantly about the biological clock screaming in their heads. She had read about it. Studied it. But before now, it didn't click. Sugary innocence and unadulterated trust stared up at her, threatening to thaw one of her dark fears. Family. Children. Parents.

"Look at you." Colby came up behind her and leaned on the chair. His presence made her nervous. What if he didn't want her to do this? What if he *did*?

He massaged the anxious knots in her shoulders. In an instant, the hefty weight of concern washed away with his meaningful caress. "Clara's addictive. Watch out for that, doll. I hate to grab my food to go, but I have to head to work."

He filled a plastic container. Watching him make his lunch made her laugh. Big, bad, tough Colby Winters—in real life, he was a baby-toting, brown-bag lunch packing, family man. Despite his lean muscles and hard-edged face, he was an honest man, trying to fix the world one tear gas grenade at a time.

"It's easy to see why. She's perfect, Colby. You're a lucky man."

Lucky. Happy. Warm.

It wasn't that she didn't think those things of herself. She was just different. Family was a foreign concept. Long ago, she allowed hers to fade to black in her memory.

Her childhood had been regimented. But even that description was an understatement. Her father had preferred to be called *The Colonel*. Her mother's indifference to The Colonel's rules and regulations came in the form of pills and booze. She never stood up for Mia, even when The Colonel put a knife to her throat to teach her a lesson or spanked her with a belt until she vomited. Welts branded her for days.

Mia shook her head. No need to go down memory lane. No need to remind herself why family life didn't work for her. All her pain was channeled to help others. Mia specialized in military families and soldiers who came home from hell. It was all in hopes that, one day, she could help a young girl avoid a home life like the one she had suffered through.

But for now, for this simple moment, she appreciated family time with Judith, Colby, and Clara.

She'd also savor the handsome man who proved so interested in being her hero. No matter where they were, or what they were doing, Colby made her blood rush at a feverish pace, crashing through her body like a stock car race. When he looked at her with those dark-as-night eyes, she felt stronger and more desirable than she thought possible. And when he didn't look at her, heck, when he wasn't in the room, the mere thought of Colby made her shiver with wanton need.

He placed a disposable cell phone in front of her. "And you, beautiful… I'll call you later. Burner phone. Another fun toy. If you have to call someone to let them know you're safe on your vacation, use this one. If you need to talk to me, I'm the first number programmed in."

Colby placed a kiss on her lips that took her breath away, stilling all the concern and apprehension she felt in his home, with his baby. And in its place, she relished the bold attraction that bloomed. She was too overcome, and slightly embarrassed, at the casual intensity of his kiss to see if Judith saw them.

Clara finished her bottle, and her sleepy eyes hung heavy. Colby scooped her out of Mia's arms and placed her up against his shoulder. The baby wore a pink flower onesie and matching footed pants with ruffles on the bottom. She was a stark contrast to Colby's combat boots, dark camo pants, and ass-kicker shirt.

Mia knew he wore his Glock tucked into a holster under his shirt and saw the tactical knife secured against his calf. Both weapons were secure and safe from the curious reach of the baby.

He burped Clara, his huge hand spanning the width of the sleeping baby, and left the kitchen. As he bounded into the kitchen again, he flipped on the switch for the baby monitor sitting on the counter. Mia listened to the last few notes of the mobile play a lullaby as he waved good-bye to her and his mom, grabbed his keys, and walked toward the garage door.

CHAPTER FIFTEEN

Titan headquarters was a fortress, a high-tech lair with Fort Knox-like security. It was cold. Impenetrable. His home away from home.

Winters stared over Parker's shoulder at the wall of flat screens. Computer systems that NASA could only dream about continually scoured through data and satellite images like electronic wallpaper. Ones and zeroes danced a techie tango. High-resolution topography shuffled from one covert location to the next. The hub monitored their operations around the world. Teams he didn't know, but would go through hell to assist, were mere blips on an observation screen and surrounded by all the intel that could possibly help.

"Where's Jared?" Winters ran his hand over the smooth war room table. Many a high stakes battle plan had been drawn there.

Parker didn't look from his wall of screens. "Most likely thinking of ways to torture people."

If Jared developed new techniques, Winters would love to try them on the fuckers chasing Mia. He'd try anything, experimental or not, if it meant a slow and painful demise.

"We need a plan of action. Otherwise, I'm just going to start picking off anyone I don't know. Titan's legal bill will spiral into the cataclysmic category."

Parker spun in his swivel chair to face him. "You're not going to like this, but I'll bet my Ducati for your new WaveRunner, he'll want to use Mia as bait."

"No. We've already been down that road, and I'm not doing it again. We can use the NOC list as bait. We can use me as bait. I'll string that bike up like a piece of NOC list meat. But Mia is a no go."

"Whoever these guys are, they'll follow her. She's the easy target."

"You'd think with all of your damn brains and Jared's 'been there, done everything' attitude, you two could come up with something more original." Winters picked at his nail with his keys. "Shit. Easy target. I don't want to hear it."

"That's a lot of whining, Winters. Bring it up with Jared when you see him. You might as well grab some grub, I'm not going to be done for a few hours." Parker put his earbuds in and turned back to the screen.

"Would've been nice if Jared mentioned that when he said to get my ass to work." Winters spun on his heels and hurried to his vehicle. He couldn't get home fast enough.

Juan Carlos Silva rang Diego's phone all morning. No answer. Several possibilities crawled through his mind. The two most promising excuses were death or prison. Death was preferable. If Diego were incarcerated in an American prison, Juan Carlos would have to kill him later.

Juan Carlos ran a hand over his smooth cheeks. He was so close to that list and that woman. How he wanted her now. A prize for his troubles. A bonus for the headache this American jaunt had caused him.

It wasn't as if he assigned an underling. He sent a capable, lethal man. Diego had never disappointed before. He'd never needed punishment, encouragement, or extensive lessons. No, Diego wanted to be in good graces. He wanted to be a leader. He'd never given Juan Carlos a reason to plan for his execution. The more things changed, the more they stayed the same. Diego might have been a pupil, his very own puppet, but he was expendable. Just like all the rest.

Juan Carlos cracked his knuckles and knocked back the last of the amber liquor in his highball glass. "Have Alejandro brought to me."

Someone always listened for his orders. His staff would find his number two and send for him immediately, though none of them would venture near the man unless requested. Alejandro looked like a gorilla, snarled like a barracuda, and stunk like a sweat-soaked gladiator under the high sun. If he weren't a valuable resource, Juan Carlos wouldn't let him within one hundred kilometers of his estates. But he was valuable, and he'd more than earned his title of second in command. Alejandro developed ways to torture that made him cringe.

Before he could refill his glass from the crystal decanter, Alejandro Suarez ambled into the room. An Uzi was draped over his shoulder like a child's backpack, but nonetheless, he addressed Juan Carlos with a reverent tilt of his head. "You sent for me, Senor."

"Diego is failing. If he's not dead, he soon will be."

Alejandro nodded. Perhaps hoping to carry out the death order.

"Do whatever it takes to bring me that woman and the list. You should fly out this afternoon. Head to Washington, DC. You can have access to any of my resources you should deem necessary."

Alejandro smiled with the sadistic look Juan Carlos knew would fix his problems. His number two wanted the woman. He hadn't given him a woman of his own in weeks. It was like tossing a meaty bone to a Rottweiler. A day later, he would be picking his teeth with a rib bone.

Juan Carlos hated to sacrifice his bestselling product, especially the assumed caliber of Mia Kensington. A little older than he liked, but she had shown fight. Men paid well for that attribute. But if Alejandro succeeded, he'd give the man whatever he wanted.

"Alejandro, *mi amigo*, if she's to your liking, you may keep her as a reward for your continued excellence." Without second thought to the tormented fate of the young woman, Juan Carlos returned to his desk to review a ledger.

CHAPTER SIXTEEN

Winters had a raw lump at the back of his throat since Mia had held Clara earlier in the day. And that kiss by the window didn't help. Hell if he'd known he craved domestic bliss. Seeing her hold his kid knocked Mia intergalactic-style past the Milky Way.

He had made his way home in a flash, driving like a man intent on sharing his newfound revelation. Now, he towered over her freshly showered body, relishing the scent of his shampoo in her hair. He resisted the urge to finger-comb it. They were in his living room. An empty house, except for the two of them. Too bad he missed another shower with her.

"This could be complicated." He rubbed a few dark strands of her wet hair between his fingers. "It feels complicated. It feels like *something*, and, doll, I'm not used to *anything*."

He broke from her, scrubbed his hands over his cheeks, hoping to push away the sinking dread. He was saying the wrong things. Mia remained mum, and he couldn't keep his mouth shut.

Without his conscious permission, his hands found her tresses again. "I'm sorry I had to drag you into this. Into my home. Into my family."

"It's not that I *dislike* being here." She tried to brush his hands from her hair, but it was no use. He couldn't keep his hands off her.

"Oh, it's not, huh?" He laughed, cupping her chin in his hand. "Tell me then, Miss Psychologist. Where does all your anxiety stem from?" *And tell me the root of mine while you're at it.*

"From places you don't want to know. Places I don't want to share."

"Why not? You know things about me. All my shit. You know all about Clara and how she came into my life. You know my biggest fear is an inability to protect my family. That my career could somehow hurt Clara one day." He took a breath. He sounded like a chick. "I showed you mine. What about yours?"

"Truth?" she asked, dripping in hesitation.

"You want to stop now?"

"Well, no." A grandfather clock shook the room. Tic. Tic. Toc. "I don't do family…"

"You've established that."

"Because, well, it'd be better if I showed you. Look at this beauty." She turned, dropped the waistband of her pants, and pointed to an old scar on her bottom.

His eyes narrowed and jaw clenched. Were those scars? *How did I not see that?* She'd been below him and in front of him, but never bottom up. One line after another. They were definitely scars. Smooth and faded but very much there.

She lifted her chin, took his angry fist, unfolded his fingers, and traced a narrow line. "And over here. They're cuts. Slices. Deep reminders in my flesh as to where I came from and what I need to avoid."

He stood furious and mute, not knowing where to take his line of questioning. Kind words and coherent thoughts evaded him. It was his turn to go silent, despite the storm that thrashed inside his chest. He'd kill the motherfucker.

"And I have marks on the back of my legs, real high up. Right under my butt. Thicker. Wider."

Thicker? Wider? He'd been so… distracted. He was a piece of shit. How did he not see this?

"Mia, baby. I didn't—"

"You wouldn't see them if you weren't looking. They're old. But nowhere near forgotten."

Deep pools teemed on the edge of her bottom eyelids, threatening a flash flood. They never fell, forced back by what could only be a will made of steel.

"Mia..." What could he possibly offer this moment? He hated himself for not having a fucking hot spring of extraordinary things to say. For not knowing how to take away the pain she must've been feeling.

"My mother drank like a fish. Or a sailor. Or whatever the worse of the two is. She chased her liquor with her pills. Pint-sized pills. Big-dog pills. Pink and blue. Yellow and white. Square and round and rectangle. She loved variety."

There were the walls. The sarcasm. It all made sense.

"She hurt you?" he asked but knew it didn't matter what her response was. Someone hurt her, someone who should have to pay in gigantic proportions.

"Oh, no. She never hurt me. She just focused on laundry, or she'd watch television. Though sometimes, on the days I thought she couldn't love me any less, she'd go for a walk. Come to think of it, that hurt more than any stupid cut."

How could a mother hurt her baby? He'd never understand it. He'd spent his life fixing wrongs others couldn't handle themselves. Mia was trying to keep it together in front of him. It shouldn't have been this way. She shouldn't have these memories and scars.

"She hurt you in my book."

"There's always that."

"Your father? He's the one who hurt you?"

She coughed out an arctic chuckle, more theatrical than comical. "You mean *The Colonel*? Yes, he was the one. He liked to inflict pain with whatever he could find. With whatever might entertain him, distract him, or pass the time in his miserable existence."

Winters would love to kill the bastard. But not before he ensured the man relived each old wound he gave Mia. Winters channeled all his rage into his fists and tried to hide them in the pockets of his pants. Ripping shit off walls wasn't going to help Mia now. Napalming an area a mile wide wouldn't help either.

He had to listen. Had to figure out what might help. A rampage would only be self-serving. He'd do it later and rain fire from the sky.

"Honey—" His chest felt tight.

"Don't honey me. Or baby. Or doll. I don't need it, and I don't want it."

He tugged at his collar. "They alive?"

"Nope."

"Good."

She nodded. "Agreed."

"All of your walls make sense." He hugged her. Not with the intention of crushing her breasts against him, or wrapping her body onto his, but with the sole desire to console her, wipe away all the hurt and pain.

Mia laughed again, this time, into his chest. She was still very much pressed into his embrace. "My walls are nothing. I became a psychologist to figure out how to fix me. Helping everyone else is just a bonus."

"We're the sum of our parts. One thing doesn't define us."

"For you, okay. But I don't know about me."

How could she think such a thing? He pulled her from his chest, holding her in outstretched arms. "No, Mia. That's where you're wrong. That's where all your schooling and studying left you hanging. You *are* perfect. You *are* strong."

"I'm not—"

"Everything about you is all shock and awe. You know what that means? Overwhelming power and spectacular displays of force. Tell me how you made it out of your childhood home to a military base? Tell me how you've made it through the last days with me, enemy crosshairs searching for your gorgeous smile?"

"But—"

"You wouldn't have made it if you didn't house a hell of a fight deep within your gut. And to top it off, you're the most beautiful woman I've ever set eyes on. Ever."

Tears slid down the perfect slope of her cheeks. Her lips trembled, and she grew prettier with each passing second.

"I wasn't asking for a pep talk."

"That wasn't one. It was the God's honest truth."

"I don't want to talk about this anymore."

"We don't have to." Where did he go from there? "Forget it all, and tell me anything you want to. Tell me a joke, or your favorite food, or if you have a pet."

"A reporter asked a sniper what he felt after he took a kill shot."

"What are you talking about?"

A slip of a smile crossed her face. "Well, it's not a joke. But it'll get a reaction. A reporter asked a sniper what he felt after he took a kill shot. The sniper looked at the reporter and said?"

"I don't know. He said… I don't know."

"Recoil. He felt recoil." She laughed.

Thank God. She was laughing. "My, my, Mia. A little gun humor. I like it."

"Blueberries. Watermelon. Sushi."

"What?"

"Is it your turn to lose your mind? You asked what my favorite foods are. Blueberries. Watermelon. Sushi. Spicy tuna rolls. Extra spicy, cucumber, and avocado. And I want a dog. After this hair-raising experience, I think I'll get one. I earned it."

"Indeed you have. What else you got?"

"After Judith took Clara for the afternoon, I was dying for you to come home and kiss me."

"Dying? That's a bit dramatic. How about mildly interested? Possibly aroused?"

She laughed. The sound danced in his ears. "You're awful."

"You like it," he whispered into her ear before he kissed her. Mia pushed up on her tiptoes to nuzzle against him.

"Yeah, I do. Right now, I want more than a kiss."

Her heat pulsed through him as she murmured against his skin. "If that's the case, I'm about five seconds away from dragging you into my bedroom."

She dropped down from her toes. "That long? I'm disappointed in you."

Hell. After that smartass remark, he lifted her into his arms and bounded the stairs. Winters kicked the door closed behind them and fell onto the bed, bracing over her with a forearm on each side of her head. *That was less than five seconds, wasn't it?*

"That mouth of yours might get you into trouble."

Her eyes danced. "You can't even begin to imagine what my mouth might do."

Oh, his imagination worked just fine, thank you. Every dream he ever stored in memory, queued up and flashed at the ready. All of his blood rushed straight to his cock, and every muscle tightened in a restrained effort. He throbbed with the thought of her mouth taking him. It was almost too much to bear. Almost.

"You can't do much pinned under me." He was as obvious and pointless as directions on a rocket launcher, reading *Aim toward the enemy*.

"Let me see what I can do about that." She licked her top lip in one slow, wet lash.

Before he knew how to wrangle that thought, her hands planted on his chest and pushed against him like he wasn't two hundred plus pounds of lean muscle. She could have used her pinky and had him flat on his back, powerless to her will. That was just fine with him.

Mia straddled his waist like a dominatrix ready to work. She drew his black shirt up, working it over his head with the efficiency of a woman on a sexual mission. Her fingers spread wide and ran though his chest hair. Her chilly palms left a trail of fire. She rocked her hips and arched her back.

"Open your eyes, Colby." Her soft order contradicted the inferno hidden in her words, and he all but said *yes, ma'am*. If she wanted to call the plays, he was more than game to give her this round.

Silken hair teased his chest as she leaned over to kiss him. Hard, wanting, greedy. Her fingernails traced an old battle scar, high and right on his chest, then threaded into the coarse hairs and tugged with a temptress's touch.

He flexed against her center, radiating heat. She met his drive, rubbing a slow rhythm, an exacting pace, demanding what she wanted of him. Wet kisses danced across his chest. In a move of perfect torture, she shimmied down his legs. Her face and lips hung above his skin, a glowing sun ready to set. She kissed one side of his stomach, then the other, leaving red-hot tracks of smoldering embers.

She unfastened his utilitarian belt. So practical, except for when it wasn't. But the leather bent to her will and loosened at her sultry command. Next, the top button popped open and the zipper released. If one could suffer in paradise, then he was there.

Mia looked pleased. Proud. In charge. With her on top, she might as well strap a block of C4 to his chest. It wasn't going to take much of an ignition to make him dissolve into a million fragments.

"I've been dying to kiss you," she paused, as he helped her shuck down his pants and boxer briefs, "just like this."

Her tongue traced to the top of his shaft. Smooth, soft, and supple. Her mouth encircled him. A snug, deep heat overtook him, and a groan ripped from the depths of his gut. Profound, harsh, more and more familiar.

"Are you okay?"

"Hell, yes. Do. Not. Stop."

Like a desperate man, he was ready to beg for her torment, borrow sweet nothings, and steal her mind, her soul, her anything that would bring another caress.

Hotness enveloped him again. *Sweet Jesus*. He buried his hands in her hair and watched as his length disappeared into her mouth, her eyes trained on him.

Damn her snug mouth and whipping tongue. Damn the springs of electricity that raced through him. Mia hummed, and he vibrated like piano strings struck by a virtuoso. She massaged him, fondled him, and straight drove him to the edge of a vicious cliff. He teetered on the threshold but would swan dive face first if it meant his climax.

"Mia, doll." He panted. He pleaded. He needed her on so many levels. What was left of his control was seconds away from dissipating.

He should pull away. An old drill instructor barked in his head: five second fuses only last three seconds.

Words wouldn't come out. Reluctant, he tried his best to slide from her. But she wouldn't let him, her intentions clear, and he didn't fight her. Winters fisted a pillow and crushed it onto his face, choking on her name as flames ripped through him.

"Good fucking God, Mia," he shouted, as he pulsed. She didn't loosen, forcing him to stay with her until he was done.

Unbelievable. She knew some tricks, and then some.

Mia pulled the pillow from him. And, oh, was she a foxy knockout. Lips slightly swelled. Cheeks very flushed. Her smile captivated his heart. *How did he get so lucky?*

"I can't compete with—"

She cut him off with a blistering kiss. Her tongue delved into his mouth, and he pulled her into a possessive hold, sparking him hot and bothered for an encore performance. He craved her. Bad.

The spicy aroma of sex filled the room. He savored Mia, then made quick work of losing her clothes. With her naked body lying beside him, their skin clinging together, Winters ached. In a perfect way. In an "every nerve tingled, screaming for him to do something about it" way.

"Mia. Mia. Mia."

His throat constricted. An invisible hand crushed the air from his lungs. He needed to make love until he was devoid of those desires, those affections and afflictions that clouded his mind and made his heart pound like he'd been eight-ballin' lines of coke.

Wait a hot minute.

Make love. Make love?

Mia's fingers ran into his short chest hair, exploring his pecs and stomach. Her damp sex rubbed his erection. He leaned forward, catching the tip of her perked breast in his mouth, cupping and sucking her, then watched the chain reaction. Her head dipped back, her back arched, driving her luscious breast into his kisses.

Mine. Definitely, absolutely, all mine.

He leaned over to the nightstand, removed a condom from the drawer, and slipped it on. Winters ran a hand into her silky hair as Mia angled herself over the tip and hovered, only allowing a moment of entry into her tight body. Such a tease. He smiled and closed his eyes.

She engulfed him, every sense infiltrated. Sight. Sound. Mind. And left her permanent mark.

"I've needed you my whole life, Mia. And I had no idea," he whispered, eyes still closed.

Was that aloud? She danced her fingertips across him. Did she hear him?

His eyes opened, staring deep into the dark, trusting eyes of Mia Kensington. *Yeah, she heard.*

Mia rode him slow and deep, rocking back and forth. Her breath hitched, her tempo amplified, and he felt larger and harder and more of a man than ever before. His day job was nothing compared to earning her honeyed cries of rapture.

Good God, he wouldn't—couldn't—dare let this end.

She rose on him, nailing the Aphrodite act. Her fingers snaked into her hair, her pussy tightened on his shaft, and she swayed to a rhythm and music he could almost hear. He palmed her hips. His cock screamed for speed. His mind prayed to bring her to the brink.

"Mia, I—"

She shut him down. "I'm here. I'm not going anywhere."

What the fuck was going to come out of his mouth? *I need you? I want you?*

"Promise me."

As if he uttered a magic phrase of Kama Sutra, her face went stormy, and her vagina clenched. He held her tight, as she came undone in his arms like a Tasmanian devil, climaxing in a dervish.

She collapsed on him. Cheek to cheek. Perfect. He wanted to feel her float back to him in bed, all ambrosial and glittering. All things he was unaware of, until Mia landed in his life, a superb bombardment.

With gentle precision, he rolled off his back, still deep inside her. Angelic hair splayed on the mattress, framed by pillows. Legs wrapped his torso. Fingers threaded his hair. Trying for the softest of strokes and failing, Winters took his entire length from her drenched sweetness, then shafted her full again.

He brushed the hair from her face and concentrated on the flawless symmetry of her cheekbones. Sweat beaded on the nape of his neck, on his temples. He skipped fingers over her clit. Together, they soared in cadence to his thrusts. Mia trembled, vibrated, pushing them both to the verge of orgasm.

She purred in his ear. The wonderful, incoherent mumbles filled his heart.

Did she understand how he felt? If she did, at least one of them understood.

He wasn't ready for it to end, intent to declare some sort of message, but yet, he was dying to finish.

"Please, Colby, come with me. I need you with me."

Against his control, a deep breath loosened. She turned his key, unlocking an unprotected passageway. He drove with her, trying to fulfill her wishes.

Mia released again, ramming a shudder from his core to the tips of his ears. Absolute and sweeping completeness. They came in unison. His moan and her cry intermixed. Panting. Struggling. Battling.

With nothing left to give, he collapsed next to her, gathered Mia into his arms, and prayed she wouldn't pull from him right now. He just needed a few more intimate minutes with her. A few more minutes of consummate fulfillment.

CHAPTER SEVENTEEN

Even as Mia drowned in comfortable exhaustion, her anxious mind sat ready to taunt her. Lazy seconds lounged into hushed minutes in the twilight-lit room. Purple shadows cascaded from the picture window. Deep oranges tempered in the setting sky. The knowing air loomed in the bedroom, a million times heavier than the emotional weight of his words.

I've needed you my whole life. His words danced in her head and seared into her memory. What would he have said if she hadn't cut him off? What did she want him to say? Something. Nothing. Everything. Who knew? Guessing made her heart and her head pound, one right after the other, seesawing in a brutal clash.

She hurt for wanting something so fleeting and so dangerous. The moments when she tried to reason away her feelings for Colby were absurd.

Absurdity was ignoring the jump in her stomach when he gave a languid smile or the warm rush when he stepped close. Absurdity was avoiding the glimmer of optimism. She wasn't destined to be alone and didn't have to feign imaginary interest in the boring and untrustworthy.

If she knew there were men like Colby Winters running around, she wouldn't have given up in a shrug of disinterest. Now, every slow kiss and every sweeping glance was loaded with potential.

Gathered into his possessive hold, his sated breaths airily contradicted every one of his unyielding mannerisms. Mia just existed in the moment. No worries. No fears. No future. No past. Just now. Him and her. She burrowed against his chest.

"I thought you were asleep," he whispered.

Scorching shivers washed across her warm skin. She could lie and say she just awoke, but there wasn't a reason. He brushed her hair with the tips of his fingers, slow and soft, like she was his to cherish.

"I feel safe." That wasn't a lie.

"Good. You should."

"I don't mean from the hell that's been chasing us. I mean from the hell that I've ignored for the better part of my life."

"Good."

"Very short and sweet, Colby."

"Baby, if you want to talk about what happened, go for it. I'm listening. But you know, I'm no angel, and I'm not finished dancing with the devil. If anyone ever hurts you like that again, there's nothing I won't do to protect you. To make sure you're never hurt again."

She nodded. He was an angel to her, no matter who he danced with.

He traced the scar under her chin. "This mark is a call to arms. This made me angry, hateful, and full of a vicious need for vengeance." He kissed her bare shoulder. "But I didn't need to see scars to know the day I met you, my world changed."

She had fought the urge to cry like she avoided his closeness. Again, tears begged for release. Her eyes burned. Her throat was raw. But, in his arms, with his words, it was finally okay to cry.

Mia didn't move. She didn't sniff or sob. But cleansing tears escaped.

"Are you crying?"

Again, no point in lying. She smiled. "Yes."

Colby leaned over, pressing her into the bed. His jaw flexed, and he locked his eyes with hers. Such intensity. Her stomach flipped, sending a rush from her head to her toes.

"Sweet Jesus, I'm sorry. I didn't mean—"

"No. No, this is… welcome." She snorted a laugh. *Very attractive*.

He laughed at her oh-so feminine laugh. "If you say so, Dr. Freud. Smiling and crying don't mix."

"They do right now."

"And why is that?"

"Because my world changed, too."

That was an understatement if there ever was one. Was there a handsome man and even a dog in her future? Years of studying psychology went out the door. None of this made sense. Nothing was practical. But here she was, a veteran gunfight spectator and kidnapping survivor. Liberated with simple words from a warrior.

Liberated. She played with the idea, turning the word over in her head. Liberated worked and was the truth. That was an accomplishment and, because of it, she earned anything she wanted. A fluffy puppy with an appropriate name like Killer or Slayer. A sexy man who wanted nothing more than to keep her safe and in bed. Life was marvelous.

"What do you think about dinner?" he asked.

"I'm not hungry."

"No, I mean, do you want to go to dinner tomorrow night?"

"Like a date?" Even as the shadows faded over the room, she saw him blush.

"Yes, like a date, doll. Like candlelight and roses."

A date with candlelight and roses? He surprised her when she least expected it, though that was the exact definition of surprise. A suit and dress shirt on his solid body might be her greatest weakness. Would she be able to hold a decent conversation while admiring the view?

Her heart sunk. So close and she was going to ruin it. "All I have to wear are your mom's sweatpants and shirt. Very sexy."

"We can remedy that hiccup."

"What? You're going to be my white knight fashionista?"

"I'm your whatever-it-takes-to-keep-you-happy-*ista*."

Whatever it took? She should define that so he wasn't left grasping at assumptions in the proverbial dark.

"I can run out tomorrow morning and pick something out," she said.

"No sweater sets. Or khaki pants."

She could hear the smile in his voice. "I don't always wear that. I just didn't plan on more than one outfit on my excursion to Louisville."

"You need something short and tight."

She laughed. "Making requests?"

"And low cut."

"Colby!" Her cheeks heated. "I can dress myself, thank you very much."

"Just letting you know where my mind is. Are you all done with your smiling tears?"

Her nerves tinged. Was all this to make her stop crying? "You don't have to take me to dinner to make sure I'm not crying on your watch."

"No you don't, Mia. No rebuilding those walls."

"I'm not—"

"The hell you aren't. I'm taking you out because you like that stuff, and I like you. Simple. Don't you shrinks know how this stuff works? All that *making you happy, makes me happy* bullshit?"

"I'm not a shrink."

"But you *are* missing the point. On purpose, I'd assume."

"I don't have my credit cards or cash. I need to—"

"Cash is in the drawer in the kitchen, next to the surveillance camera you kept eyeing. Cars are in the garage. Take your pick. Keys are on a peg board next to the door."

"I'm not taking your money."

"You think I care about coin after dodging bullets with you? But if you'd rather just go to dinner in my mom's sweats, cool by me, doll. I don't care. I was just giving you my wish list. As long as you're there, I wouldn't notice your clothes."

"Uh." What to say to that?

"Tell me when and where you want to go, and I'll make sure I'm there. Or someone from Titan, for your protective detail. I have to work sometime in the morning, but after that, we'll do whatever you want."

"Thank you." Whatever she wanted? Staying right here was top on her list. Mia leaned up and kissed him. "Do you still have the NOC list?"

"I do. It's safe."

"Why do you still have it?"

"I'm only going to give it to my boss. He wasn't there, and I didn't stick around."

"After we get rid of it, I'll be safe?"

"In theory."

"Very reassuring. How about in reality?"

He didn't answer. That was several versions of concerning.

"Colby?" Worst case scenarios would begin forming if he didn't answer soon. Heck, in the back of her mind, they'd already started.

"In reality, the fuckers will be pissed. They'll want to do something about it. We'll make sure they engage Titan, not you, and we'll all come to an understanding."

"I don't know what that means."

"It means we work out an agreement. You won't be worth pursuing, because the cost will be too high."

"The cost?"

"Their resources. Their men. They're all the way in South America. Once they know they can't get that list, anything they do will be out of retaliation. But they're businessmen. Everything has a price. A cost of what their time and interest is worth. Eventually, they move on. It's dirty dollars and cents."

"So more people will get hurt. You can get hurt." Her voice sharpened.

"We've already had that conversation. I won't get hurt."

"Now, I'm calling bullshit. You *can* get hurt. You *can* die." This wasn't what she wanted. She wanted to forget the nightmare they survived and live it up in a fairy tale world. But no, he wanted to go play cops and robbers again.

"Honey, this is what I do. It didn't change because Clara came into my life, and it's not going to change because I'm all wrapped into you. I'm sorry." His fingers drew down her arm, around her elbow to her wrist. "This is complicated, but I promise I'll keep you safe, and I'll always come home."

The room was dark, with the setting sun long gone into the night. Moonlight bathed them, casting a milky glow across the light carpet.

"When this is over, when you don't have to protect me, do you still want to see me?" She draped her arm over her face, hiding from his answer. If he said no, the moon would drop from the cloudless sky, leaving it sad and inky.

"Of course I do. I'm not making up the things I say for your benefit," he said, rubbing her arm.

"You're making it up for yours?"

He shook his head, coiling his arms around her. "Silly girl. Let me rephrase. Everything I've done is *for* your benefit, but I've never lied to you. We have something special. So let's play it out one day at a time and see if it works for us. Maybe you'll hate me on our date. Maybe you're just using me for the sex."

"Maybe I am."

"Well, it wouldn't be the worst thing that's happened to me."

His phone rang from the nightstand. He unwound himself from her and answered. A few short words later, he was back by her side.

"So that was the bad guys calling in their surrender?" She laughed softly.

"You're cute when you say bad guys. But nope. I have to be at the office at stupid o'clock in the morning."

"What?"

"Early. I have to head to Titan way earlier than I wanted. So when you wake your adorable head up in the morning, you'll be all alone. Sorry about that."

"I suppose now you'll tell me we have to sleep while in bed."

They laughed together. The moment was so comfortable and fun.

"Guess so. But there's an upside. I can vouch these sheets are softer and cleaner than that motel room's." He kissed her nose. "Besides, I need my beauty sleep. Hot date tomorrow."

"Oh, me, too."

"Must be one lucky bastard." He gave her another kiss. "Sweet dreams, princess."

If she had penned all her dreams and wishes and desires, this wouldn't have made it on to the top one hundred list. It wouldn't have made it on to the world-is-ending-time-to-make-a-list list. She wasn't creative enough and didn't aspire grand enough.

Never would she have envisioned a battle-tried hero offering a fantasy date and calling her princess. Never would that man fall asleep with her in his clutches. Twice. In a row.

Never.

But he was here. And this was happening. It was her unknown dream come true.

CHAPTER EIGHTEEN

The road noise didn't dull his thoughts. Nope. No luck for that, as they roared and complained along with the whirl of his speeding tires. Winters drummed his thumbs on the steering wheel and picked up his burner phone a dozen times wanting to call Mia.

It was still dark out, and with dawn yet to break, what was the point of disturbing her? He cursed at blameless drivers observing the speed limit as he maneuvered his way to Titan headquarters.

He woke up holding happiness. Her sweet smell still clung to him in his truck, and the last thing he had wanted to do was slip away from the warm bed. If this job didn't revolve around Mia, he might have told Jared he was taking a vacation. Time like that accumulated. He must have weeks available. When he busted through the door, question numero uno would have to be, *Where's the company handbook?*

Surely that existed. Right?

But would it have a section entitled Don't *Do* the Job? He had a date with *the job* tonight. A very hot date. No corporate set of rules would change that.

He snarled to no one and pulled into Titan's secure parking. Before facing the guys, he had to lose the whole just-woke-up-with-a-naked-woman glow. It was too early in the morning for a razzing, and he hadn't had nearly enough coffee or Dots to ease into his day.

He squeezed his eyes tight, took a deep breath, and walked to the first door. Code entered. Locking mechanism disengaging. Another door. Retina scan. Another door and another, jumping through whatever hoops Parker had going right now. Goddamn security measures. Good thing he appreciated them.

Winters blew through the ops nerve center, straight into the kitchenette, hoping to hell someone had brewed a pot already. Nope. No luck. Not even a leftover box of candy in his stash. Christ, he felt like a chick. Mood swings. Candy cravings. He needed to cut that shit out.

"What's your problem, Winters?" Parker eyed him when he stalked back into the computer hub. Despite the heat pouring off hundreds of thousands of dollars' worth of electronics, the room was icy cold. "You blew out of here yesterday like you were avoiding enemy fire, and today, it's like you have the shakes."

"I had places to be." Guess clearing his mind didn't work. "Where the fuck is everyone? I thought this was an ops meeting, or was I wrong?"

"When did you start wearing a watch?" Parker spun round in his chair, regarding him with even more curiosity.

Shit. Should he just wear a sign that said *hook, line, and sinker,* or just fess up that there was a woman in his bed he wasn't fond of leaving. He rubbed a hand over his face.

"Never mind. Just ready to wrap this up. This job's been a headache."

"Dude, *you* are a headache. Since when did you give a shit about complications? I thought you fed off pandemonium."

There were Grade A assholes who'd fucked with him and Mia. He could forgive someone going after him. But not her. Messing with her earned a place in his crosshairs.

Winters flashed Parker a shut-the-fuck-up glare when Jared walked into the room, filled to his eyebrows with the usual piss and vinegar. He was an Army Ranger and had been trained by the best to be the best. The military got all they could out of him before he took his Chief Motherfucker in Charge attitude and turned into a very tidy profit for all involved.

"He has a point, Winters." Jared studied a topography map on the table.

"What? That I don't wear a watch? Or that first one in didn't turn on the coffee?" Winters glared at Parker.

A few other men shuffled into the room, and they all took seats around a large table, bitching about the ungodly time of day. Parker spread out a handful of glossy papers, and everyone shuffled through the pile. Jared nodded to Parker, signaling for him to begin.

"I retrieved shots from the traffic cameras, toll booths, and security footage at the places Winters stopped." Parker took some photos from the men and arranged them in chronological order. "Airport. First motel."

Everything looked legit. Parker could pull any picture anywhere there was a camera. That was for sure.

He pointed to additional shots on the table. "These two men followed Winters from the Nation's Capitol to Derby City. They're employed by Juan Carlos Silva. A Colombian cartel. They trade mostly women and drugs."

Jared growled. "I'm sick of cartel kingpins trafficking girls."

Aren't we all?

Parker tossed out another photo. "This ugly fucker is Diego Cortes, reportedly one of Silva's top men. He was behind the grab at the airport. Probably panicked after you dismembered his team and hired a couple of street punks to fill ranks. He also came after you at the second motel."

The guys were shuffling through the eight by ten glossies. Winters didn't need to see them. He lived it. He caught a smirk from Parker.

Parker laid out another photograph, very deliberate, and tapped it. "Here's the karaoke bar where Winters engaged them. Police records indicate Cortes and another man were found dead in a car trunk."

Like a donkey kick to his gut, Winters saw a shot from a security camera, Mia pinning him to the wall. Goddamn, Parker. The man was going down.

Someone in the room made kissing noises. Someone else laughed. They were all going to get a beating.

Winters looked at the glossy again. It was defendable. A variation of a honey pot scheme: the operative must act otherwise engaged to lure in the enemy. The maneuver worked every time and was in all their book of tricks. But it wasn't a move that needed a Polaroid. He would kill Parker later. Knock him out cold.

Every man in the room focused on that photo—with Mia's hair loose and wild around her shoulders, her lips very much pressed against his neck, and his face showing just how into that lip lock he was—he'd never live that down. Ever.

He'd have to kill everyone in the room.

"Fuck you very much, Parker."

Parker laughed and rolled his head back. It'd be better if it just snapped off.

Winters groused and tried to move forward. "So what's the deal? More of Silva's men are on their way? They think the NOC list's still in play?"

"Chatter on the wires says that Juan Carlos Silva is furious. If you hadn't killed his man, he would have done it for you. Silva wants the NOC list and the girl. He's offering her up as an incentive to his men."

An incentive? Oh, hell no. Give me the coordinates. I'm going in.

Jared cleared his throat, silently issuing him an order to stick his ass to his chair.

Parker poked his finger on the war room's large flat screen. "We've heard that Silva's men have showed up here, here, and here."

His fingerprints left smudges everywhere he touched.

Bring on the assholes. Winters was ready to end this shit.

Parker pulled up a new map on the big screen. Bright white dots blinked along his path from Kentucky to Virginia. "Everything shows that the Silva teams followed you back to DC. They're likely already here again and have searched Mia Kensington's office and home."

"Which safe house did you stash her at?" Jared asked.

"She's not at a Titan safe house." Winters tried to add an uninterested inflection and focus on the screen of illuminating dots.

He could hear the wheels grinding in each head around the table. All stilled. Every set of eyes narrowed on him.

"Pray tell, Winters. Where might little Miss Mia Kensington be if she's not a *Titan* safe house?" Jared arched his eyebrow.

Winters had heard of a slow clap before, but this was a slow laugh. Each man coughed a chuckle, then another, until it was a full-scale assault. Fuck them.

"She's at my place. Leave it alone."

"With Clara?" Parker piped in for good measure.

"And your mother?" Jared asked, though his rigid tone was the same as always. Boss man lifted an eyebrow, even smiled a little.

Winters pressed his lips into a tight, thin line. "I might just kill all you fuckers. What's it to you, anyway?"

Now even Jared laughed and leaned back in his chair. "Well, hell, Winters. This is kind of cute. What do you think, boys? Winters found himself a girl?"

They all drum rolled on the table and hollered.

What did he expect? Of course, they'd find out. He wasn't trying to keep her a secret. But the safe house revelation didn't need to come on the heels of the honey pot photo.

"Screw you all." It was the only thing he could think to say when he wasn't cursing them each by name. So he said it again, and again, and again, only making the room more and more raucous. *Damn it.*

After what Jared apparently determined was the appropriate amount of misery, he settled into his normal gruff self. "All right, all right. Enough with Winters's bullshit. Silva will go after that list again in DC. It's his last chance to get it before our client destroys it. We'll arrange for Winters to do the drop off. Parker, you and lover boy will ensure Mia's safe when she matriculates back to the real world."

Winters's phone beeped, and dread sunk to the pit of his stomach, landing hard. Knowing what the sound meant before he looked at the phone screen, he interrupted Jared. "We've got bigger problems."

"Yeah, your phone is set to annoying," someone called from the back of the room.

"The perimeter alarm at my house was breached."

He pushed the stored number in his phone, reaching out to Mia. No answer. He hit redial. *C'mon, c'mon.* All he wanted was a quick hello. Still no answer. He hung up and punched each number into the phone to make sure the number dialed right. More ringing. Nothing. He pressed the end call button and dropped his head, muttering a prayer and a promise.

"Winters, don't you have an alarm on your gate?" Parker asked. "And sensors on the fences? If those didn't go off, then it's just Mia triggering it. I mean, if no one has come on to the property—"

"Don't be stupid, man. It can be done. Even with as good a system as I have." He hit the redial button once more. Just to be sure. "Something's wrong. Parker, hack my security system. And don't bullshit me. I know you can do it."

Parker looked at Jared, who nodded, and Parker pushed away from the war room table to a keyboard under the wall of flat screens. Winters checked his phone while anxiety blossomed. It was early, but Mia would be up by now. She should be answering the burner phone. His fingers jabbed as he dialed his home number. Same result. She wouldn't pick it up anyway.

"Where's the NOC list?" Jared asked.

Winters pulled it out of his pocket and handed it to his boss, readying to hightail it back home. "You take it. I've got business to attend to."

"Hold it, Lone Ranger. If there's a problem, we've all got business to attend to."

He wanted to argue. Hell, he wanted to ignore him and walk out.

Jared could read his mind. "Sit your ass down, Winters."

Parker's fingers flew over his keyboard. Without stopping, he'd occasionally asked Winters a question. With a few flashes of pixilated grains, several of the security cameras in his home now broadcasted on monitors in front of the men. Parker flashed through several feeds and stopped.

The feed was clear as if he stood in the room. The kitchen was empty. A coffee mug shattered on the hardwood floor in the kitchen, coffee splattered. Parker skipped through other camera angles. Nothing was out of the ordinary in the living room or hallways or nursery.

"Parker, I have a camera pointed into the crib. It's in the corner. Get that shot."

Parker clacked on the keyboard. Winters's stomach ached worse with each loud stroke, until one screen blinked, showed snow, then an empty crib.

"Fuck!"

Winters dialed his mother. She picked up on the second ring. Without giving her the chance to say hello, he said, "Do you have Clara?"

"What? No, she's at home with Mia. You said—"

Winters clicked the phone off. He summoned all of his training, and all but ordered Parker to queue back the footage. Parker worked. Winters paced. The live images halted, then skipped backward in sixty-second increments.

"Keep going."

"Dude, I'm working on it."

The screen skipped backward in two-minute increments. A blur of activity flashed and Parker hit stop. The image was clear. Mia was at the table with a cup of coffee in one hand, a sleeping baby in the other arm, and a half-empty bottle on the table.

"Make it play right now." Jared wasn't interfering in Winters's orders to Parker. None of the men interrupted. Winters's lungs ached. His body warped into warrior mode and ignored the terrifying paralysis edging at his mind.

Every pair of eyes watched as Mia turned to the kitchen window. Her face pinched in surprise. Her mug fell and shattered. The baby startled awake. Mia grabbed the bottle, stuck it in Clara's mouth, and the panicked look on her face made him ill. A heartbeat later, Mia took off at a run out of the kitchen.

Parker's fingers flew across the keyboard, and Winters yelled at him. "Find her. Where did they go?"

"Looking."

"Look faster."

Black flooded the screen. The motion detector lights flicked on as Mia and Clara rushed through a door. Parker switched the footage to the large flat screen in the center of the room. No one breathed. They watched Mia finger the keys on the pegboard wall. She selected a set and stretched out her arm. His Hummer's lights flashed as it unlocked, and she ran to the vehicle's backdoor. She jumped in with Clara but came out alone. She ran to the driver's door, cracked the tinted windows, ran back around, and to peek in the backseat at the baby.

"What the fuck is she doing?" Jared asked. Mia swiveled her head, a terrified expression plastered on her face. "Is she leaving?"

No one moved. Everyone watched. She flew back toward the house and manually turned off the lights.

"What did she do with Clara?" Jared was pissed.

"Car seat." Winters mumbled.

"Car seat?"

"Yeah, asshole. She just rat holed my kid."

Every guy in the room gave a collective oh.

Winters interrupted the stunned mumblings. "Can you get me a shot of what she saw outside?"

He needed to be there but was too far away. He couldn't get home. Whatever they watched was History Channel by now. Nothing was worse. His head spun.

"Working on it," Parker muttered. "Until I find that camera feed, keep watching this."

It played in time and a half. Mia ran through several of the shots. The kitchen. The hallway. Up the stairs and toward the master bedroom.

"Has this woman gone mad?" Jared asked.

"Damn, boy." Parker directed them to a different monitor in the corner. Parker rewound the screen, then hit play. A chopper landed several hundred feet from his house. That explains the perimeter alarm.

Men piled out. They took their lazy-ass time, knowing no escape was possible. They sauntered past the exterior camera. Parker clicked to the entrance camera feed. His front door exploded open. Two men stepped through. Others remained outside.

Every man watching the screens had to wonder where the hell they would go first. Winters had no idea. This was like reality television, the nightmare edition.

He didn't know what to do, so he issued orders. "Fast forward. Go. Go. Go."

Parker held up his hand. "Wait. Watch."

Mia flinched in the upstairs hallway, then went to work slamming every door. She waited, then screamed. She dragged their attention straight up the stairs, and they took the easy catch, running toward her ruckus.

They were on her in seconds. She flayed and kicked, her nails clawed for their eyes, and her knees aimed for their nuts. Winters knew those moves all too well. They gagged her mouth and bound her hands, despite the throws of her fists. She bucked the entire time. A visible look of relief crossed her face as they pushed her out the busted front door.

"Good night." Jared blew out a telling whistle. "That woman just baited those men away from Clara. Parker, what's our elapsed time?"

"They were in and out in three and a half minutes."

"Find me that helo." Thank God Jared was barking orders, because Winters needed to dry heave.

He heard Jared on the phone, issuing orders for another team member to get out of bed and to get to Winters's place post haste. He ended the call with a command to *secure that baby*. God willing, Clara would be sleeping. *Please let her sleep. Please.*

He hit the speed dial for his mother again.

She picked up on the first ring. "Colby, what's going on?"

"Mom, we had a problem. Clara's fine."

"Oh God. What happened?"

He took the phone away from his ear. He didn't have time to explain. "Hey, Jared. Who's headed for Clara?"

"Brock."

He put the phone back to his ear.

"Hello? Colby Winters, you get back on this phone," his mom yelled.

"I'm here. Look, you know Brock, right? He's going to bring Clara to you. I need you to take her for a few days at your place."

"Can you tell—"

"I can't. Kiss that baby for me. Call you later." He ended the call and dropped to a chair, unaware he'd been pacing.

"The baby will be fine," Jared said. "That girl of yours pulled off quite the stunt. Are you pussying out of this, or can you get your shit together? We've got some cartel motherfuckers to find."

Pussying out? The hell with that.

"More ready than I've ever been." He was resolute. Jared would never question him again where his family was concerned.

"First things first. We need to figure out where they've taken her. Parker, have you tracked down that copter yet?"

"Almost."

Winters spun to Jared, remembering he had intel to offer. "She has a skin tracker on her. Long story short, she has a bio-tag on. We've got about eight more hours to get a signal from her."

"Kinky," his buddy called from the end of the room.

"Shut your face, Cash." Winters scowled at Parker. "Can you find that tracker?"

"Trying. Two minutes. Tops," Parker said.

Jared turned to Winters. "Glad to see the company resources are so well used."

Winters rolled his eyes. "I can't handle how slow this is going. Come on already."

Parker closed the security footage except the live feed of his darkened garage. Winters sat and watched the dark screen, transfixed. Parker went back to his keyboard, numbers and code streaming across the monitor in front of him. A flash on the screen and a GPS location began to read.

"They're stationary. Fairfax County, Virginia. Not far from here. Satellite images coming in three, two, one…"

A small compound appeared on the flat screen. The chopper sat on a helipad. A decrepit mansion stood in rough shape, shutters hanging off windows, cracked white paint peeling from the clapboard, and a half-boarded front door.

"What's that place?" Winters asked.

"Land records say it's the business address of Silva Enterprises. Five pesos says it's a front for the Colombian, where they launder money. That place hasn't seen anyone in long time."

"That's advantageous. Security will be nil." Jared nodded to a different screen.

Brock entered Winters's garage. He paused, then moved straight to the Hummer, opened the door, and cocked his head to the side. Winters's phone rang, and he answered before the screen showed Brock grabbing his phone to dial.

"There must be a five second delay in the feed," Parker said.

"The kid's asleep," Brock said. "I don't know how the hell to get her out of her seat. She looks… secure."

Thank God. Relief was an awesome poultice right now. When Winters found Mia, he'd get on his hands and knees, thanking her until the end of days for protecting Clara.

He gave directions to Brock to meet his mother. Maybe he should call her back with a rundown of events. She was likely to interrogate Brock until he broke.

Jared cleared his throat. "Now that we're done with all of that, it's time to kick some cartel ass."

CHAPTER NINETEEN

The tactical room buzzed as Jared barked orders to his men, readying to rendezvous at the target point. Never had an assault been more important. Winters pulled his shirt over the Kevlar vest and tightened the vertical strap securing his leg holster.

Jared's phone rang, and he snatched it off the table. "What?"

There was a pause. Something was wrong. Times like this, Winters wished stone-face Jared had a tell. A sign of any kind.

"Goddamn it." Jared slammed the phone down and pinched the bridge of his nose. That was a tell if there ever was one.

The room stilled. Winters stood with his teammates, each in varying stages of gearing up, and waited. If the tanker-sized knot in Winters's stomach were any indication, Jared would have zip to say in the good-news department.

"Change of plans. We're in a holding pattern," Jared said.

Winters strode over to him, barely containing the acid that churned in his gut. He shoved tight knuckled fists into his pockets. No need for two battling rams to go at it. Punching Jared would accomplish headaches and busted ribs for both but not help his situation. "What do you mean we're holding?"

"They're on the move again."

"So we move toward them." That wasn't the smartest action, but it *was* action. And right now, Winters needed to expend energy. "We search and destroy."

"Every ship can be a mine sweeper once, asshole. This isn't your throwaway team, and that's not much of a plan. Use your head, Winters."

"We've got six, maybe seven more hours on that tracker."

"Roger that. We've got a solid idea where they're relocating. Give Parker a few minutes to confirm. There's no way we can intercept them before they take off again—"

"Take off? Again?" Winters was furious.

"They're moving fast and southwest. Straight toward a private airstrip. My guess, they're choppering to a jet."

Winters slammed his eyes shut, trying to calm down. "Christ, man. If they go wheels up, she'll be in Colombia in six hours."

"Parker is pulling flight plans and Silva real estate holdings. Both here and in South America. We'll narrow it down fast, find satellite feed, and see what's up."

"You're wasting too much time. We know they're headed to Colombia. Have Parker feed us a destination after we're in the air. Do it."

"Watch yourself, Winters." Jared stood square. Shoulders back. Eyes narrowed.

Winters didn't care. "Do it. Make the call."

Jared paced one turn of the room and muttered, then looked back at the men. No one moved. Not even Winters. No, Winters prayed. Prayers for a quick call to action. Prayers for blood soaked vengeance. He bargained with God, asking that his bullets meet their intended target, and offered…everything.

Jared stopped and motioned to Winters. "All right. We'll bring the fight to them. But we do it my way, understand?"

Thank the Lord. His ruthless prayers were answered.

Shaking, Mia couldn't control her muscles, and she couldn't wipe away her tears. Her hands were bound, and she was terrified. Her abductors had left her on the floor. She rolled across the cargo plane like a ragdoll. Each burst of turbulence nauseated her, only worsening her fear. They'd been in the air for hours, but now, they descended. The engines roared. The flaps moaned and the wheels extended. Destination reached, wherever that was. She wanted to vomit.

Mia's teeth jarred at the hard landing, which jarred her across the dirty floor. She struggled to open her eyes under the blindfold. They taxied over bumps and jumps. Each drop smashed her bruised cheekbone onto the splintered floor, re-scratching her scabbed-over scratches. She tasted dirt and blood.

It was the second flight since they jammed a gun in her back at the rundown mansion. They hollered at her in Spanish, and she could only guess at their meaning. *Move. Run. Sit. Stop.* Her high school teacher always said she should study harder, because it would come in handy. Nope. She'd been busy drowning her miseries in book after book, all in English.

The cargo plane halted hard, as if the pilot forgot a happy medium existed between go and stop. Her chin hit a metal hook jutting from the floor. One more scratch to go with the dozen other newbies. This ride was nothing if not an opportunity to scar up more of her body.

She couldn't see anything, but judging by what she had rolled over and into, cargo planes had a lot of bells and whistles in the tie down department. They certainly didn't have chairs and seatbelts. Her first flight was on a business charter, and she had a chair. It had been an unknown luxury. No view with the blindfold, but the chair was appreciated. Mucho appreciated, if she wanted to speak like the locals. Which she didn't. Crap. She was cracking up again. Time to check back in with her DSM-IV.

Such cruel irony. She thought she'd see Colby in a suit over a candlelit dinner. The deck was stacked against her. She knew it.

Cut the woe-is-me act. I have to survive.

A loud noise grinded, and she heard the back of the cargo plane open. Light burned through her blindfold. Heat and humidity poured into the airless belly of the plane. Rough hands grabbed her. Mia tried to keep up, but unable to see the ridges and snaps on the floor, she tripped more than walked.

The blindfold came off with all the finesse the pilot had taken with his landing. She blinked, desperate to acclimate to the sun's vicious glare. They were definitely not on US soil. Her captors chatted, paying her no attention. They didn't hide their faces, or their weapons, or their complete disinterest in her survival.

She glanced right, then left, scared to move her head. Men patrolled the airstrip with automatic weapons slung over their shoulders and large handguns strapped to their hips. *This could be a Hollywood movie set.* But, it looked real, because it was real. No one noticed how out of place she was because no one cared.

A man gripped her arm until her fingertips tingled.

"Move. El Jefe has a place for you," he said in broken English.

His rancid breath hung close. He stank of stale sweat and cheap liquor. Another threat of vomiting loomed, and his uniform, reminiscent of soldiers captured by the evening news, might be where it landed. This was a hell zone.

Disoriented, Mia took in her surroundings. Lush vegetation on all sides. *The rainforest*. She had collected pennies to help save this stinkin' place when she was a kid.

In the distance, she saw white-capped mountain peaks. A wood shack with boards peeling back from the posts and white paint flaking off was dead ahead. More uniformed, armed guards stood watch by the broken front door.

They walked toward the shack. A cold shiver rocked her like she'd stepped through a ghost. Nothing good happened in that shack. Mere feet before the door, she was released and catapulted forward. Palms first, Mia broke her fall in a scuffled cloud of dust. Pain vibrated from her hands to her neck and echoed back. Her teeth slammed together at impact, and, again, the taste of blood seeped into her mouth. She ran her tongue over a slice where her front teeth had cut her lip.

As if she needed the help, a boot landed firmly on her butt and pushed her into the windowless shack. The place was dark, and it reeked of death. The humidity did nothing to erase the dirt floating in the air. It caked the corners of her mouth and irritated her eyes. A metallic click. Chains rattled. She was safe and secure from the monsters. At least until they unlocked the door.

What would Colby do if he were here? Probably fashion a bazooka out of a bamboo shoot and blast his way home in time for dinner.

Pieces of Spanish and the smell of cigarettes filtered in to the humid dungeon. Colby would know she was in danger by now. He had to know, and he would come with guns blasting.

White knight, round four. *This is what he does for a living. He saves people.* Extraction. Explosions. Extravaganzas.

He'd come.

Please come.

Outside her shack, armed men jeered. Insects crawled on her skin. Hungry animals of all sorts lurked nearby. She could hear them but didn't know what posed a graver danger—drunk men with a serious lack of morals, or the all the howling, growling wildlife that the rainforest had to offer.

Drunk heckles sloshed into nasal laden snores.

The night warmed to dawn. Mosquito bites pocked her skin. Her sweatpants and Colby's shirt clung to her sweat soaked body. Her knotted hair stuck to her neck and face. She hadn't slept a hot second.

Time passed slowly until heavy footsteps crunched near her door. Keys jangled. Mia scampered back to a corner, finding it hard with her shoulder. She shook. Terrified, she crouched, awaiting her future.

A stubby man with an evil scar across his face, grabbed her, and bound her wrists before he wrenched her upright and dragged her in tow. How many of them were there? Too many to remember. This one, Senor Scissor Face, would be hard to forget.

With silent pleas, Mia begged for help. For escape. For Colby. *Where is he?*

Senor Scissor Face released her, and she crashed to the ground. She swallowed twice against her parched throat. No reprieve.

A handsome man stood a mile high in front of her, and her terror morphed into anger. He oozed self-important power. His white silk shirt and pressed linen pants looked obscene, given where she'd spent the night. He was clean-shaven with perfectly gelled hair. Not so much as a wisp was out of place. He smelled exotic and spicy. *El Jefe.*

She blinked once, then again and again. Words fled. But he didn't appear interested in a conversation. Mia stood, as if for a presentation.

"Ah, Miss Mia Kensington. Thank you for joining us here in beautiful Colombia." He motioned to Senor Scissor Face. The painful bindings were cut with a quick slice of a knife. "I apologize for the measures my men took to ensure your safe arrival. But it was for the best. Are you hungry? Can I get you anything?"

What the...what?

Yeah, a private plane back to the States. With a chair.

His English was perfect with the flair of a beautiful accent. There was no other way to describe him other than... exquisite. He appeared, sounded, and smelled expensive, and was striking in impeccable clothes.

"Who are you? What do you want with me?" She knew who he was and wanted to sound tough and menacing. Heck, she wanted to channel her anger into something useful, shocking him as much as he did her. Cartel dictators shouldn't be perfect and polished.

"Miss Kensington, I have been pleasant and welcoming. Your attitude will not help you." He pursed his lips, and his tanned face crinkled in entertainment at her expense. "I think we should start over. A new start between newer friends, Miss Kensington. Now, welcome to my paradise. Please join me for lunch."

He moved away from her, and Senor Scissor Face gave her a hard push to follow. They walked toward a shaded cabana. Billowing swaths of fabric danced in the heavy air as they hung to a pergola and flowered trellis. A wooden table and chairs draped in a brilliant tablecloth was protected by armed men.

Armed guards flanked El Jefe. The back of their heads rotated side to side in search of an eminent threat. *His name is Colby Winters, and those goons have got nothing on him.* El Jefe paused with ridiculous grace and motioned for her to join him in a manner befitting a cotillion teacher.

An older woman filled both their glasses with ice water. In an instant, the tall glasses began to sweat. Mia was dying for a tall drink of anything cool and wet, but she didn't dare go for the glass.

"My name is Juan Carlos Silva. I understand that you interfered with my business in your country. Is that correct?" His accent made the sinister accusation sound elegant.

Mia shook her head. Tendrils of uncombed hair stuck to her sweaty forehead and cheek, and she made no move to push them back into place.

"My dear, please do not lie to me. Would you like a fruit salad? I am sure you have not snacked during your visit." He snapped manicured fingers.

No, she hadn't snacked. Asshole.

The older woman placed a crystal bowl of fresh fruit on their plates.

"The food and water are fine. You will not get sick from them, and I will be insulted if you do not join me. I believe we also have a delicious plate of sandwiches for lunch." He took a bite of pineapple. "Simply delicious. Please, go ahead, and start."

She analyzed his behavior, his gestures. The delusion and extravagance he offered in this meal was narcissistic and self-absorbed. That didn't bode well for her chances. Mia picked up her heavy silver fork and speared a piece of green melon. Juan Carlos watched as she took a cautious bite and swallowed.

"Excellent, my dear. Now, please drink up. You are in the Colombian jungle. The heat and humidity will kill you if you do not stay hydrated."

Dehydration would kill her? Not likely.

He played up his accent when he pretended to care. Interesting. She took a sip of water, holding back the need to guzzle the glass empty. Sweat dripped down her breastbone and shoulder blades, and dirt caked her hands and under her finger nails. He didn't seem to notice.

"Thank you, Mr. Silva." She had no idea what else to say at this point. Maybe her manners upped the odds of survival.

Juan Carlos's lips quirked with an understated smile, and he tilted his head. "No, thank you. I appreciate the respect and civility. Truthfully, I was unsure as to how an American woman would behave under these circumstances. And after our first exchange, your tone nearly solidified my concern."

Mia nodded, again unsure how to respond, scared she'd say the wrong thing, and die before Colby showed up wielding that knife he strapped to his leg. Colby would make sure El Jefe's gelled hair went unkempt, and those clean clothes were sullied. She focused on that daydream.

"Miss Kensington, tell me why you stole my files."

His pleasant smile and placating conversation evaporated. The veins in his neck popped.

The fork shook in her hand, and she accidently clanged it against the crystal bowl.

"I don't know what you mean." No way would she fall into his trap with such ease.

"Let me see if I can refresh your memory, my dear. My men followed that disk to America—where that soldier stashed it. Very clever of the young man, telling his trusted therapist. But here is where my annoyance grows. You took it. You and your counterpart. Your compadre. Now, I did not send my best men to retrieve it. That was my mistake. But they were not amateurs. Somehow, you evaded them with the help of your partner. You are here, and that man will come here to barter some deal for your life."

He knew a lot more than she thought he did. Time for a different tactic. She shook her head. "Mr. Silva, if you know what the disk has on it, then you know he won't trade me for it. I'm collateral damage. He isn't going to come. His job was to secure it. I'm sure by now, it's secure." God, please don't let that be true. Let Colby come as soon as possible. Please.

"I think you underestimate him, Miss Kensington. Men like him, they walk a very dark line. But one they consider honorable. Men like him live for the fight, but they do not leave a woman to die. They help. That is what they do. And, I hate to be so blunt, but unless your friend and I work out a business deal, you will die to prove my point. It is all business, my dear. I hope you understand that."

"Well, thank you for being honest with me." She smirked before she thought better of it. The oppressive heat skewed her judgment, and she needed to be smart about this. She could talk her way into more time, increasing the likelihood Colby could save her.

"The sarcasm is not necessary." Juan Carlos showed his impeccable white teeth in a garish smile, extended his arms as if welcoming her to the family. "I promised you to my second in command. However, if you have something to offer, if you can bring your man to me, then I will spare you that unpleasantness."

Mia couldn't think straight. Her head pounded. "I don't understand. What do you want from me?"

"Stupid woman." His hands slammed on the table in fisted balls, and the table settings jumped with a loud crash.

The noise startled her. She shook to attention. "Your men grabbed me at his house. By now, he'll know I'm gone." *Tell him what he already knows. Buy time.*

"I am not an idiot. You will speak to him, tell him I will consider a trade. You for the file."

"I just met him. It hasn't been a normal few days. I have no idea how to get a hold of him." More or less, that was true.

Silva raged and slammed his hand on the table again, making her jump at the clatter. "If I can find his hidden house, I can surely track down a phone number. Do not waste my time."

"I'm not. I promise." Tears welled in her eyes.

"Miss Kensington." He calmed a degree but still spit fire. He took a long sip of his ice water and dabbed at his lips with his napkin. "You will agree to my request, or I will hand you over to Alejandro, my number two."

For the first time, Mia noticed Alejandro a dozen yards away. He stood savage. The gleam in his eye turned her stomach as he sneered his vulgar face. Alejandro licked his lips, and his fingers flexed against his thighs. He looked one defiant order away from losing his restraint and salivated like a junkyard dog, frothy spittle at the corners of his mouth. His face was pocked and sunburned, greasy and hairy. He looked heavy in the gut but strong in his arms. Sweat dampened his pits, and stains marked his pants. That was his number two?

Mia shook her head, her eyes glued to Alejandro. "Mr. Silva, I'm not worth that trade. He won't agree to it."

"Alejandro does not look like much, but he is very important to me. To my enterprise. You would be his reward for his continued excellence."

Alejandro licked his lips again, this time, with more tongue.

An involuntary shudder rippled through her. “Wait.” She didn’t know what to say. They would kill her but not before torturing and raping her. Her tough girl act faded, and she whimpered. “I’ll do it.”

“Of course you will.” Juan Carlos motioned for the sandwiches to be served. With an expedient delivery, several types of tea sandwiches were placed on the fine china plates with the crusts removed. Such contradictions. Dainty sandwiches as she dined with a monster in hell. Narcissist was too weak a description. She should tack on sociopathic, pathological, and deranged.

They sat in silence as he devoured his finger sandwiches, and Mia picked at hers with polite intention. She would follow his requests, be demure when she needed to, and play to his psyche. She would do whatever the hell it took to live until Colby showed up.

Dabbing his mouth with a linen napkin, Juan Carlos eyed her up and down. “If he comes for you, it will be on my terms. But just in case either of you try to deceive me, you will stay in the main house with me.”

With him? Less scary but not encouraging.

He stood with a smooth air about him and walked away, a gaggle of armed guards in stride. Alejandro and Senor Scissor Face stalked toward her. They bound her hands again and pushed her down a path. They rounded a bend, then stopped at a pickup truck with a partial canvas cover. Senor Scissor Face tossed her onto the truck bed and jumped in, perching above her, while Alejandro got in the truck cab.

With every divot in the makeshift road, her body slammed onto the hot metal bed. They traversed further into the jungle. Mia closed her eyes and wished Colby could read her mind. Until then, she was alone.

CHAPTER TWENTY

The pickup truck rumbled to a stop before an imposing wood gate with a half dozen armed men guarding it. A stone fence surrounded the compound, soaring at least twenty feet high. The guards did a bored once-over of the truck until they saw Mia. Laughter and catcalls followed. Animals. They were all animals.

The gate opened and closed, caging her inside the sprawling estate. They stopped in front of a Spanish mission-style mansion, with stucco walls, wide sweeping arches, and an expansive manicured lawn. It looked straight from the pages of Architectural Digest. Immaculate and pristine, minus the armed guards crawling around like ants in their colony.

Senor Scissor Face pulled her out of the truck and toward the mansion. They stepped to massive wooden doors, which clicked open. Cool air conditioning washed over her body. It was heaven.

Mia looked around, breathing in the chilled space. The air was fragrant. It reinvigorated her. Marble floors gleamed, the high ceilings soared, and expensive tapestries hung in each corridor. Decadence. Perfect for a maniacal narcissist with trafficking money.

They moved up one side of the grand double entryway staircase and toward the last room at the end of a bricked in corridor. His boots echoed down the unfriendly hallway. After unlocking the deadbolt, he pushed her in, a hand tight on her back, then shut the door behind him with a resounding thud. The latch clicked, and Senor Scissor Face stood against the only way out.

The windowless room was lit by a small light bulb, casting a heavy amber glow. There was a bed, a blanket, and one small closed door. He untied her wrists and pointed to the door.

"Shower. Clean up. Now."

He leered, but left, locking the deadbolt from the hall. Shudders ran down her back. Silence caved in on the dank room.

A lot of atrocious acts had happened in this room.

She made her way into the bathroom. A dress was folded on the barren counter. No mirror. No lighting. She left the door open for a slice of light and got in the shower.

Raw welts encircled her bloodied wrists. Bruises throbbed across her body. Bug bites itched. A cold shower would clear her mind. She needed a plan. Think like Colby. What would Colby do? But his course of action didn't surface. She closed her eyes to bite off the tears.

Someone pounded on the door, which sounded as if it would cave into the room. It brought her back to her cruel reality.

"*Vamanos. Vamanos.* Let's go," a man shouted through the door. Fear churned, slushing up the fruit salad in her stomach. She slammed the water off and wrapped the towel around her fast, praying the voice would stay outside. She ignored the raw burns and scratches, and shimmied the dress and her worn underwear on seconds before the deadbolt unlocked and heavy booted footsteps walked in.

Alejandro flanked her side in an instant. He huddled over her, harshly breathed her in. Mia's stomach catapulted, and she braced for the worst, but he laughed and forced her into the hall. They moved through the labyrinth and arrived in a polished sitting room. Juan Carlos sat on a spotless white couch, sipping out of a demitasse cup. Spicy cologne and the aromatic coffee intermixed. Everything was flawless. Everything except that Alejandro drooled over her, and she looked like a wet dog in her cartel-gifted sundress. Her legs quaked, and she tried to lock her knees to hide her reaction to the men.

"Are you ready to contact your friend at the Titan Group?"

She didn't know whether to hang her head or not. Mia opted to meet his gaze and hold her head high in faked confidence.

"Of course. Yes, Mr. Silva."

Tapping his fingertips together, he didn't respond, and Alejandro left them alone. A nervous flutter ran rampant through her stomach. Silence. Juan Carlos needed more from her. What did he want?

"Thank you for the shower."

A surprised glint flashed on his face, and he nodded in acknowledgement of her *gratitude*. Alejandro walked back in and signaled to Juan Carlos, who then picked up a nearby phone and handed it to Mia. She pressed the phone to her ear. It rang.

An automatic answering system picked up. *Hello, thank you for calling the corporate headquarters of The Titan Group. If you know your party's extension, please enter it now. If not, please hold for the operator.*

"I don't know the extension," she whispered.

Juan Carlos didn't respond. She sucked on her lip. Apprehension tugged her thoughts. Unsure what to do, she did nothing. She didn't know much about Titan Group, but of what she did know, it didn't seem like they had a receptionist sitting at a front office desk. The phone rang three more times.

"Hello?" a man answered.

"Um, hello. Is Colby Winters available please?" She shook, trying to pull herself straight.

"Mia?"

"Yes."

"It's me," the man said.

No, it's not. Who is this? His delivery conveyed a trust invoking quality. It didn't give away any concern or interest.

"Sorry. I've never heard you on the phone before."

"That's okay. I'm glad to hear your voice. Where you are? Who are you with? I saw someone take you on my security footage."

Mia covered the phone with her hand enough to show Juan Carlos that she wanted his permission but her position allowed Titan to hear as well. "Mr. Silva, he would like to know who I'm with. And where we are."

"You may tell him that you are my guest, and that you are not hurt. He can figure the rest out. Your friend will know what I want, and I am willing to negotiate."

She turned her mouth back to the phone and moved her hand ceremoniously. "Winters, I'm fine. I'm Mr. Juan Carlos Silva's guest at his beautiful white home. The gardens are gorgeous."

Juan Carlos slammed his hand down. His accent flared. "Enough. I did not say details."

Tears welled in her eyes. Of course, Juan Carlos would realize she tried to reveal her location. "I'm so sorry, Mr. Silva. I wanted to convey how lovely you've been to me. The food. The shower. Thank you."

He looked convinced of her genuine thanks. "Fine. Go on then."

"Yes, sir," she said before speaking back to the phone. "I'm not hurt. Mr. Silva is willing to negotiate for what he wants."

"And he wants?" Titan's man spoke in an even disinterest.

"The list."

"Of course he does. And I assume you're the pawn in this exchange?"

"Yes."

"But he doesn't want to talk to me?"

She offered him the phone. Juan Carlos shook his head. "No, not now. He needs to think over the possible consequences."

Putting the phone back to her ear, she said, "Not now."

"Don't you worry. I'll see you soon. Just relax, and listen to Mr. Silva. You'll be safer that way. I promise."

Oh thank God. Who was that? He had to be one of Colby's team members. But why didn't he put Colby on the phone? He'd see me soon? A tickle of hope bled through her veins.

"Oh, that's great. Thanks."

The line disconnected. Shoot, she hadn't meant to sound hopeful. Mia passed the phone to Juan Carlos and found him studying her.

His fingertips tapped again. "What is great?"

"Nothing. He just re-assured me everything would work out."

With a disgusted grin, he groused. "How cute."

Her fingers pleated into the skirt of the sundress. *Now what*?

Juan Carlos took a sip of his coffee and beckoned to Alejandro. "Return her to the room. And do not take her yet. Damaged goods won't help me get that disk."

She felt damaged already. But the wounds on her skin weren't what he meant. The lust in Alejandro's eyes didn't bode well for Mia. He seemed to weigh the options—listen to his boss or deal with the consequences, and he didn't appear too concerned about the consequences. Mia fought to swallow the terror choking off her airway.

CHAPTER TWENTY-ONE

The satellite phone rang in the jet somewhere over the Caribbean Sea. Winters would've answered it if he could've, a thousand questions at the ready. Instead, he was sentenced to a flight where every man trained their gaze on him, unsure if he'd ratchet down his fury. Their plan was based on strategic assumptions and scientific wild-ass guesses, but cartel kingpins didn't always behave according to plan.

Jared hit the speakerphone button. "Give us something good, Parker."

"Good? Hell, I'll give you fan-freakin'-tastic. Mia called our headquarters. I'm sure she knew I wasn't Winters but never let on. She kept her cool, described her location, and I checked a few things out. You guys are headed to the right locale."

His girl was alive. Could he get an *amen, hallelujah*?

Jared shot a confused glance to Winters, who shrugged.

"Why did Silva have her call?" Jared asked.

"He wants to deal with Winters and thought he was still stateside."

Winters paced the length of the airborne war room. He paused, then drummed his fingers on the corner of the table.

"So we've got the element of surprise," Jared said. "Given that it's five men to their army, we'll need that. Anything else?"

"What? A location confirmation and proof of life isn't enough?" Parker asked.

Proof of life. Winters never should have left her alone. This was his mistake. That realization struck him numb, and he raked a hand over his jaw.

"What's our timeline for Winters to make contact?" Jared asked.

"I think our boy should give him a ring." Parker paused. "Offer up the NOC list in exchange for her. I think Silva wanted it to sink in before they chatted."

"Sink in?" Winters asked.

"I got the vibe Silva wanted Winters to sweat it. He's not pulling the standard operating procedure for a ransom request."

"What a prick. All right. Patch us through to wherever Mia called from." Jared pointed at Winters with a ready sign.

He nodded back.

"Roger that," Parker said.

A ringing sound echoed in the belly of the plane. Each long pause in between ate at his sanity. On the fifth ring, a woman answered.

"Colby Winters for Juan Carlos Silva. He's expecting my call."

"*Si*." The phone went silent. He raised his brows, silently asking if they still had a connection.

Invisible boulders weighted his shoulders and his mind. He needed to stretch. He wanted to fight. But more than that, he braced for every appalling outcome.

"Ah, Mr. Winters." A voice, iceberg cold, filled the galley through the overhead speakers. "I trust you found time to consider the gravity of your situation. You must be interested in your lovely friend's safe return."

"Safe is preferred." Games worked both ways. He'd play.

"So you do realize she can come home in several different ways. A plane. A box. One piece or two."

"What's it going to take, Silva?" His fingers flexed with the urge to reach through the phone and rip the fucker's throat out.

"Of course you know. I want that list. You hand it to me, I hand you your girl. And she is *your* girl, isn't she? I have an eye for these things. It makes me superior at my job."

Ripping his throat out would be too easy. Too fast. Disembowelment first. Skinning him alive second.

"She is exquisite," Silva said. "Even with the bruises."

Winters's teeth gnashed. If he hadn't willed them apart, they would have shattered.

"She's not yours to touch. Unmarred and unhandled, or no list." He hid his rage, storing it for Juan Carlos Silva. No warning of his caged fury slipped through his measured cadence.

"Her injuries were accidental. Nothing more will harm her if we can make a deal. If not, I promised her to one of my best, albeit most fiendish, men. I am sure things would not end well for her in that predicament."

Anger thumped in his chest. Each guilt-drenched breath ached. Juan Carlos baited him. Winters knew it.

"The list is yours. But hear me like your world depends on it, Silva. Because it does. If Mia so much as sneezes in your care, I'll make you pray for death."

"Mr. Winters, no need for threats. My offer is true. If you make the exchange, she will be returned. Unharmed. If I do not receive the list, then…she will be harmed. *Comprehende?*"

The things Silva would comprehend when Winters was finished with him would be innumerable. *First lesson. Don't fuck with my girl.*

Winters diverted his attention from mapping out lesson number two. "How do you want to do this?"

"Fly to Medellin via private charter. I expect you will arrive by midnight our time. I will have my driver escort you to my home. Come alone. Do not bring any men. Do not bring any weapons. Any failure to follow my directions will result in catastrophic repercussions."

Following the rules was never his forte. "Where will your men take me?"

"What does that matter? Your ground transport will be arranged."

"I'm supposed to trust you will return us to the airport. No harm? That sounds like a load of Colombian crap to me."

"Such language. I have no need for either of you. Whether you like what I do or not, my reputation is sterling. My word, solid gold. If I speak, if I promise, you should listen."

Winters bet Mia was psychoanalyzing the hell out of this piece of cartel trash.

"Besides, what other choice do you have?" Silva asked.

"We'll meet on your terms. I'll be in Colombia midnight, local time."

Adios, motherfucker. He sliced at his neck. Jared punched a button. Parker cut the connection. No one spoke before the line disconnect was confirmed.

Winters forced his muscles to relax and whistled a death march. "He doesn't have a clue we're on our way, does he?"

Jared pursed his lips. "He might. If things are going too easy, we're walking into an ambush. Silva didn't rise to the top by being slow to the game. By now, he should know more about Titan. I'd say you two just did a sparring two-step."

Winters crumbled a scrap of paper from their table and threw it into the trash can. "Fuck him. I'll quick step all over his tango face."

"You're going to follow orders."

"Yeah, yeah. I get it. It's your rodeo, Jared."

"You're goddamn right. Now, if you don't mind, let's finalize the details." He flipped the remote and shuffled through the satellite images. "The tree line here, overlooking the gate will be our best for surveillance. Cash, you set up a protective watch here. You'll handle any unexpected men during our entry and cover our asses on the way out."

Cash nodded, his cowboy hat pulled low. He grabbed a set of printed images and turned to study them.

"Brock, you'll handle diversions at the front gate." Jared pointed, analyzing the screen. "Rocco, I need you on wheels. We should have an armored Range Rover ready when we land. It's all yours. Our contacts in Colombia will have staged anything at our rendezvous point that wouldn't pack in that vehicle. C4 and charges. Extra guns and ammo. If you don't see something you need, tell me."

Brock and Rocco knew the deal. Jared turned his focus. "And Winters, I'll kick your leatherneck, devil dog ass from Colombia to the States and back again, if you run in there like your dick's on fire."

Winters grunted. He didn't respond to Jared. Didn't even look at him.

"I'm not messing with you, Winters. If you don't get yourself under control, I'll bench you on this one. You'll sit your ass on this plane until we get back, like a little bitch. Hell, I'll let Brock sweep in and rescue your girl."

Brock cocked half a grin and raised an eyebrow. "I'd be down with that, buddy."

"Fuck you." Winters turned from one man to the next. "And fuck you, too."

Brock laughed and slapped Winters on the back. "I've never seen you worked up like this. Who the hell knew it was possible?"

Jared cut in. "All right, all right. Winters, you'll be the same cold asshole, as always."

"Yeah, yeah. 10-4." Winters glared and cracked his knuckles. "I'm focused."

"Glad we have this all under control, lover boy."

CHAPTER TWENTY-TWO

Alejandro flashed too many teeth, the cadence of his breaths too quick for their short walk. As he guided her toward her room, his fingers flexed into her arm, cascading in a deviant rhythmic massage. Alejandro stopped at an open door. His rancid odor surrounded her. *Please, walk away. Leave me alone.* Her heart slammed into her rib cage.

With a disgusted shove, he shut the door on Mia, enclosing her in the windowless room, alone. She'd take any small miracle. Alejandro abandoning her now would qualify as one.

The lock scraped closed and seemed to seal her fate. Alejandro was perched inches away, only a thick wooden door offering protection. Too bad he had the key. She could feel his evil aura. His boots didn't retreat. Each heartbeat thumped in her ears, marking the anguishing passage of time. He wasn't leaving. Her mouth went dry. Panic bubbled like acid in her stomach.

Go away.

The scuffing sound of movement dialed back the oxygen in the room. It was hard to breathe. Was he turning to her? Or from her? A shuffled step. Her mind played tricks. The sounds bounced. Her ear ached to hear what direction he would go.

Silence.

Please go away. Please.

Another footstep. Toward her or away? She still couldn't tell.

Her lip trembled. Her hands covered her mouth to drown any wayward weep. Was she strong enough to handle whatever depraved plundering lurked in the sick depths of his psyche?

A sound again. It moved away, as he did. Every ounce of petrified anxiety tore from her chest, a heaving breath escaped. Mia doubled over, holding herself. Hot tears streamed down her cheeks.

Just kill me now. This was more than she could take. The room closed in, suffocating her. The air somehow thinned. She gulped at it. She was too weak. Nothing like Colby promised she was. How had she fooled him? It was pitiful how easy it was to back into the corner, begging for the easy way out.

Still holding herself, Mia sunk to the floor. The dim light illuminated the room, but her sight blurred through her sobs. She sniffled and wiped her nose with the back of her hand.

This sniveling stuff had to stop. *Channel shock and awe. Find it. Do it. Now.*

She traced a finger on the cold tile floor. The hysterical tears slowed to a stream. She could blink them away. Force them to stop. She had no choice. How the hell was she going to get out of this? She hadn't come up with anything close to a bamboo bazooka.

A wisp of hair tangled over her wet cheek. Mia blew at it, banishing it back to place, but it stayed put. She didn't make the effort again. Exhaustion weighted her eyelids, already puffy and swollen from irresponsible, self-pitying wails.

Juan Carlos and Alejandro yielded no information to aid her struggle of survival. She should have studied their interaction, searched for weaknesses, and built a psychological profile. But she didn't.

Where was Colby?

Tracking her to Colombia seemed impossible. How would he know where to find her? She tried to pass along a clue to the man on the phone, but how many white houses with gardens were in this country? A lot.

Colby would have to play *Where in the World is Mia Kensington?* Only with automatic weapons instead of a red trench coat and hat.

Mia winced after she made herself laugh. He was a tough guy with a soft heart. He'd find her.

I've needed you my whole life, Mia. And I had no idea. His words echoed in her mind. Just when everything seemed so fresh and safe, so outrageously optimistic, life laughed at her plans. It had been foolish to fantasize about fairy tales.

The scrape of footsteps drifted under the door. Did she hear Alejandro? Or was that Colby? Her brows pinched, desperate to hear again. The sound of silence blared. Her eardrums nearly exploded. Her mind was Looney Tunes' playground, laughing at her struggle to remain awake and coherent. Was this dehydration? No, this was delusion.

She should have devoured those stupid sandwiches. Guzzled that water. All she could do was beckon sleep. Her forehead pressed against her folded arms. She scrunched against the floor, trying hard to melt into it and away from here. Colby would come. He would. She hadn't found him just to let him go. He needed her. Didn't he? Colby...

The door clamored open, and she jerked awake. She couldn't get her bearings, feeling near comatose. A monster loomed ginormous. Most definitely not Colby. Teeth glowed in the dark. Foul odors smacked her conscious. A hand grabbed her, forcing a caustic rag against her raw lips.

Mia jerked away, scraping her fingernails into his knuckles. They were so rough, she could've ignited a match with a strike to his grated skin—it had to be Alejandro.

He lurched her out the door and sloshed her through the hallways. One confusing turn after another. The fumes from the poisoned rag seared her nostrils. Bitterness abraded her tongue. Her stomach rolled, convulsing. Her eyes slinked side to side without her control, as bright trails from hallway windows decorated her drugged vision. *Oh, this again.*

She slammed into Alejandro's armpit, smashing to a stop. Her eyes moved hazy and lazy, searching for an answer.

Juan Carlos Silva.

She tried to focus. Tried to study him at his desk. Stupid coffee cup. Stupid cologne. Did he want another phone call? Her lips tingled. She couldn't feel her tongue or her face or her… Lots she couldn't feel, but sleep she could, even standing up. The hum in her head lulled her asleep.

Rocco adjusted the steering wheel in the Range Rover. Winters sat in the backseat, sandwiched between Brock and

Cash, and tried to spread out. The last thing he wanted to do right now was knock knees. Anxious adrenaline raced its course. How did he end up riding bitch?

He ran his fingertip over the recently sharpened edge of the tactical blade. Its serrated claws gleamed. The metal was warm in his grip. He had toyed with the knife handle since they started their steep descent. His hands itched for action, while his mind fucked with him. The job had never been personal, and this was far past that level. Doubt and anger battled, leaving a bitter aftertaste in his throat.

Winters coughed for attention. "If anything goes wrong, if something happens to me, you bring Mia home. No questions."

Jared ignored him.

Cash rolled his eyes. "Christ, Winters. Nothing's going to go wrong. We didn't fly across the globe just to bail on your girl if your pretty ass takes a bullet."

He couldn't keep his mouth shut. "She's an important person."

"Yeah, we gathered that."

Winters sheathed his knife and ran his palms over his thighs. Too much energy. Too many what-ifs.

Jared turned around in his front passenger seat. "Listen, man, do whatever you have to out there. And we'll do the same. We know somewhere in your pea brain, she's important to you, so she's important to us. End of conversation."

Jared finished with a curt nod and swiveled forward again. They bumped along a makeshift path. Branches hit the windshield. Winters wasn't entirely sure Rocco was using a road. But whatever the quickest way from point A to point B was, he was cool with it.

Rocco pulled up hard, parked the vehicle as planned, and they fell out. Cash slipped into the vegetation. Gone. Damn snipers, and typical Cash. Sneaking in. Sneaking out. The man melted into shadows.

Brock had the trunk open and unloaded a cadre of explosives.

Jared moved past Winters. "Let's go. On my six."

They hoofed it to the fence line, barreling to the main gate like they were running toward Satan's open jaw. On the other side, hell waited, machine guns on the ready.

Brock broke off with a hand gesture from Jared. Winters checked his watch. Time wasn't moving fast enough. They dropped to the ground. Waiting. Calculating. Preparing.

Blast number one hit. The front gates exploded. Shards of wood and fragments of concrete rained down in a cloud of smoke and fire. Before the vibrations stopped, blast number two, smaller and less obvious, rolled through the outer wall. Alarms shrieked. Guards bellowed. Confusion penetrated the perimeter.

Jared and Winters crawled to position, rifles up, scanning their opening. Uniformed men ran toward the main gate, positioned in defensive formations, and ready to take on an enemy they couldn't see.

Time to duck and hustle. Jared and Winters sprinted forward, reached the side of the main house, and breached a door. They pushed in. Uniformed maids ran past them, eyes averted. Obviously not their first attack. He swept a harsh gaze back and forth. No tangos worth a bullet.

A quick hand gesture later, Jared veered down a winding hall. Winters listened with angry intent for signs of life, oncoming attack, and Mia through the constant pulse of warning alarms.

The house sounded empty. Jared was on stealth mode. Undetectable, then he disappeared.

Winters moved forward, one cautious step at a time, long gun ready, finger on the trigger. Seeing no traps, he sidestepped around a corner, focusing in the now dark hallway. Sirens still blared.

Winters pushed down a hall, spot-checking each room. Another corner. This place was a maze. A muffled feminine sob stole his breath.

Only one closed door left.

"No!" Exhausted pleas homed him to her. He readied to burst through the door, but instead, tried the handle. It swung open to his real-time nightmare.

Juan Carlos Silva held her by the neck and shook her limp body as he pointed wildly to something outside the window. A number of foreign curse words were tossed at her, and she had the thousand-yard stare of a battle weary soldier. Silva moved her with the ease of a child playing with a doll. Her arms hung flaccid, and her legs wobbled.

Winters's try-the-handle-first tactic gave him the element of surprise. Silva never even looked his way.

"Get your hands off her neck, Silva." Winters roared so deep, his voice was unrecognizable.

Silva spun Mia into a choke hold. A knife glinted in the other hand. Mia faced Winters but gave no acknowledgement. *Shit.*

Hell, she couldn't even focus in his direction. Her head lobbed forward before Silva shook her back to consciousness. The need to kill burned in Winters's veins.

"How are you in here?" Silva looked around.

All his guards were busy. Big blasts would do that. *Thank you, Brock.*

"Pure fucking magic, asshole."

"Stay where you are." A nothing-to-lose gleam shined in Silva's eyes, and his lip curled in contempt.

Winters lowered his weapon.

"I'm surprised. Did you really not expect us? That I'd leave her to a wolf like you?" Winters clucked in mock disappointment.

Silva pressed the knife against her throat. Mia seemed not to notice. "She is yours if you hand me that disk."

"Nope." The simple word stoked Winters, made him even more ready to end this with bloodshed.

A blast rocked the floor, followed by the pop of gunfire. Winters smiled. Jared was on the move, clearing their way out.

In more of a show than was necessary, Winters clicked on the live feed of his mic, "Tango located. Second floor. Third room north of center."

No response in his ear, but he was sure he transmitted. The team was out there. Always watching. Always listening.

"You do not scare me, Winters." Silva spat his name out.

"Then you're a moron. You have seconds to make a choice before you die." Winters backed up to a large wooden hutch, and with an angry shove, he barricaded the door. "Now, you have no way out."

CHAPTER TWENTY-THREE

A sharp sting tore her neck, dragging her from a dizzying unconsciousness. She was standing, and no longer in that windowless room. Flashes of Alejandro charging her, hand outstretched, made her double-check she was still breathing. A cold sweat shivered across her body. Her arms and legs did nothing she asked of them. What was happening?

The room came into focus. Brighter than *her* room. Loud clanging reverberated in her head. A massive migraine swirled behind her eyeballs. Tears further blurred her vision, then leaked down her cheeks.

Murmurs. Far away, whispers. She fought to focus. To shake the cotton from her head.

"Mia."

How familiar the voice sounded. Her name. His voice echoed along with the pounding of her headache.

She closed her eyes tight and tried to swallow against her dry mouth. Instead, she hacked up a cough. Her throat stung again. Burned. Worse this time.

Bitter, ferocious garbles. It wasn't English.

Silva. Captivity. *Oh shit*. Everything was so slow, but the mental freeze thawed. Just like after the gas station.

"Mia."

Colby. His words were far away, in a dream.

She tried to focus again. Colorful blurs lined up. Images sharpened. Sensations collected, aligning themselves in her mind. The room was bright. It smelled like smoke and cologne.

Mia rolled her head to the side. Juan Carlos Silva wrapped his arm tight around her neck. The horrible, familiar feeling of a knife slicing her neck sent flashbacks of The Colonel screeching into her head.

Life has now come full circle.

She pulled away from the recognizable lick of a blade. She heard Colby. She felt Colby. He wouldn't let Juan Carlos slit her throat. She blinked, and there he was, in all his superhero glory.

He was miles away, yet her arms reached for him. His steely eyes paid her no notice. He looked like a raging bull. Larger than she remembered. Incensed and ferocious.

Juan Carlos shook her with powerful pumps. Her arms and legs shimmied like gelatin. He launched her toward Colby, then yanked back. The vicious cycle was on repeat. Their words jumbled. Their disagreements were loud, yet empty and meaningless.

The door behind Colby bucked and bent. Thunder plowed through the room. Vibrations waved one right after the other, catapulting her to full consciousness.

Juan Carlos yelled over her shoulder. "My men will blast through that door. Both of you will die."

"Take the knife from her neck." Colby narrowed his bloodthirsty stare to Juan Carlos, morphing into a giant of a man. A killer, perched to attack.

"I will kill her now." Juan Carlos rocked her limp body again. "You'll never get out of here alive."

He brought Mia to the window, and she saw carnage. Smoke drifted from the fence line and a fire was in the gardens. In the distance, gunfire pulsed. Colby had brought an army. Juan Carlos cursed in her ear.

He pulled away from the window, and she caught sight of Colby again. In spite of it all, she smiled. It was too short a moment. Juan Carlos dragged her back to the window again.

The black smoke drifted skyward. She could taste it. Alarms still sounded. The men outside looked like children's toys. They were so far away. Was this a dream?

The window exploded inward, launching them in a furious surge. Warm, sharp, and red. Juan Carlos released her. Mia was mush. Her legs were like stilts in quicksand. They sank fast into a numb thud. He landed on her. Hot ooze. Sick metallic stank. A faceless man, eyes open, blood macerated, covered in glass, and dead.

Dead.

Colby stormed her. He scooped her into his arms and threw her over his shoulder. It was too fast and jarring. The horizon slipped sideways. Her stomach fell. Her headache felt like it hit her toes. Everything throbbed, but then she caught sight of Juan Carlos Silva, deader than dead on his beautiful carpet. Surrounded by blood and glass.

Relief was missing. Where was it? A feeling. An emotion. Something, anything. But nothing surfaced. Her mind was empty and foggy. A sticky mess coated her hair and face, and a sick stench of blood permeated the air. Her hands clawed at her face. Bile rose in her throat. Revulsion attacked from the inside. This was the blood of a madman.

She was still over his shoulder. Her face was planted firmly against his back. She didn't need to see the door explode open. She could hear men crawl through, their grunts and threats ending with the pop of Colby's gun.

He kept her still with a palm on her backside. As he moved to the door, he kicked the dead bodies out of the way and scraped furniture aside.

Each of her muscles flopped against his hard body as he bounded down a set of stairs. She jostled as he took each step. *This should hurt more than it does. Something's wrong.*

He stopped and shifted her off his shoulder. Her head swayed in a circle, and she pinched her eyes closed. His hands dug into her armpits, keeping her righted. *That* she felt. Her weight was too heavy to bear. She was too tired to help. Too exhausted to escape.

"Mia." Colby reached to her, pushing through the dense fog, calling her to focus.

She'd reach back. Later. When she felt stronger.

"Mia. Come on, doll. Right here. I'm right here." He was more urgent now. Firmer. A pain in the ass if she really thought about it.

His hands cupped her chin. The rough pad of his thumb ran across her sticky cheek. She opened her eyes to slits. His handsome face stared hard, worried eyes probing her.

"Colby." Her faint breath escaped over raw lips. His name revived a miniscule portion of her will. Not much, but enough to focus.

"Hiya, doll. I'm getting you out of here."

He sounded so calm. Perhaps he needed to sleep, too.

Behind him, bright lights flashed on and off in the dark hallway.

"We gotta roll. Hang tight."

Angry yells came from somewhere closer than she could establish. He lofted her back over his shoulder. Blood rushed to her head. The smell of his sweat and gunpowder intermixed, and she struggled against unconsciousness.

With a dizzying step and spin, he rounded a corner and pops reverberated from a gun. He moved forward, took a couple of hops, and slid back against the wall. Mia saw the blood on the white carpet. Three bodies, arms and legs splayed, and eyes wide open.

Oh.

She balanced on his shoulder. He reloaded his gun. A boom echoed through the house.

"Got the package," Winters whispered. "Ready to roll out."

He wasn't talking to her. His team was here. Somewhere.

"Repeat. Ready for cover. Over."

He let loose a quiet string of expletives and pulled across his chest. A snap sounded from his mouth. Winters lofted a throw and hustled them back around the corner. A boom followed.

Oh, a grenade. But where is the bamboo bazooka?

They moved fast again, and she was just along for the ride. If she had anything to vomit, it would have happened. The spins and turns, the hasty pace and quick moves made her queasy. Sick, however, was preferable to dead.

A loud explosion ripped up the hall. Smoke and dust engulfed them. Her eyes burned like they'd been peppered. Coughing required energy. It was much easier to fade away.

But her body jarred, forcing her eyes open. He bounded toward the smoke. Each step dug her ribs into his shoulder. Fire lit the doorway, and, with a swift kick, the remnants of the smoldering door fell as they pushed through.

Fresher air. Fresh with a hint of burning building. She breathed deep but was unfulfilled. The humidity didn't help. Her diaphragm couldn't expand over his shoulder. Her lungs couldn't quite fill. But still, the air was clean. They were closer to making it out alive.

Gunfire popped. Colby dove. He landed hard, unable to break her impact. Mia flopped on her back. Her head knocked on the ground, and she felt it bounce. Her lungs were forced empty, unable to breathe in. Terror tortured her. Her heart thumped. She heard it. Felt it. But nothing kick-started.

Finally, she gasped. Her body allowed a pant. Her lungs tried for their cadence. She wasn't dying, at least not at that moment.

Cool grass cupped the back of her head and caressed her arms and legs, reviving her.

"You all right?" He perched on the balls of his feet, peeking over a small stone wall on a patio. Statues stood yards away in the garden, and the distinct sound of a water fountain splashing played throughout the gunfire.

"Your guys can't hear you?" Her throat burned. The words croaked. She was more and more conscious. Keenly aware of her surroundings, none of which she liked. Whatever had knocked her out was fading fast from her system.

"Don't worry. We plan everything for a reason." He gave her a wink and a half-cocked smile. Just another day in the life of Colby Winters. He wasn't flustered or scared. Bullets whizzing was business as usual.

He checked his clips on his belt and reloaded his gun. A quick look up, then he grabbed a knife strapped to his leg and let it fly. A short scream of pain followed.

"Asshole," he grumbled and finished loading his clip. "Mia, we're going to have to make a run for it. Soon as we get around that bend, we'll have sniper cover. But we'll be easy targets for a minute. Can you run? I'll be able to shoot with both hands if I don't have to carry you."

Mia nodded. Adrenaline revved her blood. She had more of a fight in her than to lie in the grass and count smoky clouds.

"That's my strong girl. Tell me when you're ready."

"Now. I'm ready now. Get me the hell out of here." She gathered her feet beneath her and steadied. As she balanced on her toes and fingertips, she nodded again.

Winters stood, guns in both hands. "Go."

He moved fast, arms outstretched before him, and she trailed him, trying like hell to keep speed. The corner of the mansion was near. That was her goal.

Gunfire surrounded her. Coming for them, shooting away from them. They fired. He fired back. The burnt gunpowder floated behind him, blazing into her nose and eyes. Still, she pushed, moving as he moved, tracing his cross-hatched steps, ducking when he ducked. A shadow behind the man.

She heard a thump. He growled and missed a step but didn't stop moving. Brilliant red blood sprayed onto her. He didn't slow. Her legs burned keeping the pace.

They rounded the corner, and he pressed her against the stucco wall. His blood stained her. It painted the wall and covered his hands. Vehicles came their way. Armed men poured from a hole in the perimeter fence like ants from an anthill. Fireballs from the jungle hit the vehicles. Violent explosions sent deadly fireworks into the sky. Rubber and diesel burned hot. Black smoke billowed around the armed men running toward them.

The heat, humidity, and smoke would have slowed a lesser man. So would a gunshot wound. He scanned the vast lawn.

"We have to make it past that hole in the fence. There's a vehicle waiting for us. We've got a sniper in the trees, and two more men on the ground. When you see someone dressed like me, you run like hell toward him. Got it?"

"You're hurt." She wanted to run her hands across his skin and stop the bleeding.

He ignored her. "Say it, Mia. Can you do this?"

"I can." She gave him a strong nod, exacerbating her headache. She didn't care. Colby was here, and she'd do whatever he needed her to do.

"You got this. Let's go."

He gave her a small push in the right direction. Bullets sounded around her. Men ran toward them, guns pointed their way. The shots hit the grass, spitting up dirt, and slapping her face. She tasted blood and grit, and felt the filth in her mouth, which caked her lips and teeth.

White-hot pain rocketed through her. A dizzying flash made her stumble. He grabbed her upright.

"Flesh wound. Keep going," he shouted above the noise. His teeth were gritted together. He huddled beside her, pulling her. "There's Jared. Run!"

Another thump. He was hit again, as he shielded her from the rain of artillery. One by one, men advanced toward them and were dropped by a sniper. But as one went down, another appeared.

She heard another bullet hit. Winters dropped to his knee, pulled Mia under him, and cursed violent threats. His sweat and blood coated her. She felt it through the layers of clothing and vests. He scooped her with one arm and crawled behind a statue.

"How bad are you hurt, Colby?"

"Doesn't matter." His labored breaths worsened with each passing moment.

"How bad, damn it?"

Winters stopped laboring and laughed. "You're unreal, you know that?"

Mia glared at him.

"Bad. But I think Kevlar got most of it. Everything heals. I'm not worried. Jared's twenty yards ahead, picking them off. We have to go for it right now. Or we don't have a chance. You got it, babe?"

"I can do this."

"I know you can. Run, baby, run." He took off at a limped sprint, acting as a barrier from the fire again.

His leg went out from under him. The whiz of bullets went to slow motion, the sound ceased. Mia dropped on bent knees, watching him on the ground.

"Run, goddamn it," he shouted. His veins popped out of his neck as he fired into the distance.

The world came back, loud and furious. Her legs moved, even though her mind was numb. Jared appeared out of nowhere. He jumped from his perch and snared her with an arm, dragging her into the vehicle.

"Wait. Colby."

Jared threw the vehicle into gear and spun tires as he tore down the makeshift road. Branches and jungle leaves scratched at the windshield.

Mia launched at Jared, hitting his shoulder.

"Colby's hurt." Tears and terror filled her throat. The very depths of her soul ached. Her screech turned to a pleading whisper. "Please. Help him."

"They were right on your tail. They've got him by now."

Dread ricocheted through her head. All the pain and loss pressed onto her. Suffocating despair ripped her apart. Tears streamed down. Rapid breaths came fast. Too fast. She tried to cut them off but failed. All went black.

CHAPTER TWENTY-FOUR

Winters used his last bullet with perfect accuracy. It hit his target, dead center. But his one bullet to their many men was more vengeance and habit than any intelligent course of action.

He pulled himself to cover. Nothing left to fire. Not even his knife to throw. And he bled from three of his four limbs. They had him. He knew it. They'd know it soon as they listened. None of the gunfire was his. Until then, he had a few minutes.

While he was sheltered by an obscene amount of marble statues, each one a naked Greek goddess reaching for the sky, he ripped off his shirt. His chest was now only covered by the Kevlar vest. With quick rips between his teeth, he made three tourniquets. He had to tie off his bicep, thigh, and calf until he could assess his wounds.

Juan Carlos Silva was dead. He owed Cash for that shot. *Sniper fire will get you every time.*

Silva's number two, a man they called Alejandro, was nowhere to be found. Winters didn't see him when they breached the house. Didn't see him on the way out the door. Didn't see anyone resembling a leader in this firefight.

Did the cartel soldiers know they lacked a commander?

Diversionary tactics may have worked to enter the house undetected, but surely, they had a succession plan. Alejandro must know by now he was no longer second in command. No, he was now El Jefe. And pesos to popcorn, they still wanted that NOC list.

Milking that hope was his only chance to survive and escape.

Winters pulled the third tourniquet tight with his teeth and grimaced though the hot pain. His blood raced in a mad dash, but it wasn't flowing into the grass anymore. He needed a slow breath in, slow breath out to ramp down his heart rate. The pain might lessen. His mind might clear. But most importantly, he'd keep more blood than he'd lose.

The armed men slowed their pace from charging to a careful hustle. Tentative footsteps neared. Muffled arguments sputtered in Spanish. He almost laughed. They didn't know what to do with him. It was his move to make. His only move possible.

Surrender. It'd keep him alive.

He rolled onto his back and slowly raised his hands, giving them the chance to take him alive. Damn, his arm throbbed. This surrendering shit sucked.

Winters watched plumes of smoke drift through the air. The gunfight was over. The carnage ended. Titan would be far enough away. Mia was safe. That was all that mattered.

An armed man approached, with an automatic rifle directed at Winters's head.

"Up. Up. Stand up," the man shouted with a thick accent.

God, Winters hated these fuckers.

"All right." He kicked his empty weapon away and rolled to his knees. Blasts of agony tore through his muscles. The tourniquets accomplished their goals, but he'd need medical treatment. *Rapido*, that was for damn sure. Chances were slim to impossible it'd happen.

"*Hasta.* Up. Up." The man jutted the business end of the automatic rifle into Winters's chest. Better his chest than his head, though his vest couldn't do anything about point blank rapid fire.

His head spun, and his vision fought from fading to lights out. Bright explosions fired, and he saw stars. He closed his eyes tight against the splashes of color. If he passed out, he was a dead man.

He gulped smoky air, tasting gunpowder, and pried his eyes open, snarling. He felt like a gutted animal. Shot up, cut open, and bleeding out. Pain bubbled. Blood seeped as he hoisted himself up to stand.

Motioning to his loosening leg tie and fresh blood. "May I?"

"*Si.*"

They didn't want him dead. At least this second. "*Gracias.*"

Gracias? Gracias, assholes would've been better.

He tightened the fabric ties, wobbling and bobbling. *Stay up right. Stay clear-headed.*

The man jabbed him in the chest again, and his legs buckled against a loss of balance. *Shit.* Things were worse than he thought.

The head asshole-in-charge motioned to two others, let out a string of commands, and turned away. Two men grabbed him under his arms, lifted him like a bag of shit, and hauled him along.

Hell, this was far from ideal. His ties could handle only so much abuse. Their group moved through a gaping hole, where a front door once hung, and into the house. Smoke stained the walls, and blood soaked the carpet. It was silent except for their bump-bump-bump of boots beating over expensive flooring.

They moved up the stairs. With each jarring step, his pain didn't register. Fuck. That was a bad sign.

Finally, they stopped. No words exchanged. No explanation, threats, or pat downs. A simple push into a black hole, then a lock scraped secure. He smacked the tile floor. His eyes screwed shut. Lightning strikes reverberated through his limbs, circling toward his nauseous stomach.

After a long list of curses, the agony subsided, and he propped on his elbows. It was hellhole dark. He stretched forward, hoping to find a wall and define the room. After failed attempts, his fingertips found plaster, and he propped against a rough wall. With his uninjured arm, he found a switch and flipped it. A light glowed orange.

A small room. A bed. Another door. He crawled toward the door with the energy required to run a marathon.

It was a bathroom. With towels and a place to assess his wounds.

He pulled up to the counter and tried the faucet. Success. Winters splashed water on his face and draped himself over the sink. The dim light burned in the bedroom, and shadows fell long in the bathroom. The plumbing leaked on the floor. The estate was old, and the plumbing didn't have a chance. But the water still ran from the tap. Thank God.

He soaked a towel, then wiped the debris from bloody wounds. His arm was only a flesh wound. It bled but didn't need a tourniquet. He released the wrap and flexed his bicep. More blood leached. Pressure was still needed. A bandage. Some dressing. Anything to clot the hole in his arm. He grabbed a flimsy, threadbare towel, tore to the right size, and wrapped it around his bicep. Makeshift Band-Aid number one, complete.

His legs burned, shaking when his weight pressed down. But he could stand and crawl. That ruled out bullet-shattered bones. And he was still conscious. More or less. So no major arteries were hit. He couldn't complain about that luck.

Winters examined his right thigh. A through and through. Both openings leaked. The tourniquet helped, but more blood loss wouldn't sustain an effective escape.

His left calf pulsed blood, despite the tie off. An entry hole but no exit. *Shit.* He looked around the sparse bedroom and bath. The accommodations sucked. No first aid kit, not that he expected one. He leaned back on the counter and rubbed the nape of his neck.

A headache pounded, gaining violent momentum. First requirement to stay alive, he needed to hydrate. Drinking the South American water wasn't high on his list of things to do. But adding dehydration to the list of shit gone wrong was futile.

He spun the metal faucet handle, stuck his head under the stream, and drank. The water eased the unrealized flame in his throat. It reinvigorated him. He stood upright on throbbing legs. The room spun. *No good.* More water, then time to figure out how the hell to fix his legs.

He sucked down another gulp and rose, slower this time. The bullet lodged in his leg had to go, and he had to patch it. His eyes darted around the cave of a room. Nothing would help.

Get creative or die.

Winters's gaze landed on the bed, and he hobbled over to the cheap mattress packed full of lumpy filler. It had a subpar metal frame, little more than cross-hatched chicken wire. All the money in the world, and Juan Carlos Silva outfitted this dungeon for his captives.

Winters wrapped his fingers around the frame wires and pulled. They dug into his skin. His muscles shook with effort. The wires mined into his flesh, threatening a laceration. He pulled again, summoning strength that he didn't possess.

Come on. He needed this like he needed to live.

One wire sprung free.

All of that exertion and a speck of progress to show for it. But he'd take specks. The woven wired started to unwind. He dropped to the floor and breathed in scampered gasps. *This shouldn't be so hard.* Maybe he was worse off than he knew.

Like pulling the string from a metal sweater, he used both hands to untwist each wire. The length of the wire loosened. Chain reaction. The next one did, too. The tension was gone. He was surrounded by a mess of medium gauge wire. Pliable but sturdy.

This was going to be awful. On days like this, he needed a stuntman.

He doubled over the end of a wire. Then again. A zee with a long end. Really a vee. It was the shittiest set of forceps a man could dream up. This was going to be really fucking awful.

He struggled to the bathroom, wire forceps in hand, and looked for the remaining scraps of the torn towel, then turned the water on. He hoisted himself onto the counter, tore his tactical pant leg open, and shoved the remaining pieces of the towel in his mouth.

He'd only removed a bullet from his muscle once before, and even then, it was under better circumstances. More apprehensive about the pain than he was about the act, he jabbed his finger into his left calf and felt for the bullet.

Holy shit.

He screamed into the towel. Sweat poured down his back and chest, down his forehead, and into his eyes. That goddamn bullet. It was there. Not too deep. But still under his skin, burrowed into the top of his muscle.

He heaved breaths like a woman in labor. One right after the other. No longer thinking. Just doing. Trying to breathe. His nostrils flared as he grabbed the forceps, roared, then pushed into the wound. Fiery explosions ricocheted. Spasm panged. His hands shook in his strangle grip.

Slippery blood seeped, covering his hands. Metal found metal, and with a silent prayer, closed tension around the bullet. It surfaced and popped loose. Metal clanged on tile. Bullet and field-made forceps. He heard them plunk before he saw them in a puddle of his blood.

Step one complete.

This shit show was only half over. He took methodical, blood slowing breaths, and concentrated on his sky-high heart rate. Blood covered the rickety counter and tile floor. His splatter decorated the plaster wall and dried under his fingernails. *Talk about a bad day at work.*

He lumbered off the counter, and the world swam. A quick catch braced him against the wall. Flashes of pain scorched him. He sawed his teeth together, as his healthy shoulder bore all his weight.

Too much blood loss. His head fell forward, rolled, and swayed. He was so close to finishing this off. Rallying energy he didn't have, he staggered to the angry, red floor, and grabbed the torn towel. Each threadbare piece systematically rolled into fabric stoppers. He plunged one in each hole, stymieing the flow. Shutting down the blood loss. Giving himself the only shot he had to survive.

He fell to his side, marinating in his blood. Each gasp sounded in the thickening gel. It was too much to handle. His delirious mind was strung tight as a trip wire. He was one misstep from kaboom.

Sleep and survive.

He wiped his face and led the charge back to the sorriest excuse of a mattress he'd ever seen. It'd be heaven if he could get to it. Half-dragging, half-overpowering, he struggled until he accomplished his goal, and schlepped himself onto it. He rolled, face first. No position alleviated the misery. He slouched sideways, unable to control his limbs, and his hand tumbled toward the floor.

He didn't touch tile or wire or blood.

He touched clothes.

His fingers danced across the soft cotton.

Mia.

She'd been here. And thank God she was gone. How long since he'd held her? He pulled the clothes to his face. Soft. And smelled faintly like her.

He would get home to her. She'd do family. He'd do family. They'd figure it out. Her sweet kisses could wash away his hurt. Her embrace would ease the pain flowing like lava through his veins. Mia coaxed him to the black oblivion, lulling him to nightmarish sleep.

CHAPTER TWENTY-FIVE

Mia woke up with her face cemented to the leather seat, drool crusted over the corner of her mouth, and her throat far past Sahara dry. She squeezed her eyes shut against the flashbacks. Colby's orders. Jared's arms. She lost her man.

Screw them both. Mia excised her cheek from the seat and glared at Jared. He left Colby. Left him for dead. Why didn't he get him? Wasn't that what they did? Save people?

"Hey, Jared, or whoever you are. Why are we sitting here?" Her voice rumbled, hoarse and desperate. Her question should have been why was he sitting here and not loading up a torpedo launcher.

Jared gripped the steering wheel with enough strength she thought it might break. They weren't flying through the thick jungle underbrush. The slapping echo of vegetation slashing against the windshield no longer drowned out the roar of the engine.

"Mia." He could crush asphalt with his voice.

"Jared," she said, both scared and angry, and fairly certain this was Jared.

The dome light clicked on overhead. Jared jumped out as if he needed a calming stroll in the park, and he beelined to a small shack in a clearing. Wood boards hung gimp and gaped. Peeling paint clung to an occasional plank, while others were sun-blistered and bare. It was larger than her last shack, but that wasn't saying much.

Mia reached for the door handle to follow but instead whimpered. Everything ached. Her forehead to her ankles. And her arm, that was the killer. It was the first time she noticed the bandage.

Vivid flashbacks again came at her like a skipping movie. Juan Carlos Silva, gruesomely dead. Her flesh wound. Colby propping her up and pushing her through hell.

Jared could run away, but he couldn't get too far. She pushed through the roar in her arm, opened the door, and set the stumbling pace of a discombobulated woman on a man-saving mission.

Heat drenched her, humidity cloaking her in a jungle second. A wave of nausea smacked her clear across her face. Food. She needed something in her stomach. She tried to ease the stomach rolls.

Nausea punched her again. No, food wasn't the best idea. She'd just throw it up, preferably all over Jared. She swallowed against the queasy ripples. Water might be the prudent plan.

With the concentration required for brain surgery, Mia placed one foot in front of the other, hobbling as close to Jared's path as her stupor-slicked mind could manage. She stumbled through the egress into a gang of mercenaries, all who looked like they ate rusted nails for Sunday brunch and bent steel for fun.

Her awful cartel-gifted sundress, splattered in blood and dirt, stood out as strangely feminine in the sea of muscles, guns, and testosterone. Mia fingered the scab from Silva on her neck. She apparently presented a shocking image. The room hushed soon as they caught a glimpse of her.

A blond in a cowboy hat tossed her a package that crinkled before it went airborne. Somehow she caught it, unaware of what *it* was, and her arm hurt fierce from the motion. All eyes locked on her, then hers pinned on Jared's.

"Wet wipes," Blondie said. "Like a soldier's shower. Use whatever you need."

She pivoted and looked at him. His face was painted in greens, grays, and blacks. Smudged and sweaty. Brilliant blue eyes beneath it all. Somewhat human compared to the others.

Mia cleared her throat. Her gaze stole back to Jared. The sinewy muscles in his jaw flexed, and he took a step toward her but didn't open his mouth. Her chest felt tight, anxious energy flooded her fingers.

She had nasty things to say to him. Things to order him to do. But her mind couldn't string them together. Threats loomed close to her tongue, but her mind didn't comprehend reason or issue rhetoric.

Unable to complete menial oratory tasks, she rushed at him, fists balled, teeth cemented together, and slammed him dead center in his chest.

The impact was like she ran fist first into the side of a mountain. Sheer physics would have bounced her off and onto her butt if he didn't grab her forearms. Other than his hands cuffed on her arms, Jared didn't acknowledge her tirade.

What kind of assholes did Winters work with? Anger pulsed in her temples. Her molars hurt from gritting her teeth. She pulled from Jared, struggling and vibrating with rage. He loomed impenetrable. Not flinching. Not reacting. Nothing. Not a single expression.

"What's your plan?" Finally, her vocabulary returned.

The steadfast boredom on his face stoked the embers of her irritation further. Red-hot anger choked her. Shit. She couldn't breathe. Suffocating heat. Insufferable assholes. It collided into a stifling, strangling grip on her chest.

"Calm down, Mia." His words were condescending. Patriarchal.

She'd calm down just to tell him to kiss her ass.

"Shove it." In her mind, it came out like words launched from a flamethrower. In reality, she wheezed. But wheezed loud. That was something.

Again, no reaction from a void-faced Jared, but Blondie laughed so deep the shitty shack quaked. With focus like a laser beam, she drilled into him.

"Jokes." She arched her brows and shook her head. "You think this is funny? Why don't you take your face painted butt and get a move on, cowboy. Go find Colby."

Blondie-the-Cowboy doubled over in near hysterical cackles. If she had the strength, she'd have stalked over and kicked him.

"Man, this explains everything." He leaned up enough to extend his dirty hand. "Mia, I'm Cash."

She cut him off. "I don't care who you are."

Were those tears in his eyes? What was so funny? She'd knock sense into them all. After they helped Colby.

"Oh, honey. I know you don't."

He *was* laughing so hard he had tears. Now, it was his turn to gasp for breath. This was ridiculous. These lethal warriors needed to march their behinds back into danger.

Jared and two others watched her watch Cash the Cowboy. Blondie. Whatever his name was, the jerk. They were all jerks. God, this was frustrating.

"Honey, we're going after your boy," Cash said. "But we don't want to get killed doing it. Give us a minute to strategize. There are a helluva lot more assholes with automatic weapons set to rapid fire rock-n-roll than we'd planned to tangle with."

Silence ticked by, one second after the next. The sweltering Colombian heat made the air heavy. All their eyes bore down on her.

She crossed her arms, trying to make sense of their assumptions. "This explains what?"

"What?" Cash asked.

"You said *this explains everything*."

"It does."

"Stop screwing with me, cowboy."

He laughed. "There you go again. The only woman who Winters could ever fall for would be one who tries to push around Ballbuster McGee over there, then strut around, calling men cowboys and shit."

"He hasn't *fallen* for anyone." She smirked at Cash, then to each of them, one by one. "He's just…important."

"Yeah, we've heard that one before, hon. You've got him so wrapped up in you, he doesn't know his asshole from his elbow."

Eyes narrowed, she looked at them again. Jared still showed no expression.

"I, uh…I don't know what to say to that."

Jared cleared his throat. "There's nothing to say. But we need your help. Recount everything you saw, everyone you met."

"Let the girl clean up or something," Cash said. "Jesus, dick."

"You can do two things at once. Three." He grabbed a bottle of something red. "Hydrate. Now."

Wasn't he the Prince of Manners? Then she thought of Juan Carlos and his absurd etiquette. She'd take Jared any day, and twice on rescue day.

Mia took a big sip and gagged on syrupy fruit punch, warm and fizzy.

"Bug juice." Cash laughed.

He laughed a lot. No, he laughed *at her* a lot.

"This is disgusting."

"That'll keep you alive, hon. Just the way Winters requested."

Mia opened the package of wet towels, started on her face, and systematically moved down to her feet. She dug at the grime under her fingernails and ended with a mound of towelettes on the dirt floor.

Jared peppered her with question after question after question. None made sense, but then again, she wasn't used to planning an offensive attack. She couldn't wait to do whatever came next. Hell, she couldn't wait to finish this bottle of bug juice. She took another huge gulp and shook in disgust. Lord only knew what was in bug juice. She didn't need to know. But if she finished it, maybe she'd earn a bottle of water or protein bar or anything edible.

Last sip down, and Mia crushed the plastic bottle and held it up. Proof positive she finished the awful thing. "Can I get something else now?"

Jared nodded.

Cash opened a bag. "We've got beef stew, beef bbq, beef—"

"Don't offer her the shit you don't like." A man she didn't know rolled his eyes.

"All right, jackass." Cash tilted his head and snarled. When he wasn't laughing, the face paint made him look like a bulldog ready to tear something apart. "Mia, spaghetti with sauce, cheese tortellini—"

"What are you talking about?" She shook her head, sure they were making fun of her.

"MREs, babe. Bag o' nasty. Meals rejected by—"

"She gets the point, Cash," Jared said. "Shut it."

"Spaghetti it is." Cash threw a pouch at her.

Every camo-clad, weapons-strapped man watched. Would the MRE be that bad? She ripped the package open. The contents looked like spaghetti and sauce. Smelled like…plastic. Whatever. She was starving. They didn't offer a fork, and she didn't expect it. The taste was as appetizing as the bug juice.

She looked up. There may have been a crumb of approval in Jared's grumbling face.

He blinked it away before she could confirm, then he spoke up. "So, this is the team. You already met Cash, sniper to the stars. Thinks he's a funnyman. You can also thank him for blowing Silva's brains all over you. Rocco's our wheels guy. Brock, you can thank for not eating beef tonight. He blows shit up, and says there's an art to it. And you talked to Parker on the phone. Tech guy extraordinaire."

"And you?"

"Me?"

"Yeah. If everyone has a specialty, what's yours?"

"I'm a master at everything."

Of course. She glared at him. "What about Colby?"

"Winters?"

"Yeah, that's his name. What's his specialty?"

"Escape and evade. He's a survivor. He can stay alive when most men beg for death."

"What is it with you guys? He's not invincible." She rolled her eyes but was secretly praying Jared was right.

"Give him credit. With a handful of help from us, he'll be home playing house with you soon enough. Unless…" He shrugged.

Her breath caught in her throat. All the air vacuumed out of the shack. Dread shook in every cell. His simple indifference made her head spin. She'd wring his neck. No matter if he was master of everything.

"Easy there, Mia." Jared's lips twitched. "Unless he shows up before we bug out. It wouldn't surprise me if Winters dragged his busted ass through this door."

"Oh." Mia's cheeks flashed hot.

"So, if you're done with dinner, let's get down to business. Silva's gone. Our intel says that Alejandro Suarez, his number two, would take over. Seen him? Heard of him?"

"Yeah. I was *his* if Colby didn't turn over the list." The memory caused a cold sweat in the jungle heat. She pinched her eyes to fight off the revolting reaction her body produced when thinking of Alejandro.

The men fidgeted, obviously unaware of how much she knew of her almost-fate.

"So you met him?" Jared asked. "He's on the grounds?"

"He's there."

"And is he a leader? Or is he a fall guy?"

"Not much of a leader. Nothing I'd think a cartel number two should be." Mia wrung her hands together. "Not that I know much about it, I guess."

"Give us something. Your file says you're a psychologist. What can you tell us?"

Deep breath in, out. She blocked her repulsion and analyzed her memories. "Where Juan Carlos was a narcissist, Alejandro was a need-driven fiend. His interest lies in what they called their *product,* and Juan Carlos kept him in line with promises of...well, of me." She took a deep breath. "He may have the brawn to keep men in line but not the brains. And he knows it, too. Strategy won't be his thing. But torture? That's his modus operandi."

"Good job, Mia. That's great."

"Why would that be a good thing?" Mia scrunched her forehead.

"Because Winters can handle a little torture, and he's smart as they come."

"But he's hurt bad. He told me so."

"He'll do what it takes to make himself ready for our arrival. He knows the drill." Jared turned toward the table and their drawings. "All right. So they have a leader. They have plenty of men. We need another blitz attack to confuse the hell out of them again. We figure out where our boy is, grab him, and hightail it on home."

Mia cleared her throat. "They kept me in a room that looked like it was for…captives. Top of the stairs and down a long hallway, locked from the outside. No windows."

"Smart girl. So we get into that room. Brock, I need diversionary explosions here, here, and here." Jared pointed to the schematics on the table. "A fiery blockade near this section, where his men congregate."

"Roger that." Brock narrowed his review on the map.

"Cash, position here," Jared said. "I want you to cover me on the way in, pick off anyone you see in the house, and provide cover on our way out."

Cash gave a chin lift. His cowboy hat rode low over his shaggy hair, piercing eyes, and camo-painted face.

"I want wheels here, Roc. Double-check that armored Rover. I gave it a hell of a beating when Mia and I hauled ass out there."

Rocco cracked his neck right, then left. "Ain't nothing gonna take that Rover down. But I'll give it a once-over."

"Brock, you'll go in with me. Rocco, you follow behind."

"What about me?" She hated interrupting him, but he edged her out of their discussion.

Jared didn't skip a beat. "What about you?"

"What will I do?"

"You'll sit your behind on this chair." He tapped the back of a ratty chair. "And wait for us to come back with your boy."

"I don't think so." She puffed out her chest and straightened her shoulders. Anything to make Jared change his mind.

He coughed a sarcastic laugh. "I'm not giving you an option here, Mia. This isn't a game, and you'll do as you're told."

"I didn't say it was a game." She took a step forward. "I'm just supposed to sit here and wait?"

"No two ways about it. You'll stay put. The rest of you, let's go." He motioned toward the door.

"I could—"

"You can't."

Mia slapped her hands onto her hips. "You don't even know what I was going to say."

"Honestly, I don't care. We don't have time to debate this."

"Prick."

He cracked the tiniest smile. She saw it, but it faded faster than his shutdowns. "Call me all the names you want. But if you went back out there and got hurt, Winters would have my ass."

"Yeah, you're so scared of him. I see that."

"You don't get it, honey. He's not here, and it's our job to make sure you're safe. We watch out for our own, and that means you don't move. He'd have every right to take a cheap shot at me if one good-looking hair on your head gets hurt under my watch."

"You're still a prick."

"And you're a subordinate. Sit your cute ass down."

Cute? Jared speaking in anything other than black and white seemed a deviation. Mia rolled her eyes but didn't respond. Cash ambled by her and winked. At least she had a friend in him. Jared was a jerk. And who knew about the others.

They filed out the shack door. Jared turned to her before leaving. "Sit down. Don't move. Don't leave. You may hydrate. That's all."

She hated him. Frustrated tears burned her raw eyes, but she wouldn't let them fall. She hated losing control. Hated her emotions when they ran rampant. But none of that mattered as she sat alone.

Insects buzzed throughout the shack. Mia ignored the rickety chairs and packed dirt floor. In the corner of the room was a makeshift bed. Really, just a thatched mat.

Exhaustion clawed in the silence. It overpowered the nerves that tormented her stomach. The bed called to her with burden-easing promises.

CHAPTER TWENTY-SIX

Winters blinked against the reverberations. Bursts and pops sounded dull in his cinder block cage, yet not too distant. He blinked again, registering blistering pain and chorusing excitement. Titan has arrived. Thank the Lord.

And if Titan was close, Mia was safe. Somewhere, somehow, they had secured her. They wouldn't stage an assault if she weren't.

Sweet, sweet, Mia.

Or instead, poor, sweet, Mia.

He blew a hard sigh, strong enough to empty his desperate lungs. What the hell had he brought into her life? Nothing but danger, trauma, and brutality. He was to blame for every perilous misstep she'd had since the kidnapping at the airport.

He should have left her alone on day one. Smoky-eyed and tear-gassed. She was a smart girl. She could have talked her way out of that motel room when Louisville's finest arrived, lights gyrating.

Shit, any five-oh, assuming they were red-blooded and male, would have tripped over themselves to take her statement and offer her comfort. And all he did was toss her in the backseat of his truck.

What kind of dickhead was he? The kind who selfishly exposed her to hell.

His life was too dangerous. His judgment was inherently disjointed when it came to her. Clara, he could protect, but Mia... She was different. She had a life, a job. Maybe even a mortgage. Everything was fine before he came along. And now? Very much not fine.

She was rat-holed in a jungle safe house. A deep ache, worse than the field mended gunshot holes, festered in his stomach.

Dread. Terrible, gut-wrenching dread. He squeezed his eyes shut. The realization was a knockout punch to the temple. He needed to protect her from evil and violence. And from him.

He'd have to walk away.

His mind double-timed. A shrapnel-snarled explosion ripped his heart to pieces. He didn't deserve a woman who sacrificed herself for his daughter. He sure as shit couldn't handle the responsibility of chancing her life again.

Losing her would be the hardest battle he'd fight. Ever.

Nothing good ever came easy. Or some shit like that. He'd be miserable, but that wasn't the point. She'd be safe. That was the damn point.

Winters pushed onto his elbows, cursing his fatigued muscles. His head spun. The blasts were closer. He needed to put on his cartel-surviving game face, if he was going to hobble out of this prison.

He rubbed his eyes and ran his bloodied hands through his gritty hair. He needed a few vacation days after this clusterfuck subsided.

A booming shout bled through the solid door. "Hey, Sleeping Beauty, back the fuck up."

Had he ever been so happy to hear angry Jared? The deadbolt exploded. A thump of a boot later, and the door flung open.

"About time you showed up. Lazy asses."

Jared huffed. "You're more trouble than you're worth. I swear."

"Mia's safe?"

"Safe and sound, and a pain in my ass."

He smiled. Mia'd busted Jared's balls. He'd pay to see that entertainment.

"Ready to get your pansy ass back to your girl?"

His girl. Not anymore. He couldn't let this happen again. "I'm ready to bug out of here. That's for damn sure."

Boss man eyed his injuries. "Can you move?"

"Enough with the Mother Teresa act. I can move fine." *Maybe.*

"Right." Jared pulled a subcompact weapon from his ankle holster and handed it to him. With a smooth inspection of the magazine clip, Winters reinserted it, then nodded. Jared clasped his bicep, gave him an arm up, then they exited out the door. Each step behind Jared torpedoed pain. Winters's arm burned, leg throbbed, and everything in between ached. He gritted his teeth and kept pace. They stepped over downed bodies and blew past the front door.

"We're coming out. Ready for cover," Jared said into his mic, then turned to him. "We got most of 'em. New Jefe weaseled out. The money, the guns, all gone. The safe room is empty."

Jared pressed his earpiece, listened, and nodded for Winters to follow. They made their way into the darkening night. Fresh air and open heavens gave him the push he needed to keep stride with his debilitating limp.

They reached the gate, rounded the corner, and moved fast to an idling Range Rover. Brock popped up behind them, running backwards and firing cover. Ahead, Rocco ascended from a defensive position, weapon pointed forward until he slid over the front hood, then he jumped in the driver's seat.

With everyone piled in, Rocco sent dirt flying when he slapped the shifter into drive, jumbling hard down a makeshift road.

Winters was breathing way too fast. Pain was a nasty mistress, screwing him in ways he couldn't have imagined. He tried to compartmentalize it and block it out.

Then his stomach bottomed out. "Where's Cash?"

If Cash got hurt hauling his ass out, he'd be pissed. Pissed at Cash for doing something stupid. Pissed at himself for a million different reasons he didn't have time to list. Pissed at everyone.

"Relax, lover boy. Sniper's out doing his sniper thing. We didn't have eyes on any cartel leadership, so he's doing some recon to confirm."

"Stop it with the lover boy." Winters cleared his throat. "Got any water in this rig?"

"Touchy. Touchy." Rocco laughed from the driver's seat, not necessarily looking out the windshield.

"I was wrong to pull her into this shit. The last thing that lady needs is me in her life."

Jared turned from the front passenger seat. "That lady? Dude, you realize we just traveled halfway around the globe for *that lady*. Your lady."

Brock reached behind them and grabbed Winters a bottle of water and the first aid kit. He took a big swig of the water. "I need some penicillin. I pulled a damn bullet out with a bed frame."

Jared rolled his eyes. "Cry me a Colombian river."

"Christ, man." Brock pulled the vial and a syringe from the kit. "What do you want for pain?"

"I don't care. Something over-the-counter. Nothing narcotic. I need to be clear-headed."

"Coming right up. Tylenol for the tough guy. Or is it Motrin for the moron?" Brock dug through the kit, laughing at his joke. "The warrior games are over. Feel free to stone it up."

"Nah. I need to think," Winters mumbled to himself but realized everyone heard him. Silence hung thick and heavy as Rocco bounced them through the rainforest. Bushes slapped, underbrush dragged. The Range Rover revved, piercing the white noise.

So this was self-doubt. Or was it self-pity? Either way, perfect timing.

Jared turned again and trained his eyes on Winters.

"I'll say this once, so it'd be in your best interest to smarten up and listen. That's your girl. Not some lady. No one you need to be clear-headed around. I don't particularly like telling pretty girls to shut up and sit down, but I had to 'cause she wanted in on this little rescue op. I don't know the first thing about love or any mushy shit like that. But I know Mia's your girl. So man up, and handle your shit. Handle her." He glared at Winters. "Christ, I feel like fucking Oprah. And oh yeah, asshole, you're welcome."

The muscles in Winters's face contracted against his will. He flexed his fists in his lap, trying to control gurgles of sanity-busting rage and emotion.

That lady. He called Mia *that lady*. What the fuck was wrong with him? It didn't matter. She was just too precious for a man like him.

Tight pain seized Mia's wrist. Her eyes shot open, terrified. The scratchy mat, the rickety shack. Everything came into focus, including Alejandro's twisted smile and the trails of sweat pouring down his temples. It was a sick vision.

She bicycled her legs, trying like hell to scamper away. Escape was futile.

"You are awake." His breath stank of rancid milk and rotted flesh.

"Help!" She pulled and kicked. "Help me!"

"They left you. All alone without so much as a weapon to guard yourself with. Tsk, tsk. Not smart on their part."

She didn't even know he could speak English. Now, he taunted her. Breathing her in. Licking his teeth.

"Please don't—"

He yanked hard enough her arm to make her shoulder joint pop in and out of place. Tears of pain, desperation, and exhaustion rolled free.

Alejandro shook her again. "Wretched slut. Shut up."

"Help—"

"You were promised to me."

Mia's lips trembled. Her heart screamed into her throat. Bile surfaced on the back of her tongue.

"I am in command. I am in control. And I will take my reward," Alejandro shouted, almost releasing her to beat his chest.

Thick fingers toyed with her sundress strap and snapped it, forcing it loose. His gnarly tongue licked his chewed lips, and he pulled her close to his face. She shut her eyes tight, pushing hard away from him.

"No. Don't do this." He was going to rape her in a jungle shack. Her life was over. She didn't even wipe the cascading tears. The fear, the terror boiling in her mind and gut overpowered planning an escape. Her fate was sealed.

Alejandro cackled. "My favorite part. Every time. Every girl. I get to see how much you fight. I watch your will to live drain like a gutted pig."

She whimpered. The tears obscured her vision. She wasn't sure if her pleas were verbal or frozen in her petrified brain.

Alejandro released her wrist. She dropped on the scratchy bed mat, then rolled away, slamming into wall. The shack swayed, as if breathing in and out, trying to decide if it should remain upright. His gaze raked over her, sending ice-cold shivers in the humid heat down her spine. He scraped the wooden chair on the dirt floor, leaving a trail in the dust. The devil flashed across his face.

"Sit here. Now."

She shook her head. Tears flew off her cheeks, landing on her shoulders and collarbone. Her fists clawed into the mat, bracing for his wrath. Blood thumped in her ears, drowning out his grotesque breaths. Her pulse pounded faster and faster, swimming her head dizzy.

A howl rumbled from Alejandro. He balled his brawl-scarred fists until his cracked knuckles changed color, off-white and fleshy-red. He wore a tight black shirt and black cargo pants with loops and pockets. A knife was strapped to his thigh, and a gun was holstered on his hip. He looked like an immoral, repulsive adaptation of Colby.

His calloused hand wrapped around her neck, and in one swift move, she was in the chair. The force toppled it onto the back two legs before it slammed back to earth. He yanked her one arm, then the next behind the chair, tying them secure. Too tight. It stung before both hands went numb. Pins and needles crawled up her forearms.

Alejandro radiated heat. "I was mistaken. I thought you might have more fight than this sniveling."

He bit down on her shoulder. More of shock than pain caused her to recoil. She railed against her hand ties, kicked her feet, aiming for the crotch, but as usual, that did nothing.

Alejandro slinked in front of her, just out of toe's reach. She still tried like hell to get him. To keep his deranged, lust-dripping self away. He cackled again and stepped forward, ignoring her attacking knees. One disgusting finger traced a path from her temple, down, down, down, until it hovered between her breasts.

Mia strained away from him. The tears stopped. Anger and hatred rushed in their place. He wanted a fight? She'd fight. She'd stay alive and intact until Colby and Titan returned to kick his ass for her.

She gritted her teeth against her disgust, drew back, and spit into his face.

"You whore!" He slapped her face.

Stars exploded. Her vision went white, then black. Her head bobbed, searching for equilibrium. Then she found it. "Screw you."

"With pleasure." He rubbed his hands together and leered at her. "So you do have fight."

"Untie my hands, and I'll show you." She jutted her chin toward him, itching to stay away from him but knowing there wasn't another option.

A wicked smile curled his lips. "Let the fun begin, whore."

He pulled the knife from its holster, tossing it from one hand to the next, dancing it between his fingers. As if he couldn't contain his excitement, Alejandro flashed behind her, cutting the blade into the bindings. The ties fell to the dirt floor, and her tense arms dangled numb and asleep. Completely useless.

"You promised a fight. Do you want to run?" He laughed.

The cold metal blade pressed against the back of her neck, its tip scratching her skin. She was sick of men with knives on her neck. Sick of the memories. The Colonel. The Cartel leader. And now this fiend. Sick of it all.

"You're in charge now? You are El Jefe?" she asked.

"You try to distract me? To patronize me?"

"No." She was trying to buy time.

"Liar. You spit in my face. Promise a delightful fight. And now talk business. Run. Try me."

Fist wrapping into her hair, he yanked her head back, then stepped in front of her. Mia drew her knee into his crotch. *Finally.* Caught off guard, he hunched over, covering himself with his hands. This was her moment to run.

Her feet pounded the dirt before her mind realized she was pushing through the underbrush. Leaves were so thick, she ran blind. Branches hit her face, stinging her skin. The air smelled fragrant and felt thick as she sucked it in. Clueless as to where to go, and how to get there, she pushed through aching muscles and scattering thoughts.

Far too close to hope for survival, Alejandro's angry voice bled through the vegetation, intermixing with the birds and insects, threatening and promising her worst nightmares.

Everywhere, each direction, brilliant green branches and bright flowers. New shadows from the barely setting sun cast purple hues. Her breaths and gasps burned. The sundress clung to her, sweat-soaked. Thinking her lungs couldn't manage one more wheeze, Mia pressed up against a thick tree and slumped to bended knees, damp hair hanging around her.

Her heart pounded loud enough that she wouldn't have been surprised if Alejandro pinpointed her exact location. Sweat dripped into her eyes and slipped into her mouth. She ignored its salty taste. An inner strength bubbled strong. She would do whatever it took to stay alive long enough to watch Colby slice his throat.

Nature surrounded her, deafening her. Cacaw. Cacaw. A loud bird screeched overhead. Prickled awareness hit, and her scream fought to escape, but a hand slapped her face.

No.

Another hard hand clamped her shoulder. Fear erupted inside her. She lashed out, clawing, biting, and kicking. She bucked, and she prayed.

No.

She wouldn't go down this way. Not after everything she'd survived. But she hit the ground anyway. Hard, face first, with inflexible hands holding her down, perhaps in her own grave.

CHAPTER TWENTY-SEVEN

The Rover slid to a stop in front of the shack. All the men fell out, except Winters. He stretched one leg, then the next. Raw agony weighed heavy on every level. Mental. Physical. Emotional.

Brock turned around. "You need a hand?"

"Nah. Just give me a second."

Luck had kept him alive to this point. Hopefully, penicillin would do the rest and keep his busted ass free of nasty infection. But his molasses-like moves had everything to do with his wounded heart and not his GSW hatchet job.

Mia was feet away. The only thing he wanted to do was gather her tight in his arms and kiss every gorgeous inch of her body, starting with her beautiful face. He wanted to worship her brilliance and strength. He wanted to thank her, relish her, and care for her.

But no matter what he wanted, he knew better. She was an innocent. A perfect woman meant to make a *normal* man happy. A man who came home every day for dinner, who pushed paper and typed on a computer, nine-to-five. Someone whose most dangerous decision would revolve around day-old tuna salad at the corner deli. Normal, everyday problems.

His problems weren't in the same hemisphere as normal. His daughter sprang from a sex trafficking ring. The woman he was boots over ball caps for, he'd met because he'd kidnapped her. He tangled with professional assassins and warlords on the regular. A habitual dinnertime just didn't exist in his world. What woman would even want him?

Not a smart one. And Mia Kensington was the smartest woman he'd ever met.

Fuck this awful stomachache. He'd take gunshot wounds any day over this shit. He felt hot and cold. Cloudy-headed and incredibly, desperately sure of his sub-par value to Mia.

The slower he plodded toward the shack, the more he hated himself for holding back. If he went any faster, it would only serve to hasten the pain. What a catastrophic conundrum.

He was the last to enter the shack. He took in the small space and his brothers-in-arms. Jared, Brock, and Rocco. Faces pinched and etched with concern.

"Where is she?" Winters looked around the bare room. He kicked the dirt floor, and his leg retaliated with an intramuscular fire. "Where the fuck is she?"

No answers. Jared bent over and picked up a plastic handcuff, smacking it against his palm.

Winters stalked to a lone chair and threw it against the shambled wall. His arms roared. His wounds throbbed. The chair took out a few of the rotted wood wall slats. It splintered and scattered on the dirt floor like kindling.

"Calm it down, Winters." Jared didn't sound like he was listening to his own advice.

Winters didn't plan to either. His fists balled tight. His fingernails dug into to his skin. This was why he should have stayed the hell away from her. How many times had the poor woman been attacked since he stepped into her life? Goddamn it.

"We're going after her. Now," Winters said with a level of anger he didn't know existed.

"Go where? We need a plan."

"I'm sick of your slow plans." He stormed toward the door.

"You stop right there, soldier. What are you going to do? Canvass the entire jungle?"

"There's that strategy to consider."

"You've got shit for brains where this chick is concerned. Brock, if Winters rolls out of here, you grab him and nail his ass to a chair."

Brock glared at Jared. "Yeah, thanks, man. That'll be like catching Niagara fucking Falls with a fly net."

The hand over Mia's mouth tightened and her heart raced. Adrenaline fueled her. She snapped her teeth open and shut like a crazed piranha, hoping to bite flesh and gain her release. Her elbow arched back and slammed into a brick wall of solid muscle. Her attacker wasn't fazed.

No. No. No. She refused. This wouldn't happen.

Summoning power, fortitude, and brawn, Mia bellowed in exertion, pushed off her hands and knees, and slammed the back of her skull into his face. His teeth tore into her scalp, but his hands didn't let go.

The tiniest whoosh of a curse word danced in her ear. An English curse word. No accent.

The man pinned her legs beneath her and pulled her close as though she were as fragile and delicate as an egg. "Mia. Stop. It's Cash."

She opened her eyes, seeing all the dark around her. Her nostrils flared open, closed, open, closed, as she fought for breath and to understand what was happening.

Cash. Titan.

"I'll move my hand," he whispered. "But you can't make a noise. Got it?"

She nodded like her life depended on it. She had to tell him she was being hunted. His tight grip relaxed, but she was still pinned. Cash rolled next to her, dressed in a pile of leaves. His face paint blurred into his costume.

She mouthed to him. *Alejandro*. She pointed ahead. No, wait. To the right. Shit. Where was he?

Cash cupped her hand. "I got this. Stay put. I'll come back to you."

"Don't leave me. *Please*."

He scanned the area, then moved to her ear. "You stick close. I'll scout him out, then he's done. You okay with that?"

Mia's lip pursed into a tight line, but the tears spilled over. His eyebrows bit together, and maybe he was more scared of her crying than finding Alejandro. Whatever the reason, she was glad to stay near him. "Thank you."

He lifted onto his elbows, tucked a rifle into place, and drew his legs beneath him, motioning for her to do the same, minus the gun. "Ready?"

Mia nodded, but she was suction cupped to the wet ground.

"Look at me, Mia."

Mia stared straight ahead in the dark, then at him. His face was a shade above invisible. This should be easier. All she had to do was follow Cash. Then Alejandro would die, and she could run back to Colby as fast as her legs would take her. But her body ignored her awesome plan.

"Mia, honey." He redirected her attention with his thumb and forefinger, tilting her chin toward him. "Focus on me. We've got a good man to get you back to. Winters oughta have my ass that I haven't killed that fucker yet. Put all your fear into a box. We've got places to go. People to snipe."

"A reporter asked a sniper what he felt after he shot someone." Now wasn't the time for nervous chatter. She was losing her mind. But it was the only thing she could think of in this moment.

He laughed quiet as the wind. "And the sniper said recoil. And honey, you ain't even going to feel that. Ready?"

A smile crossed her face. "Yes."

"Well, alrighty. Get your butt up, and on my six." He dropped his hand from her chin, and readied his rifle.

He slinked forward, looking more like foliage than a man. She was inches away, scared if he got too far ahead of her, he'd melt into the night. He paused. She held her breath. Nothing sounded. No birds. No insects. No scary night animals. The last of daylight abandoned them, and they were surrounded by the blackest of blacks.

He pivoted quickly. She had no idea why. Her ears burned to hear something, anything. His silent steps crept forward as though following a well-laid trail. She sounded like a freight train pushing through a rail yard.

What looked like a leaf-covered branch motioned her down. She dropped to all fours and flattened on the still warm earth. Wet leaves pressed against her cheek. An insect crawled across her skin. She suppressed the urge to react and prayed for resilience.

A soft flick sounded, followed by a click. Mia couldn't hear Cash breathe. Couldn't see the leaves move. Time passed as she recited grade school limericks over and over, pretending she was anywhere else.

The world around went brilliant for a spark of a second. A muffled pop punched the night. Cash didn't move. Neither did she. The night stilled after the momentary burst of artillery lighting.

Another soft click. He rolled onto his back and sat up. "You all right?"

"He's dead?" Her ears pounded with racing blood.

"Yeah."

She strained to hear any other dangers. "You sure?"

"Did you just question my incredible cartel sniping skills? Seriously?" He snorted a laugh.

"Sorry, Cash. Didn't mean to offend you."

"I'm just playing. 'Course he's dead. And I don't see any other fuckers out there. Including our boys. There will be hell to pay when I find them."

"We're way out in the jungle. How would they know which way to go?"

"You weren't that hard to track, honey."

"You think there's a problem?"

"Hell no. I think they figured they'd had a long day, and I'd take care of this. Bet you they've wrangled a bottle of liquor and are waiting for us to mosey on back."

"Well, let's go. I need to see Colby."

"Yes, ma'am. Anything to see ole Winters wrapped around a girl's finger."

CHAPTER TWENTY-EIGHT

Mia peeled through thick bushes. Wide leaves obscured her view. Spiderwebs caught on her skin, netting her face. Insects used her as a landing zone before vaulting into the dark abyss. It had to be the dead of night, but it felt like the sun was high overhead. Cash marched them toward the shack, and with each step, she made a list of things she'd say to Colby. The list started with *don't get hurt again*, and ended with *let's find a shower. Together.*

One more step and Cash cleared the shrubbery, holding back a large branch for her. She slipped into the clearing. A huge beam of relief surfaced. This horror story was over, and all she wanted to do was crawl into Colby's arms to sleep.

Less than a dozen yards away, that stupid shack stood waiting for her return. But this time, she wouldn't be alone. Amber light shined between the slats and glowed at the front opening. Pure joy energized her faster than a red-eye latte. She'd seriously have to re-evaluate what made her happy when she was back on American soil. Shitty shacks shouldn't make her so giddy. But a wounded warrior who liked to lounge in her bed… that'd be tops on her list of the super happy. Minus the wounded part.

Angry, male complaints poured out of the shack. She picked up her pace, craning to see the problem.

Colby careened around the doorjamb, arm overhead, middle finger reaching for the moon. He was backlit and illuminated, and he didn't see her or Cash ahead. He looked colossal. Perfect and heroic. She needed in those arms and couldn't get to him fast enough.

Behind him, Jared cursed and shouted. "No one else falls for a chick. Ever. Again. No one."

She slammed into Cash's backside. He was bent at the waist, laughing. His jungle suit hung off his torso, rifle dangling in one hand. He was always laughing, and she had no time for a roadblock. Mia bounded around him, lunging out of the shadows for Colby.

Torment and relief. His face played a quick variety of emotions that she could name, but she didn't want to play psychologist. She just wanted him. His arms wrapped tight around her, and his wonderful lips found hers. She wanted everything to be all right and would only believe it when he said the truth.

"Hey there, doll." His voice cracked.

"Thank God, you're alive." She palmed his cheeks. "Don't ever leave me like that. And don't get hurt. Ever again."

First thing on her list. Check. What was number two? She had no idea, 'cause all she wanted to say was *kiss me.*

He didn't say okay, and he wasn't nodding.

"Did you hear me, Colby? Don't leave me like that ever again."

He hooked an arm around her waist, and she went on tiptoes. He swiped a wisp of hair and tucked it behind her ear. The pad of his thumb traced her cheek as he cupped his giant hand around her chin. The world slowed down. A gentle buzz ran through the air. Electrical pulses quaked around them. If it hadn't been for the blood, the sweat, the violence, and the depravity, this might have been the most romantic moment in her entire existence.

Cash cruised by them. "You're welcome, buddy. I'll let you know how you can repay this teeny favor later."

Colby folded her into him, sighing and breathing against her ear. The sizzle of his breathy clasp shivered down her spine. Thousands of nerve pathways burst to life, crackling to her core. His forehead dipped and met hers, and the touch burned. They breathed in unison. No words. No explanations.

She swayed into him, and he stifled the quietest of groans.

"Oh, I forgot. You're hurt." Mia struggled to detach herself, but his grip was firm, unwavering, cementing her against his broad chest. "Let me go, Colby. You shouldn't do that."

"Just give me a sec." A heartbeat later, he ran his hands over her face, down her neck, and settled his grip on her shoulders. "God, you're beautiful. You deserve so much more than this."

"Yeah, I deserve a candlelit dinner. Put it on your list of things to do. Come on. Let's go inside. You need to rest."

"Just let me feel you for a minute. I need this. To know you're okay. That you're safe. You against me, baby. That's what I need."

She stopped struggling and all but disappeared into his arms, which were the size of tree trunks, hiding her from the world. She pressed against his pecs, listened to the rhythmic thump of his heart. "I can't believe you worried about me. You were shot."

He relaxed around her, caressed her cheeks again, and tilted her gaze to his. His eyes glowed in the night.

"Colby?"

His lips touched hers. Delicate and soft. Not at all how she thought he might kiss her right now. Nothing she'd expect after their awful adventures. He was sweet. Careful. Savoring.

He stopped, but his lips still moved against hers. So quiet the words, she almost missed them. "I'll never forget."

Hell, she'd never forget this either, but a sentimental Colby Winters was something altogether new to her. Another facet to the man. Every day, she learned more about him. And, thanks to him, about herself, too.

"Mia—"

"Enough is enough. Get your asses in here," Jared called from the shack, a short distance away.

Colby smiled, straightened, then winced. She could tell he was in far more pain than he admitted.

"Let's go. Move your stubborn butt. You need to sleep and eat." She pulled back and gave him a wink and a smile. "They've got bug juice."

"Bug juice, huh? What do you know about that?"

"I know it tastes like the ugly step-brother to watered-down Kool-Aid mixed with day-old seltzer."

"That's an accurate description."

"And they've got edible plastic that looks like spaghetti."

"MREs? Well, aren't you the seasoned field grunt?"

"You know it."

"What do you have, Winters?" Jared shouted out the door. "A case of the dumbasses? Collect your woman and move in."

"What do you say, woman? Ready to be collected?" He scooped her into his arms and tried to hide the flex of his jaw and the sawing of his teeth with a closed-lip smile.

"You're insane. Put me down. You're hurt. I'm not."

"Tell me what to do because I'm hurt one more time, doll, and we're going to have a problem."

Without waiting for a response, he limped them to the shack, brushed past Jared, and set her down by the table, bracing a hand on it. He breathed heavy. Sweat sprouted fresh on his brow.

"You okay, Winters?" Jared eyed him, wary.

"Yeah. Dehydrated."

Jared continued to study him. "You take something for the pain?"

"Yeah. Something."

Brock, a few feet behind Colby, shook his head. Jared noticed. Mia noticed. Everyone but Colby noticed.

He cracked his knuckles against the table and shifted his weight. "I just ripped out the bandages in my cuts and doused it with cauterizing powder. Hurts. Blazing pain. Not in the mood to dwell on it. That okay with you, boss man?"

Jared didn't respond. The guys looked concerned, but whether it was because he challenged Jared or his spectacular wound care decisions, she didn't know.

Mia broke the tension. "Well then, let's get you some water."

"Bug juice," Jared said.

"Bug juice," she said more for Jared than Colby. "Cash, you mind?"

Cash tossed him the bottle. They loved to throw things. Why was that? They were an arm's length apart. It had to be some unwritten code of dudedom.

Colby cracked the cap and downed it in a few swigs. "Got any Dots in this shit shack?"

Cash chuckled. "Nope. But we've got beef stew, beef bbq, beef—"

"Cash." Mia glared at him.

"Learning their tricks, doll?" Colby asked, eyebrows raised.

"Two of them, I have pegged." She pointed to Jared, who grumbled, and Cash, who threw his hands up in innocence. "These other two, we'll see."

"Pays to have a couch doctor around. She'll get into your brains." Colby pulled his shirt from his ripped stomach and mopped the sweat on his face. "How is it a million degrees here, but I'm freezing? I need to shake this off."

Jared eyed him again. "That bug juice helping?"

"Yeah, might be." Colby grumbled under his breath.

Not wanting to tread on Jared's steel-toed boots, but not wanting Colby to topple over in a pile of rock-hard, shot-up muscle, Mia said, "Why don't you get some rest? Lie down on that bed over there. I'll keep you company. That bed isn't so bad. Scratchy, but you won't even notice."

He nodded and stumbled over. Cash and Brock took an arm to help him down, then he shut his eyes. She scooted by the guys and plopped beside him. His eyes pinched tight as if in tremendous pain. Sleep wasn't helping. His harsh, jagged snores couldn't find an even cadence.

Mia stood, found the packet of moist wipes, and went back to the mat. He didn't stir as she wiped off his face, starting at his forehead and working down to his chin. Fresh sweat bubbled up, creating a pathway of droplets from one temple to the next. His scruff was now a full beard, and she tried to smooth it down.

He looked like hell. Like his twitchy body revolted against his offered peace treaty of sleep. His shirt was drenched. The pants, torn and shredded, clung to his huge thighs. One pant leg fell open at a tear, showing a very red, very raw, wound.

"Jared." She waivered, not wanting to interrupt the men now bent over the table, working on their extraction plans. No one heard her. She didn't want to do anything to slow down plans to get the hell out of Colombia. But her gut said *emergency, emergency.*

She approached cautiously. From the part she heard, a chopper would be there the day after next. It was running an unexpected extraction for another team. A few more days, she could handle it. Bug juice and MREs. One mat and a bunch of grumpy, stinking men who'd probably been awake going on thirty-six hours. And then there was the uncomfortable dilemma of communing with nature. They didn't seem to have a problem wandering off. She, on the other hand, did.

Jared hadn't been a fan of her interruptions when he ordered men around the shack. And an interruption while in the midst of strategy and plans, Mia would've bet huge money that was a worse offense.

"Jared." She cleared her throat. "Something's wrong with Colby."

"Yeah, he extracted a bullet, ran a marathon through the rainforest, and has to deal with you. He needs to sleep. He'll be fine."

Deal with me? Jared was a tool of the lowest order. But she was in the right, and he needed to at least check on Colby.

"I wouldn't bother you if I didn't see a change."

Jared rolled his eyes. Did he do these things just to make her spitting angry?

"You think I want to slow our departure? That I like peeing in the woods, or sitting around with all you smelly men? You think I don't want a dang shower? Take a look at him. Something's wrong." Jared brought out the worst in her. Had she ever yelled at one man so many times?

Jared tilted his head at Brock. "Humor her."

Mia would have kicked him if she thought it'd help her argument. Instead, she glared at him, pursed her lips, and silently cursed him every way she could dream. And lately, her dreams had been particularly mean.

Brock, who was balancing on the back legs of a chair, let it fall, and put down the map he had been reviewing. "Stubborn ass should have taken a pain pill."

He pushed his hands off his knees and stood. Mia wanted to grab him by his belt loops and drag him over to Colby, but Brock didn't seem the type to be pushed around by anyone. Not that their off-putting grumbles brought her to a full stop before. Still, she was going to give him a hot second before she forced him into gear.

Brock ambled to the mat and dropped down to a knee. Mia hovered over him, ignoring his annoyance. He put the back of his hand on Colby's forehead and took it away. Placed it again, then moved it to the back of his neck. "Shit."

Two fingers on his neck, Brock waited, taking his pulse. "Shit."

Two shits? What did that mean? Would he say something besides shit?

Jared raised an eyebrow. "What?"

"We've got a problem." Brock's hands moved back to Colby's forehead.

"What is it, asshole?"

"His brains are cooking. He's got a hell of a fever. He's sweating his ass off and shivering."

Jared stalked over, his face stern. "What the fuck, Brock? I thought you gave him some heavy hitting antibiotics. Penicillin so strong, it'd stop the plague."

"I did. Something's wrong."

Mia felt tiny in the room of raging testosterone but spoke up anyway. "Well, yeah, he's been shot."

"No, Winters gets shot all the time."

Oh, of course he does. What the hell?

He must have seen something on her face. Brock back peddled. "Well, not all the time. But enough that he knows how to handle it. Let's see what our boy missed."

Brock pulled a knife out of his back pocket and flipped it. A blade shot straight, and before she could wonder why he had it, he cut Colby's pant legs straight to the waistline, sheathed the knife, and inspected his legs. Colby didn't stir.

He took the knife out again and repeated the cut on the front of his shirt. It sprawled on each side of Colby, who now vibrated with the shakes. His teeth chattered. His brow pinched tight.

Brock motioned to Rocco. "Help lean him over. I need to see his back."

Rocco stepped forward. Cash and Jared followed. Rocco and Cash braced a shoulder, lifting him up and on his uninjured side. Colby didn't wake up. His body was limp, and his head rolled forward. Brock cut the remaining remnants of his shirt off.

"Son of a bitch."

Mia tried to see around the men. All the cussing did little to explain what was happening. They conversed in shits and bitches, and she was left clueless.

"What's the deal?" Jared asked.

Well, at least Jared had a taste of her annoyance. He hadn't translated the shits either.

"Shrapnel. Right near this GSW. Probably couldn't feel the difference. He's had way more blood loss than originally estimated. It's all still in there. Best case scenario, dehydration and nasty infection. Worst case, septic shock. We gotta get him out of here, like now. Or he's done."

The analysis hurt deep in her chest. Physically made her flinch, cringing away from the men. Jared cursed a Colombian mile wide, grabbed the radio handset, and strutted out the shack door.

"This is bad, isn't it?" Mia mumbled but already knew the answer.

Nobody responded. No words of comfort. No lies. The hush answered her question.

She swallowed past a knot of despair. "Well, what are we supposed to do? Guys? Anything?"

"With what we have, not much we can do." Brock moved to a backpack. "This is the last of the antibiotics. But we need to cool him down. I don't see anything to do that with. We need to keep watch."

"Watch for what?"

"To make sure he keeps breathing."

Tears leaked. Her throat seized in pain. "And if he stops breathing?" The words barely passed her lips, and the prickle of cold sweat beaded on the nape of her neck.

"We'll cross that bridge when we come to it, Mia."

"I don't give a fuck what I said before." Jared's bark streamed into the shack. "Get me that helo now, or my man is good as dead."

CHAPTER TWENTY-NINE

They landed at an airfield outside Washington, DC. The last day was a hazy blur, and Mia had yet to sleep any length of time. Short bursts of shut-eye here and there, whether she realized it or not, were all she got.

Whatever Jared did to re-route a helicopter worked. She heard whispers that another team needed it as bad, and she hoped they survived. But it didn't keep her from thanking God they were choppered out of that godforsaken jungle.

Her fingers interlaced with Colby's limp, nonreactive fingers. He was in a coma. A helicopter ride to a field hospital, then a private jet ride, and Colby was still out, under medical supervision, and scaring the shit out of her.

Brock, who had some sort of medical training, monitored him on their supersonic trip back up to the US. He wasn't a doctor, but Mia could tell he was the Titan go-to-guy for all things health related. She was also convinced he had more practical experience than the collective knowledge at the field hospital in somewhere, South America. Hospital was a very generous term. But they were gracious to Colby, so she kept her mouth shut.

A red medevac chopper stood on the ready, as they landed and taxied on American soil. She watched out the oval airplane window. Their flight crew jumped out and scurried to open the backside of the transport helicopter.

She looked back into the belly of their plane. Titan's jet came with an exterior opening to allow the transportation of bedridden patients, similar to the backside of the medevac chopper. The opening hadn't been immediately obvious to her, but they loaded Colby in through the side of the jet and directed her to a set of stairs.

Once inside, with a few moves of collapsible chairs, his gurney was locked into place. Nondescript hooks on the wall held IV bags and a travel monitor.

Guess this wasn't their first flight with a bedridden passenger. Who outfitted their private jet to function as a makeshift hospital room? Titan did, apparently. She wondered how that conversation went with the manufacturer. *I'd like the medical transport option and a few gun racks.*

The medevac crew wore air suits with arm patches. They boarded the plane like old habit. They whispered to Brock, facing away from her. She couldn't hear what they said. Jared stood with the men, listening and nodding. A moment later, they moved to Colby's bed and opened the hatch. Clicks sounded as the gurney released from its holds. One man grabbed the IV and monitors, while the others were ready to lower him away from her.

Emotion choked her. This was where the crazy adventure stopped. Where they'd part, and she'd have to catch up with Colby later. Jared would tell her where he was going. She was sure of it. He couldn't be that terrible.

A cough caught her attention. Jared pointed at her. "This is Mia. She goes where he goes. Tell whoever you need to."

Mia's mouth dropped and hung slack-jawed. Her thoughts of gratitude scrambled to form before she pulled it together to mouth *thank you*. She didn't have the energy to do anything more, but his look of acknowledgement said she didn't need to. His eyes were very expressive. Did he know about that chink in his tough guy armor?

She stayed with the medevac crew as they loaded Colby up and ran him from the plane to the chopper. Immediately, they were airborne again. Not flying high, but they moved forward like a hurricane blast.

A crew member gave her headphones. It muffled the dull roar from the chopper blades. When the pilot talked to the hospital, it sounded so formal—their estimated time of arrival, Colby's condition, and his vitals.

Mia watched out the window, not wanting to hear his reality. The farther away they flew, the more the Titan team became tiny action figures trudging to their waiting trucks and SUVs. Just another day in the life of those guys. Parking their vehicles at a private airstrip to go battle evil, dodge bullets, and save the day.

One truck remained—Colby's—and she focused on it until it was out of sight.

What a crazy life. It should've scared the hell out of her, but it didn't. He'd pull out of this. No problem. He'd be up, ready, and waiting for another chance to chase down the bad guys. She laughed. *Tangle*. He loved that word. He wanted to *tangle* with the bad guys. Always looking for the righteous fight. This was how he earned a well-paid living, doing right in the shadowy face of malevolence. His job was an intrinsic part of him, which made her proud. He was her body-armor-clad dark knight. A silent hero. The man wagered his life in high stakes combat games. He had the training and the know-how. She'd seen that in action. He was careful and deliberative. Tough as he was smart.

When he busted out of his coma, she'd tell him how she felt. She was proud, accepting, and in love.

In love.

Her blood thumped in her neck. Her mouth went dry. When had that crept up? He was sexy and strong, with a tender heart and a caring soul. She trusted him. Believed in him. But in love with him? Love was a deep personal attachment. A profound affection. Love was something she hadn't thought possible in her situation.

But, yes, she loved him.

And, surprise, surprise, it wasn't a scary realization. Rather, it was warm and calming. Centering. She was secure and stable with him. When he awoke, those would be the first words out of her mouth. She might even shout them, shaking him completely awake at the first sign of stirrings. Until then, all she could do was hold his lifeless hand, as they floated through the air.

Exhausting minutes later, she heard the approach in her headphones before they landed at the top of a hospital tower. Nurses stood by, ready for their arrival, heads down and hair blowing, as the chopper hovered over the red and white painted landing zone. The flight crew disembarked, and the hospital nurses took over. Everyone moved fast, checking monitors, bags, and wires.

They rushed into an elevator, and Mia pressed against the wall. No one spoke to her. She was invisible in the midst of chaos. The doors opened, and they rolled into a quiet hallway, then a private suite. Such a whirlwind. She didn't know what to say or who to thank. Each person placated her with a pitying smile as they left her alone in the room. Well, not alone. Colby was in bed. The only noise breaking the silence between them was the beeping of machines.

It was only after they left that she saw herself. She was filth covered, blood spattered, and her dress had only one working sleeve. She looked like death and smelled like it, too.

A tap on her shoulder startled her out of a downward descent of depression. A man with salt and pepper hair, caring brown eyes, and a white coat stood in front of her, clipboard in hand.

"You must be Mia."

He knew her name. "Uh, yes."

"I'm Dr. Tuska. I'll be taking care of Colby from here on out. Anything you need, just ask for it."

"I'm sorry. I don't have his health insurance card, or his—"

"Don't worry about it." He flipped through the chart.

"I don't understand."

Dr. Tuska chuckled. "The Titan Group has been very, very generous to us in the past. You have to be the first wife I've met, so it's—"

"I'm not his wife."

"Whatever you are, Mia, you have the Titan stamp of approval. I'll have a cot brought in here so you can rest. There's a shower in the bathroom. I'll ask the nurse to bring you some scrubs to change into. You'll probably feel better, sleep better, if you're able to shower and relax. There's a menu card on that table." He pointed to a small table beside Colby's bed. "Fill it out, and lunch will be here by the time you're out of the shower."

She felt her eyes bulge, and couldn't shake the shock long enough to mind her manners.

The doctor tilted his head, seemingly aware that she didn't expect the first class treatment. "Like I said, Mia, very generous. I'm going to do a once over on Colby to see if I want to change anything, then I'll be out of your hair."

"When will he wake up?" *Please, please have an answer.*

"That's up to him. He'll wake up when he's ready, when his body is ready. Until then, we monitor him, make sure nothing changes for the worse, and we wait."

Not the answer she wanted. Mia saw the doctor off and eyed the lunch menu. Not the typical cafeteria fare. Right about now, anything other than MREs and the protein bars she found on the plane would be delicious. She circled grilled chicken, macaroni and cheese, and a salad. Oh, and a cookie. Definitely needed a cookie.

She walked into the bathroom. Private room or not, the bathroom still had a hospital feel. Institutional gray tile covered the floor and wall. The overhead florescent lights hummed when she flipped the switch. A stack of bleached towels were piled on a counter next to a hospital thermos, plastic-wrapped cups, and toiletries.

Mia slid her clothes off and into a pile on the floor, then stared at the oversized mirror. Dirt streaked her face, arms, and neck. Scabs and bug bites decorated her skin with varying shades of red. Her hair was a giant rat's nest. And good Lord, she smelled like things she didn't even want to think about ever again.

Mia unwrapped the plastic from a comb and started at the bottom of a handful of hair. She picked and picked and picked. With each methodical stroke, the knots tore, strands floated to the floor, but her hair made no progress. Her arms ached. Frustrated, she put the comb down. Its bristles were not straight and pristine anymore. They were bent, like the comb had given up, too.

She twisted the shower knobs. Scalding water ran into a nearby drain, steam floated into the sterile bathroom. Mia adjusted the temperature from scalding to dirt-melting. She hooked her clothes with a toe and tossed them into a trash can, stepped under the cascading water, and pulled the curtain around her.

Soul-soothing water crashed over her. It dulled the aches and pains, made her sunburn sting, and eased the torment of the itchy bug bites. All in all, Nirvana, but she refused to look at the dirty water swirling down the drain.

Somehow in her hypnotic trance, Mia heard a quick rap on the door. “Hi, Mia. Just dropping off some scrubs for you. I saw your lunch order. Thank you. Need anything else? Snacks, munchies?”

Snacks? This was like a hospital with a hotel concierge. How much money did Titan pour into this place?

“Do you have any Dots?”

Her chipper chatter replied from around the corner. “I’ll see what we can do,” the nurse said from around the corner. “I’ll be back.”

Colby would appreciate a box of Dots when he woke up.

She was far past burnt out and exhausted to the point of debilitation. After shampooing her hair, she dumped the entire travel-sized bottle of conditioner into her hair and finger combed it. More progress than with the plastic comb but still a dismal mess. She didn’t care. She needed sleep. Bad.

She dried off, slipped on the scrubs, and found a cot piled high with blankets. She’d never seen something so enticing. A few steps later, and Mia was burrowed in. Soft pillows and blankets, all stinking like bleach, but it didn’t matter. Sleep beckoned, but her wandering mind kept it a finger’s distance away. Would she have nightmares filled with bombs reverberations, knives against her throat, and the evil, accented threats of a monster?

Yeah, she would.

But Colby would wake up and kiss away her fears. He’d love her until she relaxed. She knew he would. There was something special about him. And she loved him. That was enough to drive away the nightmares.

Warm shudders ripped through her. A sweet smile hung limp. It was her first smile in days. She loved him. The realization thawed fears of family and commitment. How could she possibly not want them—him and Clara—in her life?

Memories of the Colombian carnage would dissolve. She couldn't wait until he woke up. She had to know what he'd say when she covered him in kisses, confessing how much he meant in her life.

CHAPTER THIRTY

Bright lights seared his retinas as Winters blinked awake. He blinked again. This wasn't the same view as when he went to sleep. He closed his eyes and tried to remember. He felt starched sheets that itched. An antiseptic smell registered as hospital-like. He blinked again. Definitely in a hospital.

His tongue felt furry and dry. When he opened and closed his mouth, it made a spit-less sound. He surveyed the blankets tucked tight around the length of his body except where his left arm stuck out, an IV inserted and secured with tape. The dirt and blood that he remembered was gone. He stretched his hand, and worked his fist. Even his fingernails were clean.

Winters scanned the empty room. The private suite, vitals monitor, IV bag, and furniture were decidedly not Colombian. The television played the nighttime news in silence. Muted and American. A whiteboard on the wall said his doctor's name was Tuska, his nurse's name was Sandy, and his tech's name was Jeremy. He had no idea how it happened, but he was back on US soil.

A white remote with blue buttons lay next to his blanket-covered mid-section. He grabbed it and gave it a once over. Basic and in English. Television controls. Bed controls. A nurse call button. He pushed a button and rose to a sit. His mouth was still disgustingly dry. He blinked several times more to clear the cobwebs and focused on the television.

If that date and time in the corner of the news program were correct, he'd missed several days. Somehow, he left a shanty shack in South America and made it back to somewhere in the United States.

Winters pushed the call button for the nurse. He tried to swallow again and ran his tongue over his teeth. A nasty, gritty film said it'd been too many days since a toothbrush had been anywhere near his mouth. He pulled his other arm from the blanket and brushed his hands over his face, finding a beard.

A nurse walked in, chipper and bubbling to talk. He wasn't in the mood for either.

"Mr. Winters, it's so wonderful to see you awake. We've been waiting on you. How are you—"

"Where am I?" A rough, unused edge in his throat made him cough.

She handed him a large container of water with a straw. "Thought you might be thirsty. You're at the hospital—"

"Where? What hospital? Am I in the United States?"

Her eyes widened. She took a step back. He needed to ease up his method of interrogation, or he'd have to find another nurse.

"Uh, um, yes. You're outside Washington, DC. Do you know—"

"Who brought me here?" His mind and his mouth hadn't agreed yet to the terms of easing up the line of questioning.

"You're in a private suite. Jared Westin of The Titan Group made arrangements for you. We're to call him as soon as you're awake. I'm surprised no one's here. They've had someone with you twenty-four hours a day."

Shit. He'd never live this down. And Mia. What about Mia? Please let her be back in her normal life and not chasing after a man who'd asked her to run into danger.

"Were there only men here?" And did he have to sound so desperate and scared?

"No. Mia's been here most of the time, whether the other men were here or not. She was on the Titan approved list." The nurse tinkered with a beeping machine. "She's wonderful."

His head dropped against the plump, plastic pillow, and his eyes rolled to the ceiling. That wasn't what he wanted to hear. His squeezed his eyes. Why didn't Mia run from him? She should be long gone.

"Don't let her in to see me. Don't let her know I'm awake."

"What?" She shook her head, then cocked it in confusion. After a pause, she did a once-over of his IV bag and monitor, evidently concerned that he neared a PTSD freak out.

"Do *not* let her in here." He was a fucking bastard. "I'm serious. She's no longer Titan approved, or whatever you said."

The sound of heavy-booted footsteps stole his attention away from the nurse. Cash, in his best cowboy-mosey, ambled up behind the nurse. His hat was tugged low over his shaggy hair, and he towered over the woman with a half-assed, one-sided grin. Clearly, they'd been acquainted. Damn Cash. Was there any woman who didn't drop drawers for him? Cash whispered in her ear, she blushed and sidestepped around him toward the hallway.

"Well, well. Get enough beauty sleep, sunshine?"

"Cash, man, you have to get me out of here."

"Yeah, well, first we had to keep you from dying. But, all right. We'll get you out of here as soon as Doc T gives you a go. Jared will be here soon. Mia just walked down the hall to stretch her legs. She'll be back in a sec. Want me to call her?"

Winters pinched his eyes. Her name made him schoolboy twitchy. Bits and pieces of Colombia filtered back. But the one blaring memory burning up his brain was when he limped into that shack. It was empty, and the woman he loved was gone. He wanted to tear every beam from the wall, to ram through the Titan guys for no other reason than he needed an outlet. And when he saw her, safe, coming toward the shack, it was the most satisfying and gut-wrenching moment of his life. She was alive, within eyeshot, and he was the worst thing that could have ever happen to her.

He loved her, and she'd never know.

A feminine snip of exasperation echoed in the hallway and dragged him back to his conversation with Cash.

"Sounds like your girl is here. Wonder what has her in a fuss." Cash chuckled and pivoted for the door.

Winters dropped his head down. The beard whiskers tickled his neck and scratched his chin, and it was all he wanted to think about instead of ponying up the truth.

"I told the nurse to not let her back in here." He winced. It sounded even worse out loud than in his head. And it was horrible in his head.

"You did what?" Cash pivoted one-eighty back on his heels, dumbstruck.

"I asked the nurse to send her away." Winters glanced out the window instead of at Cash. But that didn't ease the guilt and overwhelming sense of loss.

"You, my friend, have a death wish. Colombian cartels are child's play compared to a woman on the warpath. That woman in particular. She pushes *Jared* around like he's a bratty toddler. Hell, she pokes him in the chest on the regular when he's not listening."

Winters sawed his teeth back and forth, and turned from the window to watch Cash take a backward step to catch the showdown in the hallway. Someone must have seen him, and he threw his hands up in innocence.

"Aw, shit. Here she comes." Cash made a move to duck-and-cover. "Mia, one. Nurse, zilch. And you're in trouble, sunshine. Adios."

Before Cash made it through the threshold, Mia roared around the corner, knocking him out of her way, and back into the room. "What is your problem, Colby Winters?"

She was red-faced, bug-eyed mad. This wasn't working out the way he planned.

"I think this might be my cue to leave. Mia, nice to see you. Winters, glad you're alive, buddy. Best of luck."

She flashed daggers at Cash, who again threw his hands up. She stepped to him and pushed him out with one outstretched finger. Then she turned toward the hospital bed. The delicate veins in her neck popped. Her narrowed eyes zeroed in on him like a predator sighting its kill.

Cash was bull's eye right. Winters was a dead man. Who knew a petite one like her could scare him clean out of his skin? Funny thing was, he should have known how well she'd do fury.

"You mind telling me what the hell is your problem?" Her hands flew to her hip. What she lacked in height and weight, she more than made up for with attitude. He felt smaller and smaller in his bed with her reading him the riot act. But he deserved it. It was a pansy-assed move to have the nurse do his dirty work.

The nurse rushed in behind her. "I'm so sorry, Mr. Winters."

Christ, could this get any worse? Someone needed to save Sandy, or whatever the nurse's name was, before Mia killed an innocent woman.

The air conditioning kicked on, chilling the room even more, wisping up the already sterile hospital smell. He hated it. The stench was stuck in his nose. Mia was yelling at him. Nurse Sandy left, no doubt calling for security. And he was trapped in the bed, tied down by wires and hooked up to monitors. Mia's warpath left no escape. He was stuck and had to think of something to say. But nothing intelligent surfaced.

"I'm sorry. I just need... some space. Or something." Not intelligent. Bumbling, stumbling idiot might've been a better description. He needed to tell her the honest truth and be done with it. This was for her. And despite whatever crazy, emotion-fueled insanity he continued to drown in right now, he should, at the very least, man up, and give her some sort of explanation.

"You needed space? You're a freakin' liar."

"Mia, look..." He pulled at his shaggy beard, wanting to tear it out and replace the pain in his chest with a different, more physical pain. "My life is dangerous. Nothing's safe, obviously. You met me, and look how your life's been turned upside down. Hell, your pretty little cheek is still bruised."

"Don't talk to me about *my pretty little cheek.* You don't have any right to wake up and pull this stunt." Her voice broke, and it hurt down to his soul. "You don't know what you've put me through."

"See, the thing is, I do. You never should've dealt with any of it."

"Colby, that doesn't matter. You and me. That's what matters." Her words were painful enough to last until his last breaths.

"Damn it, Mia. Don't you see? I'm doing this because of you. Because you matter to me. You're the only thing I can think of. I wake up wanting to see you after I dreamed of you." Admitting it only made the hurt worse. His stomach tightened. His throat constricted. He was dying to embrace her and could barely string together the words. "Mia, I… Look, I feel for you. I—"

"Excuse me? You *feel* for me? Grow a set already, Winters. Don't stand behind the lie of protecting me. When you figure out what you're so scared of, you find me. Otherwise, don't worry your heart. And you won't have to concern your nurse with keeping me away from you. I'm gone."

She stormed out, the privacy curtain trailing after her in a harsh breeze.

Shit.

That went all wrong. Nothing like he envisioned. He had to get out of this bed. He needed to chase her down and explain everything. She needed to understand he shouldn't love her. She deserved so much more than that burden.

Winters ripped the blanket off of him only to see electrical compression wraps on his calves and a collection bag for his catheter. Fucking fantastic. He grabbed the remote hanging by his bed and pressed the nurse call button once, twice, and then again.

Where the hell was she?

He tried to lean forward to release his legs and groaned. His body hurt. Every muscle was sore, weak, and pathetic. Just like him in the love life department. It might take weeks of physical therapy and training to get back to where he needed to be physically, but he was done for when it came to Mia. Some wounds never healed.

He leaned over again, undid the Velcro on one leg wrap, then moved the other. His lungs burned, and his pulse raced. He paused for a breath. How was he so out of breath? His plan to run after Mia might need to be downgraded to a speedy walk. God, he hated being sidelined.

The nurse shuffled into his room. Her concerned glance morphed into alarm as she saw him batting at the wires holding him back and working to undo his second leg wrap.

"Mr. Winters."

"Get these wires off me." He motioned to the catheter. "Take this fucking thing out."

"You've only been awake for minutes after *days* recovering from serious injuries."

"I've got places to go."

"I'll get Dr. Tuska in here. You can talk to him."

Winters struggled against his pain, unhooking wire after wire on his chest. Alarms beeped. He studied the pole holding his IV bag. "Does this thing move, or do you need to unhook it?"

"Sir. Calm down." She pulled a phone from her pocket and paged the doctor or security. Who knew?

"Sit your ass back in that bed," a familiar male voice yelled, and the nurse jumped straight into the air.

Jared's steely face was pissed. He sped past the nurse, who had one hand over her mouth and the other pressed against her chest.

"Whatever the fuck you're doing… Why ever the hell you're trying to break out of here like it's the clink, you stop. Right now. You got me?"

The wide-eyed nurse pressed herself against the wall and sidestepped toward the door. With her exit, the loud click of the large door closing echoed through the room.

"Give me a break, Jared. I got stir crazy. Needed to get up and stretch my legs."

"And I'm sure that had nothing to do with little Mia Kensington tearing out of here like she planned to kill somebody. And she probably could, so I'd watch my ass if I were you."

Winters grabbed the remote and turned the volume up on the television in a desperate attempt to ignore his boss. The news host's all-American enunciation didn't drown out Jared.

"If you want out of here, you have to earn it. I'm not going to have you almost die just to have you kill yourself."

"I didn't almost die. Stop with the dramatics."

"Oh, hell. You *are* that stupid. Miss Thang you just sent scuttling out of this hospital? She's the reason you're still kickin'. I would've let you sleep on that mangy-assed cot until you died. But nope, not her. She was all tending to you and shit. She noticed your fever. She noticed your piss-poor responses. I didn't. The guys didn't. Your ass got choppered out of Colombia, and medevacced all the way back to the States. So if you think you didn't tease the widow-maker, think again. 'Cause you're a dead man who was hooked up by Lady Luck. Or in this case, Mia Save-Your-Ass Kensington."

Winters threw the remote, hoping to hit the wall across the room, but it didn't go far. Attached to a cord next to his hospital bed, it swung back at him, and clattered against the bed rail, finally dangling inches above the floor.

"What the fuck do you want me to do?" Winters yelled, bunching his fist in the blanket.

"Get your head back in the game, and figure your shit out."

Just like Mia, Jared spun and stormed out in a fashion far more dramatic than Winters was used to seeing in his jerk of a boss. He relaxed his death grip from the blanket and ran his hands over his face, trying to clear his mind.

Mia. Mia. Mia.

Nope. It wasn't working. A hollow despair spread in his blood, pumped into every crevice of his body. Through his aching heart, to the soles of his feet, Winters mourned what could have been.

He threw himself back against the pillow and tossed his head to the side. His gaze landed on a cot, a pile of used blankets, and several unopened boxes of Dots.

Damn it. She was perfect in every way, and he couldn't have her.

CHAPTER THIRTY-ONE

Winters hung his head over his bathroom sink, despondent and depressed. It'd been three days since he was released from the hospital. He should've shaved his beard when he got home, but he had neither the energy nor the motivation. Other than Clara, nothing interested him. His mother tidied around the house, trying for conversation, and he brushed her off like the prick he was.

Unlike his mother, the guys were as subtle as whores hocking blow jobs. They arrived uninvited and unappreciated, and did nothing but pepper him with moronic questions. They started out with lead-lined softballs like *how's Mia* and ended with power-punches about his health, his mindset, and his ability to get his shit together.

He leaned off the vanity and watched the image standing before him in the mirror. Two weeks off was an eternity. He needed to work out, to train and pump iron until his muscles gave up on him. Something, anything to alleviate his tension. But exercising sounded like an awful waste of time, and he didn't want to muster the energy.

His cell phone sat quiet, charging on the vanity counter. It didn't ring a lot, but now it was infuriatingly silent. The guys hadn't shown up all day. Maybe they went out on a job. An operation Jared didn't tell him about.

With a few more splashes of water, he finished in the bathroom, then went to Clara's room. She stirred, her infant fists balled over her head in a tiny stretch. Not that he had much to base assumptions on, but Clara was an awesome baby.

More or less, she kept to a schedule. He knew, to a five-minute window, when she would wake up. Right now, he had a few moments to sit and watch her slumber. It was the only thing he could enjoy.

Her bright blue eyes opened wide with the realization she was awake. Without giving her a chance to cry, he scooped her off of her purple sheets and cradled her against his chest. She was getting to be a big girl.

"Baby girl, I missed you while you were sleeping."

He walked her over to the changing table and made fast work of a diaper change.

"I know, I know. It was awesome when Mia was here before. She'd be so proud of you." He smoothed the baby's cowlick down. "Peas and sweet potatoes. Who knew babies like that? I sure didn't."

She gurgled and reached for his face. Used to the smooth skin of a clean shave, Clara tugged his beard, intent on investigating.

"Yeah, I miss her, too."

His cell phone vibrated on his hip. They could screw off. He was busy now. He ignored two calls as he sat on the floor, watching Clara try to crawl. A pile of toys encircled them, and he fashioned two guns out of large, pink building blocks, then set up a row of stuffed animals.

"This is how you take out the enemy. First, you—" Clara stared at him, reaching for her pink block weapon. "Let me have that back."

He took a few of the blocks off. "You're too young for guns. Even pink ones. This is a pink stick, and I have no idea what you should do with it."

He pinched the bridge of his nose. What did he know about babies? Faking it wasn't fooling anyone, particularly him. He didn't know what the hell to do. Mia would know babies didn't get pink guns of the building block variety. She'd know how to turn a pile of pastel plastic into something girly and appropriate like… he had no idea.

The phone rang again, and he looked at the screen. "What do you want, Cash?"

"Three times. You made me call three times before you picked up the phone. You're acting like a chick."

"Maybe I was on the shitter."

"Yeah, maybe, but I think you're all bullshit. I talked with Judith. She'll be there in ten minutes. You and I are going out. Make yourself reasonably presentable."

Winters dropped his head back and stared at the ceiling. "Fuck that. And since when do you and my mom chat?"

"The world's conspiring against you, bro." Cash chuckled and hung up.

Winters returned to making large stacks of blocks. Pink skyscrapers or were they pink bridges? Pink sticks. Straight lines were the only things he could fathom that weren't based on violence.

Winters cracked his neck, snagged Clara, and walked into his room, ignoring the few items of Mia's on his dresser. He shimmied out of pajama pants and into jeans and a shirt.

Coffee. That was next on the list of things to do before they arrived. It might be the only way he could survive. He rounded into the kitchen and saw two vehicles traveling up the driveway. His mother, followed by Cash. This wasn't what he needed.

Winters held Clara in front of him, at arm's length. "This is going to suck."

He poured a cup of coffee and watched out the window. His mom and Cash stood out there, chatting like a couple of good old boys. He downed the coffee in few blistering swallows and poured another cup.

They walked into the kitchen, both staring with the same disapproval.

"Dude, you've got to get out of the house. You look like shit."

"Watch your mouth around the baby." His mother reprimanded Cash.

"Sorry, J. My bad."

J? Cash was past first names and onto nicknames with his mom? In what world was this happening?

"Colby, I'll take Clara for the afternoon."

"Grab your favorite gun." Cash rummaged through his pantry. "Grab more than one. You might need 'em."

Winters tore open a box of Dots and dumped in a jaw-full. Cash snacked out of various containers in the cabinet, and Winters's mom took Clara into the living room.

"By all means, Cash, help yourself. Where we going anyway?" He threw in another handful of candy.

Cash chewed and talked, mouth wide open. "You're going to lose your boyish figure eating shit like that."

"Says the man who just housed a sleeve of crackers."

"I burn carbs like you cry over girls."

"Watch yourself, Cash. I'll leave you in a puddle of your own blood."

"Nah. You'd be too worried about Clara getting in it. Move your ass. We've got places to go." He motioned to a box of cookies. "I'm taking these. I'll meet you in the truck."

Winters took two stairs at a time to his weapons stash, unlocked the safe, and selected a handgun and rifle. As he headed back down, his mom cleared her throat. Twice.

"I'm glad you're getting out of the house."

He grumbled. "I'm not."

"That's precisely my reasoning. You need to see different walls. You're a mess."

"Thanks, Mom. Exactly what I needed to hear."

He slammed the new door behind him hard and heard it shake. He was definitely the leading candidate for worst son of the year. Also, biggest asshole of the year. What other awards would he rack up? Prick, dick, jerk? He could go on and on.

Winters got in, and Cash switched radio stations, stopping on the Eagles singing Desperado directly to his sorry ass. He didn't want to be in this truck, going God knows where. Even the radio mocked him. Cash burned past the speed limit, looking excited.

"Want to tell me where we're headed?" Winters stared at the unfamiliar road.

"You needed to get out of the house, so what's it to you? We'll be there in a minute. Man, your panties are in a twist."

"Get off my back, Cash."

Several songs later, they turned onto an unfamiliar two-lane road that curved and angled. Cash drove the odd turns like he did so every day.

"We almost there?"

"Yup."

"And *there* is?"

"My secret getaway. Where all your problems will be forgotten."

They slid into a small dirt parking strip and splashed through mud. A nondescript sign read GUNS. The words dangled under a rusted, larger-than-life bison replica complete with a snarling face and a charging hoof pulled high. A few pickup trucks lined the lot in front of a one-level, brick building with bars on the windows.

"Your secret escape is a gun range? I could've shown you a half-dozen thirty minutes closer."

"Patience, buddy."

Cash jumped out and shut his door. Winters pressed his head against the headrest. What the hell? Pounding out a few rounds might help. He followed Cash with far less enthusiasm than his buddy. A security camera traced their path to the door. Cash rang a doorbell and, seconds later, a buzz preempted the door popping open.

They entered a small room. It was dimly lit and glass cases lined the walls. Handguns and throwing knives hung on the dark-paneled wall. An empty desk sat in the corner next to a shady hallway. It was dingy and hadn't shown any of the promise Cash raved over. Winters trailed a finger over the smooth countertop, peering down at a compact Beretta 9mm.

"Well, if it ain't my favorite of all my favorites. Hi ya, Cash. You come down here to play with your toys or mine?"

Winters spun around. The woman wore black leather pants like a second skin. Her silver belt buckle of dueling pistols etched over a jagged heart shined near a belly ring. Her black cotton shirt hung to right below her full rack. The lettering scribbled over her tits read *Girls Love Guns*.

Christ. Cash brought him to a whorehouse.

The smile on Cash's face reached from one sideburn to the other. "Well, hi there, Sugar. I brought a friend."

The woman wore lipstick that was far too red. Her tussled hair was piled in a way that screamed *pull here*, and she smelled like scotch and spice. Her gaze raked him up and down, lingering over his crotch, before his lips pulled off hello.

"Does your friend have a name?" She flicked a wink intended for both of them. "'Cause I was back there, field-stripping a .22 LR, and he looks handy with a long rifle."

She stepped toe-to-toe with Winters and planted a hand on her cocked hip. "It's just a little thang for range practice. But I promise, it's real smooth. Grab a couple bricks, and we can go all night long."

Cash was a dead man. This was such a bad idea. Weeks ago, she might have been what he needed to blow off stress and excess energy. But now, his inner horn-dog was annoyed and far more interested in shooting a long gun, than fieldstripping in any capacity with her.

He needed to change the course of this exchange. Winters extended his hand. "Name's Winters."

"Well, Winters, welcome to my range. I can't believe Cash never brought you here before."

"I don't bring anyone here, Sugar," Cash said. "Haven't you noticed? You're my not-so-guilty secret indulgence. I'm not one to share."

She batted her thickly-painted eyelashes and nodded to Winters. "So, what's the special occasion?"

"He's in need of a distraction." Cash laughed.

Winters growled. "Christ, Cash. Mind your goddamn business."

"Aw, Winters, don't be so harsh." She licked her pink tongue over her very cherry bottom lip. "I happen to specialize in distractions."

This stunt was borderline ridiculous.

"I think we better just pound out a few rounds." He paused, no idea how to address her. "I didn't catch your name."

"Sugar's my name, but Honey, Dollface, that'll work, too. Call me whatever you want. If you like it, I like it. But you already have my laser-focused attention."

No appropriate name popped to mind. He eyed Cash hard and ran a hand from his beard to his nape.

Cash jumped in and ambled to the hall. "Okay, Sugar, we'll just take a couple of lanes. Put it on my tab."

Winters followed, not wanting to spend any alone time with the woman. Her exotic perfume hung thick as they walked to the range.

"Think you could have warned me, man?"

"About what? She's your type, and you need a distraction."

"And what's my type?"

"Aggressive, vampy, and without strings."

"I don't need a prostitute."

"Well, Dollface back there isn't a pro. She's just a few kinds of fun." They entered a ready room that narrowed to the lanes. "Hell, they're all fun."

Winters looked around at the range. Typical tactical team types practiced shots, and a few range grunts focused on the targets. But there were women. Women like Cash's *Sugar.* Sexy leather pants, too-tight shirts, strapped with guns.

"What the hell is this place?"

"Something of an invitation-only gun club."

"And all the women?"

"What? You've never seen a lady in the lanes before?"

"This is sex on display."

"Sugar knows how to run a profitable business. Nothing out of line. Just gorgeous gals who have our type of fun and know their weapons. What's hotter than a woman wearing a belly shirt, holding a grenade launcher? She'll find you one if that's your fancy."

"Christ, Cash. So this is..." He wasn't sure how to ask him if he was mixed in a hooker ring.

"It's no different than you nailing some broad from a bar." Cash stood in front of a lane but didn't step forward. Winters moved adjacent to him, feet from the starting line.

"Cash, man, I don't need a special invite to those bars."

"It's a social club, not a bunny ranch. Dude, what's your deal? I'm not trying to lure you into some seedy, VD bordello. It's a gun range that quality females with special interests frequent. If someone catches your eye, do something about it."

He turned from Cash and stepped into the cubbyhole. After he ejected the empty clip, he loaded the rounds and donned protective glasses and earplugs. *Do something about it.* Cash was off his rocker if he thought a piece of leather-wrapped tail would do something for him right now.

He owed it to Mia. She'd never know, but that wasn't the point. Sugar wasn't appealing. Winters jumped his gaze from one lady to the next. Hell, none of them were interesting. Maybe his taste in women had changed.

Winters slammed the clip in and blew out a heavy breath. He pinched his eyes, then focused on the target twenty-five yards away. He squeezed the trigger and absorbed the kickback.

Yeah, he needed that.

He cocked another round into the chamber and fired again, and again. The kick was a relief. A constant. Something comforting that happened with every trigger-pulled blast.

"Winters," Sugar said, almost purred, seconds before he was overpowered with her perfume.

He didn't need to look behind him, but he did. Sugar wrapped herself around the edge of the partition.

Go away.

But she didn't. He took off his protective shades, took out his earplugs, and gave her a nod but didn't offer a response. Instead, he punched the button, and his shot up cardboard target raced forward on the track and came to a stop, swaying. Each gunshot landed where he'd intended. His precision was a work of black powder beauty.

"Hey, champ. That's your everyday carry?"

He nodded, curt and not friendly. "You're here to make small talk?"

"Look, we got off on the wrong shitkicker. I'm far past outrageous. I get that. Cash told me you thought I was…offering more services than I actually do."

He closed his eyes so she didn't see them roll. Cash was earning his ass kicking. "I didn't mean—"

"Of course you did. But don't sweat it. I threw myself at you. And Cash rightfully assumed I would, which is why he brought you here. I can be a distraction, I know. So, you're doing okay?"

He watched her take small steps closer. Her hips swung more than they needed to, and she flipped her now-down hair over a shoulder.

"And you're distracted from whatever you need distracting from?"

"Guess so." Firing off each shot cleared his mind. It was a first since he woke up in that hospital bed.

"So here's the deal. I'm not a pro. Nor am I insulted you thought so. You, Winters, you have a body to jump. I'll distract the hell out of you, if you're interested." She stepped close, ran a finger over his pec, and stood on tiptoes to reach his ear. "I promise you, whatever is weighing heavy on your mind will wash away."

She flicked a tongue onto his earlobe. He flinched.

"You're keyed up. I can do something for you, baby."

Her hand dropped further, cupping him.

He grabbed her hand off and dropped it. "Not interested."

She ignored him and crushed her body onto his. "It's your circus. I'm just here for the rides."

"Not interested." The muscles in his neck tensed, and he leaned away from her mouth. If she kept rubbing him, disinterested or not, she was going to get a reaction out of him. And he was, without a doubt, not interested.

She pulled back, her tongue dancing over her lips again.

"If you change your mind, I'll be in my office." She pointed down a hall at the end of the lanes then trailed her hand across his bicep. "This time. Next time. Whenever. I sense my kind, and darlin', you're my kind. It'd be fun for both of us. Think it over."

She winked at him and turned away, swinging her ass in those tight pants. He really should've thought about it. He needed his old normal. Sugar was his style and didn't ask for a morning after. That was exactly what he liked in a woman. *Right*? He shook his head, confused. He didn't know what he liked anymore.

He was tired and cranky and empty. It made him wish Mia was waiting for him at home all the more.

Winters dropped the clip from the gun, reloaded, and holstered the piece. It was time to head home. Whatever Cash was up to, he could finish later. Sugar lurked within eyeshot, and he wanted to get away.

He spotted Cash, signaled to go, and headed to his truck. The door was unlocked, and he hopped in with Cash hot on his heels. Cash jumped in, threw it in reverse, and traced their return path.

"Sugar didn't do it for ya?"

"You told her I said she was a pro. That wasn't an awkward convo."

"I didn't say pro. I said madam."

Winters glared at him. "Big fucking difference."

"So she's not your type anymore?"

"I don't have a type."

"And I call bullshit on that one. Leather, fake tits, ready to—"

"I got your point."

"No, you've completely missed my point."

"And that is?" he said through clamped teeth.

"My point is she's not Mia." Cash stared from under the low-set brim of the cowboy hat.

"So today was to screw with me. Great. Thanks. I really needed it."

"You're stupid. Connect the dots. More than willing female. Your stereotypical fuck. But you didn't care. The Winters I know wouldn't mind blowing off some steam with the likes of Sugar."

"I've got a lot on my mind."

"No, brother, you've just got Mia Kensington on your mind. And you should deal with it."

"I've dealt with it. End of discussion."

They pulled up to the front of his house. Winters grabbed his rifle and jumped out with Cash laughing behind him. Winters walked through the front door, threw the door shut but caught it just before it slammed. No need to wake Clara if she slept and make both of them miserable. He was doing it well enough for two.

CHAPTER THIRTY-TWO

Mia zoned out in front of her computer. The screensaver was blank, except for the lonely square bouncing corner to corner. A Magic Mike highlight reel could've played on repeat, and she wouldn't have noticed. Instead, she twirled a pencil between her fingers. Her last patient cancelled, and she was left with empty time.

She drank so much coffee that the next step would be mainlining espresso. That wouldn't do. Coworkers were already whispering. After the professional inquisition from her coworkers about her bruises and scratches, she decided all the cover up and foundation wasn't hiding the tired eyes and sad smile they really wanted to know about. It was too bad the frown was here to stay.

She stared at her coffee cup, debating the drawbacks of the shakes. A jittery caffeine headache would kick this defective day over to the pointless category. She held her hands out to ensure her fingers didn't tremble.

Someone knocked on her closed door. She should have turned out the lights. Disruptions weren't welcome. Her next appointment wasn't for at least another hour, so whoever it was could find someone else to bother. If she didn't move, they might leave her alone.

The door clicked open. She cringed, disinterested and annoyed. But then an infant gurgled, offering a slew of nonsensical words. Her heartstrings quivered, wanting to see the baby, needing to see Colby. She inched round in her chair, heart punching into her throat. Disappointment exploded in her chest. *Not Colby.*

"Judith." Her throat stung. Mia failed a happy smile. It was more of a smeared grin. Of course it wasn't him. Why would it be? She hated herself for even hoping he'd show his face. The man had no reason to, but as much as it pained her, she was so desperate to hear from him. Pathetic. She was steps beyond pathetic. "What are you doing here? I mean, I'm glad to see you. But, is everything okay?"

She stood, fidgeting with her shirt. *Oh...no. Something happened to Colby.*

Softness creased Judith's face. Clara knotted her hands into the woman's hair, then, excited and flapping her arms, offered Mia a conversation of sounds and syllables.

Judith waited for Clara to stop. "Hi. How are you?"

Not a big fan of lying, she shrugged. "Would you like to sit down?"

Judith seemed to hesitate. She took one slow step, then another, finally relaxing onto a leather couch.

"I'm not the interfering type. But…" Clara reached for her, and a piece of her heart broke. "I'm sorry, Mia, would you like to say hi to Clara? Hold her?"

Mia closed her eyes against the hot tears that threatened to wash away her cover up under her eyes. She blinked twice. "It's okay. I don't think I should."

I can't, because I'll fall apart.

Judith fidgeted, toying with Clara's hand. "I just want you to know, Colby is... He's just not right in his head. I don't know what you two went through, but he's never come home shell-shocked before. Beneath all that bravado, there's a guy who's just scared of losing everything."

"We went through a lot. I just… thought things were different than they were."

Judith shook her head as if disappointed in herself, or maybe in Colby. "I'm meddling. I know I crossed the line. I shouldn't be here."

"You're not meddling, Judith. Don't worry."

"It's… I'm sorry, Mia. I saw a shine in my son when you were around. He was different, and it was special. I'd hate to see him lose you because he's an ass."

"He is special. I hope he's doing okay."

"You care about my son?"

"I do."

"I'm sorry you're hurting."

Mia shrugged again. She couldn't think of anything to say that wouldn't magnify the hurt. And Clara. Sweet Clara. She wanted to hold that baby as bad as she wanted to smack Colby and hug his mother.

"He's hurting, too. His fault, but he is."

"I don't know what to do." Her voice broke. She couldn't believe she'd said that out loud.

Judith was off the couch in a second, wrapping a motherly hug around her, with Clara giggling in the middle.

This is what a hug from a mom should feel like.

"Oh, honey, me neither," Judith said. "I'm so sorry."

Mia's tears fell, and Judith kept her close. "I'm sorry to cry."

"Don't be ridiculous."

"I miss him."

"We all miss you."

Mia wiped at her streaking makeup. "Thank you for saying that."

"Alrighty, I had no intention of making either of us cry." Mia didn't even notice Judith's watery glance until she'd said that. "You know how to get a hold of me, right? Please call. If you need anything, call me."

"Sure. Thanks for coming by and for bringing Clara."

"Of course. And again, I'm sorry to interfere—"

"Please. You're not interfering, Judith. Besides, you can't compare to Jared and Cash. They've made it their personal mission to make sure I'm okay. I'm like their adopted younger sister or something."

Judith laughed.

Mia smiled. Cash had shown up, armed with jokes, and Jared had tried to act like a hard ass. He failed each time.

"I was surprised to see you and not one of them. The guys keep popping in. No idea how they're getting on base."

"They can get anywhere. That I've learned." She gave a pause, possibly thinking what Mia thought. If they can get on base, Colby could've done the same. "Those boys. They're like a nuclear, adrenaline-junkie, gun-toting family. Blowing stuff up and drinking beers together. They think I don't know what all they do. But I know. And I'm proud of them."

"Me, too." With each passing moment, she missed him more and more.

"If he ever comes around, tail between his legs, I hope you'll give him a second chance. That is, if you think he deserves it. I'll see myself out. Take care, Mia."

Clara reached her chubby fingers to Mia and called out gibberish again, sweet and innocent, as Judith walked them away.

Mia plopped into her chair, spun in mindless circles, and drifted to a stop. She shuffled papers and tried to ignore the jewelry-sized box under her desk. It beckoned to her, screaming for attention. She wheeled away from the desk and bent down to wrap her fingers around it, wishing she could crush it.

Everything happened for a reason. If nothing else, she now understood how family was supposed to feel. She deserved it. The deluxe package. A husband, kids, and a happily ever after.

She fingered the brown leather box and listened to the muffled rattle as she flipped it over again and again in her hand. Mia shut her eyes and pulled the top off, dumping the contents into her palm. Metal shards. Disfigured, corkscrewed, and hooked. Shrapnel.

For whatever the reason, Jared brought her the box with the metal fragments from Colby's shoulder. It should have been gross, but it wasn't. It served as a brutal reminder of the way Colby protected her from gunfire and explosions. That Colby would rather have died fighting than let her go down under his watch. But did he know losing him this way was just as terrible?

She tossed the box toward the trash can. The box bounced off the wall, remaining shut, and jumped to a dark corner under her couch, where it could stay.

CHAPTER THIRTY-THREE

Winters's cell phone buzzed across the table, moving closer and closer to the edge. It was a cliff over the hardwood floor, and he'd let it careen off without hesitation. If it shattered, he'd have an excuse for not answering.

He heard the front door and knew his mom arrived. Another person he could ignore. This day hadn't hit the bottom yet. She walked past him at the kitchen table and threw him a pitying smile. "Haven't seen you since I took Clara with me on some errands last week, and you're about as peachy as I saw you last. Is the baby napping?"

Winters grunted, digging at his fingernails with a tactile knife. There wasn't dirt, blood, or grit to remove. He hadn't been in the field since South America. Still, he moved on to the next fingernail. It was a nervous tic. Something to occupy his hands or his mind.

"Seen the guys?" she asked.

"You mean after that debacle you orchestrated with Cash last week? Nope."

"Seen anyone lately?"

"Nope."

She hovered. It made his skin crawl. Since he'd been home from the hospital, this was her modus operandi. Stand and watch. Stand and watch. Nothing said, but lots to say.

"Colby…"

Shit. Friendly fire was never friendly, and it was coming. Operation Stand and Watch was over. Did that mean Operation Bust His Balls was on deck?

He opted to go on silent mode and continue his weaponized manicure.

"Colby, you about ready to cut the crap?"

And Operation BHB was a go. He didn't have the inclination to sit around for a lecture, so he stood. "Thanks, Mom. You don't need to swing by if you don't want to."

She shook her head. "One day. You get one more day being a little tart before you're done."

"Christ, I don't need this from you." He fell back into his seat and stared at the ceiling.

"You do, 'cause no one's giving it to you like they should."

"Give me a—"

"You aren't the only one in this family who knows how to kick ass. And now you've been warned."

"Mom, leave it alone." Yelling at his mother was the wrong thing to do, but here he was, ready to yell. "You don't know what's going on."

"I know Mia." She stalked over to him. "She's the best thing in your life, next to Clara, and you're hell bent on ruining it. If you haven't done so already."

"She's not safe with me." Why was this so hard for everyone to understand, and why did it even matter to them? "I did this for her."

"That's baloney, son, and you know it."

He sheathed the knife and spun it on the table like a one-person game of spin the bottle. His frustration bumped up another level, into the red zone.

"What the hell am I supposed to do?" He was harsher than he wanted. An out of control panic pushed at him.

"You don't have a plan, so you sit here, watching hours drift by? That's not my son."

"Shit, Mom. I just don't know what to do." He slammed his hands on the table and pinched his eyes closed. He needed a deep breath, but all that came were escalating angry ones. He opened his eyes, and his mother had her hands planted on her hips.

"Simple. Take that fire and fix what you broke."

"Simple my ass." What would he say? Mia would tell him to skip straight to hell, and he deserved that and worse. He kneaded the edge of the table. Anxious energy toyed with him.

"Colby, you're getting one more day with your foul language. Then I'm done with that, too."

"Mom, I struggle with…" He sagged. Where would he even begin?

"Things you can't control? Things that you didn't plan? Things that haven't gone the Colby Winters way? Want me to keep going?"

No need for him to make the list. She apparently came prepared. Winters rubbed his jaw. "I'm crappy with things that I care about."

She sighed. It wasn't pitying as much as contemplative. "Oh, I don't think that's true. You're amazing with Clara."

"I didn't have much choice with Clara."

"Yes, you did, and you took it like a soft-hearted brute. Clara was the best thing that happened to you. Until Mia. Now, you've got two best things. Hopefully, one is still waiting for you."

"She's not waiting for me."

"A broken-hearted woman might wait, hoping."

"You don't know Mia. She's not the broken-hearted type."

"I wouldn't be so sure." Judith looked like she had more to say, but left it at that, and went about tidying the empty counter, picking at non-existent crumbs. "You have to man up and deal with your mess."

There she was with a stick, poking him in the eye. "Man up? Come on."

"Whatever you guys call it. Man up. Get your panties out of a wad. Put on your big boy shorts. *Grow a set.*"

"That's the last thing Mia said to me." He fought the stomachache that surfaced anytime he recounted his brilliant plan of avoidance.

"Smart woman."

"Yeah. She's smart. But not smart enough to run from me."

"Lose the pity party, son. If Clara hadn't arrived on your doorstep, we wouldn't have grown close, and we wouldn't have conversations like this. But we have, and we are. This is my opportunity to tell you that two wonderful girls are a part of your life."

"She's gone. I chased her away."

She shrugged. "I didn't take you for a wimp. And I never thought you'd walk away from a worthy fight."

"What?" He didn't expect for her to break out the name-calling. Everyone else but not her.

"You're a superhero to the world, but when it comes down to it, I guess you're scared."

"Leave it alone."

"I don't know whether to feel ashamed I raised you like this or—"

"Christ, Mom. Back off."

"You're going to let her wander into someone else's arms? There's another man who could protect her better than you? Well, if that's true—"

"Goddamn it." Angry thumps of blood pounded in his ears, flooded his veins. His chest felt on the verge of explosion. Like hell another man would hold Mia, protect her, and care for her. He'd kill any man who tried.

Judith nodded toward the garage. "I've got Clara. See ya."

Winters grabbed his cell phone and jumped from the table, knocking the chair over.

His phone buzzed in his hand. Fuck. Would people stop bothering him already? Winters grabbed the keys for his blacked-out, pumped-up truck. It suited his mood. Dark and ready to get the job done.

"Jared, what the hell do you want?" That roar should put a stop to the incessant, badgering calls. Get a clue, man. He was tired of everyone hanging on his nuts.

"This isn't Jared."

Mia's short retort slammed him in the gut, and his heart jumped clear into his mouth. Christ almighty, he missed that woman.

"Mia, where are you?"

"Why?" She was quiet. Wary. Why did she call? Hell, who cared? She called, and that was all that mattered. If he could hear her for the rest of his life, it wouldn't be long enough.

"Right now, doll. Where are you?"

He planned to go all alpha on her if she didn't fess up in seconds. He needed to locate her fast. And fast wasn't fast enough.

"At home. Why?"

"I'll be there in ten minutes. Do. Not. Move."

"You don't even know where I live."

"The hell I don't." He really should tone it down, or he'd scare her.

"You're not invited."

"Tough."

"You're at least a thirty minute drive from me."

"Time me." He checked his watch.

"I don't want to see you. Come to my office tomorrow."

Winters clicked off his phone. He didn't want to know now why she called. She could say it to his face. Anything so that he had a fighting chance. His guts churned. Need spiked with overwhelming, raw emotion, making his muscles ache and his brain fuzzy. He skidded out the corner of his driveway, sliding sideways before he redlined the truck. Ten minutes. There was no doubt.

CHAPTER THIRTY-FOUR

Mia's front door flew open. She should have known better and locked the deadbolt. Not that a deadbolt would have kept Colby out.

Bright sunlight illuminated her dark den. She had pulled the blinds, hit the lights, and bunkered down for a sobfest, complete with blankets, junk food, a tissue box, and enough sappy movies to make Cinderella forget about her Prince Charming.

She'd been heartsick but tearless until the lonely night before, after she signed the paperwork. She went to bed an emotional mess and woke up ready for a cleansing release. Today was the day for it all to come out. And because of that, she had no need for anyone showing up uninvited, and standing there, blinding her, in all his sun-drenched glory.

Colby filled the entire doorway. She should have been surprised, but really, she was annoyed she didn't expect it. Like he was just going to knock.

Mia paused her movie. The Bodyguard. What shitty timing. This was the perfect part, where Kevin Costner held Whitney Huston to his chest. If Colby barged in during her first viewing, he'd have caught her singing along to the soundtrack.

"Go away." She turned back to her paused movie, finger on the play button, ready for his departure.

"We have to talk."

"We did that already. Go away." Mia snuggled further into the down comforter and eyed the mess of balled-up, tear-soaked tissues heaped on the floor. *How embarrassing. Couldn't he just leave?* "I didn't call you to invite you over."

"I don't care."

"Glad to see we're back to snippy sentences. Just like how it started, and how it should have stayed." She picked up the spoon in the container of ice cream and took a huge bite, tasting both peanut butter and chocolate chunks. Double score. At least some things worked out. "I've got plans, and I don't want you here."

"With who? Ben and Jerry?"

"Watch yourself, Winters. You have no right to judge."

"Don't call me Winters. Can I sit down?"

"No, you can leave."

He moved closer to the couch, as if considering how to wrangle a wild beast. "Why'd you call me?"

"Well, it wasn't to invite you over." Why did she call him anyway? She had no purpose, no plan with her phone call. Thank God he went all alpha-bossy on her, because she had an excuse to hang up.

"I can see that." He sat on the far end of the couch, placing the empty box of chocolates on the coffee table. She should have addressed her heavy heart before it exploded into a calorie bonanza. She should have cried it out two weeks ago and moved on. But she didn't, and here he was. She hated him and hated herself for loving that he was within reach.

"I'm leaving." She tried to swallow away the tears and did a valiant job at holding them at bay. Accepting that already-made decision was what started her downward spiral to the fabulous party-of-one she was throwing herself this morning. "I'm moving. I rented my house out to a newlywed couple. I'm gone in a week. New job. New state. New life."

Winters's jaw dropped. "You can't do that."

"Why can't I?"

"Why would you?"

"I don't want to live in a house that was ransacked by a Colombian cartel. I came home from hell and walked into a disaster."

"Mia, doll—"

"Don't *doll* me, Winters."

"Please call me Colby." He growled through closed teeth, losing all the effect of his polite request.

"No. You aren't in a position to make requests. Deal with it."

"I'm so sick of people telling me to deal with it."

"You're not going to find any sympathy from me." Mia took a bite of her dripping ice cream instead of crawling into his lap. The substitution did zip to quell her urge to scoot closer.

He leaned over to an end table and turned on a lamp, again illuminating her movie-watching, cry-fest cocoon. She blinked, eyes adjusting to the new splash of light. His face was clean-shaven. He seemed so big on her couch. Did he always wear tight shirts that made his biceps pop and pants that molded to his muscles? Compared to her frumpy pink pajamas, she looked ridiculous, and far from attractive.

"You have every right to be angry with me."

The *right* to be angry? Hell. Anger wasn't in the same galaxy as how she felt. Anger was too simple. But she didn't feel like describing the utter remorse sickening her, all because she fell in love with him.

Instead, she pulled herself off the couch. She had things to do, and they were far away from him. He could find his way out, like he found his way in.

"I'm sorry."

Why did hearing that make it hurt worse? "Just leave."

"Mia—"

"I can't do this. Please leave." She wasn't going to beg. He had to go.

"I'm not going anywhere."

"Why?" She turned toward him, frustrated. He stood, imposing and ignoring her pleas. It was infuriating. "Why are you torturing me? You don't get to say I'm sorry. You weren't here when I walked into my ransacked house, or each sleepless or nightmare-ravaged night."

"I—"

"And every day I stayed at the hospital, holding your hand, talking to you about the future. I was a fool. You told me to leave. No, correction, you had the nurse tell me."

Pain twisted and shredded her soul. Everything between them was gone. It was irreversible. Actions had consequences, and his actions ruined her dreams.

She marched toward him, wrapped her fists in the fabric of his shirt, and did her best to shake him.

"I hate you." The words were precursory to her bubbling sobs, also uninvited. She dropped her head against his chest and bawled. "I hate how bad this hurts."

He engulfed her in a hug, rubbing her back, and smoothing her hair. Making it worse.

"Mia, doll. I know sorry doesn't do shit. But God help me, I thought I was doing the right thing. That you were better off without me. That I was protecting you."

If he thought that, then he was stupid. She had fallen for a moron. But she kept that secret and didn't move from the warm, tear-dampened place against his chest. She wanted to crawl into his cradling arms. She wanted to feel him care.

"I was scared," he said. "For so many reasons. I don't get scared. I don't know scared. But I was… I am scared out of my mind."

"Why?" she whispered without moving her head. Her hands were still wrapped in his shirt.

"Hell, I don't know."

It was like a sledgehammer of reality, reminding her of him. She pushed away and out of his arms before he could protest. "Then that's something you should've figured out before you got here."

"Mia, you're not moving. You're not going anywhere."

"Typical subject change. Resort back to orders. Classic, almost cliché."

"I'm serious." He looked serious, but he was always serious, and when it came to them, he was wrong.

"Your directives don't matter anymore, Winters."

"Stop calling me Winters, damn it."

She ignored him, needing space for clarity, and shuffled toward the kitchen. Regaining her wits, she said, "I'll call you whatever I want. Asshole. Jerk. Liar."

He stalked close. "I never meant to lie to you. I don't even know how I lied."

"You led me on. And the whole it's-not-you, it's-me spiel? I expected more creativity."

"I was protecting you."

"For God's sake. From what?" she screamed and threw a mug against the wall. "I survived crazed men and kidnappings. Plural!"

Standing in the middle of the shattered mug, he paused and took a breath. "None of that would've happened if it weren't for me. If you didn't know me, no one would have chased you, no one would have kidnapped you."

Mia wanted to run away, but the ceramic shards and bare feet kept her in place. "If I didn't know you, then I'd be dead in a cheap motel room in Louisville, Kentucky. You saved me."

They were in a standoff, need versus emotion. Their eyes locked. Her stomach tightened, electricity buzzing around their showdown.

Crunch. He stepped closer.

"Don't you dare kiss me, Winters."

"Colby." He took another step. His boot crunched more broken mug. "The name's Colby."

"Let me make this clear to you. You hurt me, and you should leave."

"I hated every single fucking second away from you."

"Get out."

His last step closed the distance. "Not a chance."

He clasped his hand under her hair, leaned over, and breathed in. Her heart stilled. Her breathing stopped. His sweet lips crushed over her mouth, and the world froze before her lips swept against his. His tongue delved into her mouth and dueled with hers. A velvet stroke. Shivers raced down her spine, but she was hot to her very center.

She drew back from his kiss, starstruck.

He looked about how she felt. "You remember what I said about you and me?"

"I don't." She wasn't entirely sure she could remember her full name. That kiss walloped a sizzle.

"Mia, I've needed you my whole life. I said it, and I meant it." He cupped her chin and brushed his thumbs over her cheeks. "But I couldn't handle it, so I screwed up."

"Oh."

"You opened my eyes. I didn't know how to need something, like I need you."

Mia wasn't sure she could speak.

"But if I had you, then lost you, I'd never survive."

She found her voice, faintly. "You did have me."

"Did." His thumbs stilled. "But now I don't?"

"I have to pack."

His eyes narrowed. "That's not an answer."

"A kiss won't change anything." She took a step back, nudging her cheek from his hand.

"It can say I'm sorry."

"A kiss can say anything you want it to, but what's the point?"

He shook his head. "Oh, hell no, hon. You're not throwing up those stupid walls just so you can kick me out and finish a pint of melted ice cream."

"You're sorry. I'm sorry. All's forgiven, *Colby.* Thanks for stopping by, but you have to go."

He stepped forward. "Bullshit."

"Cussing at me isn't going to change anything."

"Christ, Mia." He slammed his hands on a nearby wall. "I'm in love with you. Don't you know that?"

She wanted to say no, but nothing materialized.

"There it is." He ran a hand into his hair, then dropped his head before spearing her with a gaze as intense as the tension in the room. "All cards on the table. I love you."

Mia needed an escape. She had to get around him, but she was blocked in the kitchen and glass covered the floor. On tiptoes, she tried to push around him, but he countered her move. Instead, her eyes closed. "Liar."

He laughed. "Tell me I'm wrong. Tell me again it's a lie. I love you, Mia Kensington. But what's it going to be? You love me?"

She made it to the hallway without cutting her feet, but he caught her, caging her against the wall. Forearms on either side of her face served as prison bars. His impenetrable torso pressed precariously close. The rapid rise and fall of her chest couldn't be ignored. Her racing heart screamed for attention. *Love? No. She couldn't risk hurting even more all over again.*

"Mia. What's it going to be?"

She studied the scar under his eye, because she was too frightened to see the truth in his eyes. "What do you want from me?"

"I just want you." He bent forward, making his lips tickled her earlobe when he whispered. "I love you. I want to spend the rest of my life with you. I want Clara to have a mom, maybe brothers and sisters."

Her mouth gaped open. He stepped back and held out his palm. "Take my hand. Literally, figuratively, however you'll take it."

"I…" She couldn't rationalize what was happening.

"I'm praying that you love me. Do you?"

"Yes," she said on an escaping breath. Too quiet. Too easy.

"Say it. Right now. I need you to tell me."

Mouth agape and unsteady on her feet, she remained mum. This was a bad idea. Soon as she said it, she wouldn't be able to stop saying it.

"You have to say something, doll. Might as well tell me whatever the truth is."

She took a long, deep breath. The truth. She loved him more than any woman should love a man. Her mind traveled at warp speed. Words jumbled in her brain. So many things wanted to come out at once that she couldn't get them in order.

He stiffened and turned away. "Got it. Never mind. I'll just slide my ass out of here."

His boots clunked hard on her floor, heading toward the front door. What was happening? Wait, no. This was all wrong.

"Colby, stop."

He did, but didn't turn. Instead, he leaned against the wall.

She couldn't breathe. Her mind was swimming. There was a very plausible possibility she might pass out. It was too much to take in. "I'm not losing you again."

He pivoted a slow turn toward her but stayed put.

"I *do* love you. I love you so much it hurts, and I can't breathe."

He was on her in a second, pressing her against the wall, his hot mouth possessing hers. He pulled back.

"Doll, don't ever take that long to say I love you again." Then he leaned into her again, brushing his lips over her neck.

"I love you, Colby."

He smiled. She couldn't see it, but she could feel his cheek and lips pressed against her skin. "So you do need to pack."

"I do?"

"You do. You're coming home with me."

"I love you."

"You're answering every question like that?" Genuine adoration poured off him, making her all the more certain she would.

She nodded, smiling and laughing.

"That'll work." He pulled her toward the front door. "Didn't you once say something about wanting a dog?"

Now a bigger smile. "I love you."

"Then a dog it is."

EPILOGUE

The sun set on the lake. Mia leaned on her elbows and dangled her feet off the dock. Their dog ran rampant, in and out of the lake water, splashing and spraying Colby and Clara. He walked in a shallow section, the water lapping at his thighs, and Clara kicked on her daddy's shoulder. Every time he dipped her legs into the water, she flapped her arms and squealed for more.

The gold band on Mia's left ring finger felt less and less foreign. They'd gotten married in a small ceremony, with some family and several friends, in Colby's backyard. *Their* backyard, *their* home. He reminded her anytime she misspoke.

Family. The word once sent shudders of sick dread sweeping over her skin. But now, her family was lounging at the lake. Her *growing* family.

Mia had a feeling but didn't want to admit it until she took the test. She swung by the store, picked up two boxes and two bottles of water, hiding them in the cart, not even wanting to look at them for fear of jinxing her hopes. She chugged the water on the way home and ran to the bathroom. Two tests later, it was as official as a home pregnancy test could get, and she couldn't stop beaming. They were pregnant.

Colby would be just as excited. She had wanted to wait until tonight in bed, when he held her close, but the lone excitement was unbearable.

"Hey, family, come here a sec," Mia called over to Colby, as he pointed to the lake fishes flitting around his legs.

He looked up, smiling. "Come on, Mama. Don't make us stop. We're playing."

Their beautiful faces melted her heart. The minute she came home with him, he started calling her Mama. Her stomach flipped each time he said it. Not only were they family, but she was the mama. Now, more than he even realized.

"But I've got a surprise for you two." Mia couldn't contain herself, so she dropped her head back, sunning until they made their way over. Colby jumped out of the water with Clara and plopped down next to Mia, his wet swimming trunks dripping water on her leg.

"A surprise, huh? Whatcha got for us?" He adjusted the baby bouncing on his wet knee and held her in place.

"How do you feel about two under two?"

"Two what?"

"Little ones."

"You already know. Wait—" He gave a look of warning, not to be messed with. But a smile spread wide. "Are you?"

Mia threw her arms around them, squealing in his ear.

"Mama, I'm more than good with it." He wrapped his strong arms around Mia and Clara in a giant bear hug.

A husband, two babies, and a lifetime to enjoy family. It was exactly what Mia Winters never knew she wanted.

THE END

Did you like Colby and Mia's story? Pick up the next two novels in the Titan Series:
GARRISON'S CREED (Cash's story)
WESTIN'S CHASE (Jared's story)

And for sexy, quick reads, check out two Titan novellas:
GAMBLED
CHASED

ABOUT THE AUTHOR

Cristin Harber is an award-winning author. She lives outside Washington, DC with her family and English Bulldog, and enjoys chatting with readers.

CONNECT

Facebook: https://www.facebook.com/cristinharberauthor
Twitter: https://twitter.com/CristinHarber
Email: cristin@cristinharber.com

If you enjoyed **WINTERS HEAT**, I'd appreciate if you helped others meet the Titan Group also.

LEND IT. Please share with your friends.

RECOMMEND IT. Help other readers find this book by recommending it to your friends, to your book groups, and online discussion sites.

REVIEW and RATE IT. Please share your thoughts at Amazon and Goodreads on why you enjoyed this book. If you do share a review, please email me and let me know. I'd like to personally thank you for sharing the Titan love.

JOIN THE CRISTIN HARBER NEWSLETTER

Stay in touch about all things Titan—releases, excerpts, and more—plus new series info.

FIRST LOOK AT GARRISON'S CREED

Sighting the target in his crosshairs, Cash Garrison accounted for all of the variables. Wind speed and direction. Distance and range. Now the world would be free of one more bloodthirsty warlord in less time than it would take for the walking dead man to finish his highfalutin champagne toast.

Hours had passed since Cash nestled into place, high-powered rifle held like a baby to his chest. A thousand yards out from the extravagant mansion, he'd burrowed into position, melting into the landscape, and waited for this moment. Antilla Smooth, dressed like the million dollars he made as an arms dealer and unaware of the grim reaper sighting his forehead, made his way past the French doors.

Cash caressed the trigger, knowing exactly how many pounds of pressure it would take to fire the round. He monitored his breaths and heart rate. When his entire body was still, in between beats and respirations, he'd take the bastard out. One less piece of shit strutting on God's green Earth. The world would be a better place, and Cash's job for the day would be done. He and the team could find a local bar, find some local ladies, celebrate and make a night of it. *Good plan.*

He adjusted for a breeze, blinked his eyes, counted down his breaths, and—stopped. Stunned. Frozen in place. Heart pounding like a coal-eating locomotive.

A woman in a golden dress and sparkled-out jewelry that'd make royalty jealous wrapped her arm around Antilla. A soldier would sell his last bullet for a kiss from her lips. Cash saw her through his scope as though she stood a mere twenty feet in front of him.

She looked like… but it couldn't be.

His spotter spoke in his earpiece. The order: "*Send it.*"

Cash spoke into his mic. "Stand by."

His spotter whispered again. "Eyes on your target. All conditions accounted for. Go. Send it."

Nothing. Cash didn't speak.

Earpiece again. "Go, goddamn it."

The woman slunk around his bull's eye, her beautiful hair piled on top of her head, save for the loose pieces framing her face. Her smile slipped into a laugh. *I've inhaled gun oil fumes. I'm losing my mind right this second.*

"Cash, man. You there?" His spotter grabbed his attention, wrenching him back to reality.

"Here. Yeah, man. Here."

"Wind from three o'clock. Dropped to five mph. Hold. Target blocked." The woman draped over the man. This was a nightmare—his nightmare—blasting from the past and slapping him clear off of his prone position and onto his stupefied ass. The spotter spoke again. "Clear. Dial wind right, two mils. Send it… now."

Heartbeat. Breath. Heartbeat.

Fire.

And breathe.

Now, they had to move. Fast. He knew the spotter team should be slipping through the thick Maine forest. Cash paused and glanced longer than he needed to confirm the kill. Tuxedoed man on the ground. Kill shot. Dead. Panic attacked the room. People ran, most likely screaming. Security scrambled. Dogs loosed. Barks growing closer. But the woman. The golden silk-draped woman stood still, staring at the busted window pane in the French doors. No expression. No emotion. Not a drop of anything.

Cash shook his head, clearing the ghost of her image, and focused on his job. One shot, one kill. Just the way he liked it. He cleared the shell and casing from his bolt-action rifle, policed his brass, and snapped to a crouch, erasing any evidence that he had spent hours in the spot. A half second later, he beat feet, sliding down the side of the wooded hill, leaving no trail.

His spotter buzzed in his ear, confirming their meet-up point. "Rendezvous at location A, twenty-two ten." He could do it. He should do it. He powered down a hill, sliding as dirt gave under his feet. Brush slapped him in the face. Vicious barking closed in. The main house illuminated day-glow bright.

Man, he was going to hear about it for this one. He told his spotter, "Location C, twenty-three hundred hours."

"Cash—"

It took a lot for Roman to break protocol and use his name over the radio frequency, but Cash knew his spotter, his closest friend, was pissed. And an upset Roman was as much fun to deal with as the dogs Cash was about to run back toward.

Not much to do except kill an hour. Cash pulled his earpiece out as Roman cursed again. Nothing good would come at the end of that sentence. Cash laughed. Radio silence wasn't the best road to take, but it was better than coughing up an explanation of the impossible.

Nicola glided around Antilla Smooth. His lifeless face stared at the ceiling, and his perfect hair hid the sniper round's entry wound. Given the crimson puddle painting the white carpet round the backside of his brain, the bullet was a through and through, and her night was ruined. Her operation ruined, completely FUBAR.

Chaos filled the room, and was she the calm eye of the storm. Everyone and everything swirled around her. Loud noises. Screaming people. Security moved fast, but what was the point? They'd failed.

She hadn't failed, but the last few months were now crap, and it was time to call the powers that be. They'd be interested in this turn of events. Nicola put down her champagne flute and pulled out her cell. She walked away, feeling her smooth silk gown train trailing behind her.

The phone rang once, and a surprised voice answered. "It's a little early for our chat."

"We should get together for ice cream." Nicola gave the phrase that told Beth, her handler, that this mission was dunzo.

Beth didn't miss a beat. "I have to run errands first. I'll meet you after you head to the dry cleaners."

Dry cleaners. Yup, time to turn into a shadow and slink away. It was the right move, pulling her home. Too bad she had nothing to show for the months spent playing to the dead megalomaniac's ego. She'd been so close, only one or two days away from locking down the international players in Antilla's arms network.

"You've got it. I'll be in and out first thing in the morning." She walked down the hallway, and a guard looked. Apparently, her saunter was too calm, given the way other women shrieked their horror. "*Ciao*," she said goodbye, keeping up her Italian persona and put a hand against her throat.

She looked at her designer gown. No blood. At least there was an upside to this evening's party. That and she wouldn't have to feign interest in Antilla, the sick prick, then backpedal when he wanted to take her to bed.

Personal preference. Some ladies in the Agency did what they had to do without a second thought. She'd had second thoughts. And thirds and fourths. She'd wanted to screw Antilla Smooth like she wanted a root canal done by Kermit the freakin' Frog: choppy marionette hands flopping up and down.

"Gabriella?" Someone used her alias. "Gabriella, are you okay?"

Nicola saw a butler who had been friendly to her since they'd arrived at Antilla's Maine estate. Her name poured off his lips, imitating the Italian flare she used when introducing herself.

"Yes, fine. *Bene, grazie*." He looked unassuming. Who knew why the man worked for Smooth Enterprises, but looks were deceiving. Trust no one. "I need to step outside. Fresh air."

Really, she needed to get out of Maine, but why elaborate? She slipped outside. The night was daybreak-bright with the estate's security system fully engaged. Her hand caught her eye. The fluorescents made her olive skin look green, not complimenting the dress she'd fallen in love with. Nicola weighed her lack of options, knowing she'd need transportation and, for the moment, not knowing how she'd secure it.

A chill spiked over her skin as a gust blew through the forest. Someone was still out there. The same someone who took out her mark.

Pop. Flash. Pop. The exterior lights died, and she was left to her thoughts in the moonless night. Another chill rolled over her shoulders. No wind this time. She pivoted, reluctantly ready and willing to ruin her dress and take it out of the ass of whoever was to blame. Her muscles tensed. Her eyes adjusted in a flash. A man. Large. Broad. Armed. Twenty feet away at the side of the patio.

He spoke, the baritone timbre coating her in a hurt she'd hidden years ago. "Nicola."

She didn't need to see his face. His voice shattered any semblance of strength she'd mustered. Nicola braced one leg back, prepared to attack. Ready to defend herself. But who was she kidding? If he laid one finger on her, it might be her undoing. All her suffering, pointless.

"Nicola," he said again. Still as firm, but this time knowing. "What the fuck?"

This was bad news of the worst variety. She pivoted back toward the doors, ready to go back inside and hash out an emergency extraction strategy with Beth. No time to wait for tomorrow's withdrawal plan.

Reaching for the door knob, she willed herself not to run.

"It's you, isn't it?" he said.

Sweet Lord, why was Cash here? Why was the one memory she could never forget standing in the middle of her job? And why was he talking to her, armed and looking far more dangerous than the last time she saw him?

"Stop your sweet ass one second, and turn around, Nicola."

She spun on her stiletto heel, knowing she'd never be able to get to the subcompact gun tucked on the inside of her thigh. Even if she could, she'd never hurt Cash.

"No, sir. You're mistaken." She put on her best Italian accent, knowing it wouldn't fix this problem.

"Bull—"

The butler opened the door. "Gabriella, please come in. Everyone's gathering in the main hall. It's dangerous to be out here."

Cash stood in the shadows. She knew the butler couldn't see him. Yet, her pulse stuttered, and her throat tightened. She wanted to protect one man from the other. Nicola looked over her shoulder, and Cash was gone.

GARRISON'S CREED releases October 2013. Find out more at www.cristinharber.com.

ACKNOWLEDGEMENTS

There are so many wonderful people who supported me.

Lynnette Labelle, editor extraordinaire, pushed the emotion onto the pages.

My amazing crit partners: Dawn Wimbish Prather and Andrea Bramhall pushed me to better my storytelling. Victoria Van Tiem questioned every written word and held my hand as I cut my darlings. Sharon Kay's honesty honed the characters and made them come alive. Jamie 'Sparks' Salsbury—there are no words and that's okay because we share the same brain—but I couldn't have survived without her. Thank you to the Chatter Girls: Kaci Presnell, Racquel Reck, Amy Anhalt, and Claudia Handel. Your support during my mad dash to the finish line will not be forgotten.

And I can't sign off without thanking my husband and family. None of this would happen without your love.

7643048R00154

Printed in Great Britain
by Amazon.co.uk, Ltd.,
Marston Gate.